GODDESS
OF EVERYTHING

Paul DeBlassie III

GODDESS of EVERYTHING
Published by Hallowed Realms Press
Copyright © 2020 *Paul DeBlassie III*

Cover Design and Formatting by The Book Khaleesi
Editing by The Editing Hall

ISBN: 978-0-578-81368-4
Library of Congress Control Number: 2020924051

Printed in the United States of America

ALSO by PAUL DEBLASSIE III

Goddess of the Wild Thing

The Unholy

WHAT READERS ARE SAYING

"A vibrant, dramatic and disturbing novel packed with religious fervour, obsession, magic realism and horror. DeBlassie brings both the natural and supernatural elements of the desert of New Mexico alive in the mind of the reader. Passionate and inspired, Goddess of Everything makes a notable contribution to the Visionary Fiction stable."

- Isobel Blackthorn, Ph.D.
Author of The Unlikely Occultist: A biographical novel of Alice A. Bailey

"Paul DeBlassie III uses his in-depth understanding of human emotions and their healing in Goddess of Everything. He takes aim at two institutions held up as unassailable in Western culture—motherhood and organized religion. We see the dark underbelly of both. The mother who wants to control, possess, and consume the life she's produced. The church that hides sexual and spiritual abuse under the skirts of its priests and nuns. In a novel rich with Latinx mythology and a deep understanding of psychic gifts, DeBlassie plots a course for us to escape such abuse and heal. Even thrive."

- Theresa Crater, Ph.D.
Author of the Power Places and Mystic Assassin series

"Goddess of Everything, by Dr. DeBlassie, is a fascinating short read that commences eloquently with a perfect epigaph and prologue, preparing the reader for what's ahead. The book delivers a compelling, semi-poetic discernment that touches the reader's heart. One easily relates to this work as it incorporates the psychology of well-thought-out emotions. Throughout the manuscript, one couldn't help but feel a sincerity between the lines, a sentiment that deeply touches the hearts of those who long to perceive what they read. Very well written manuscript—a must-have in everyone's library."

- Dr. Hussam Atef Elkhatib
Author of Who Are We: Seeing Ourselves through the Eyes of One Another

To the Goddess

The imagination is...
both root and bough,
living between earth and sky,
in the earth and in the wind.

~ Gaston Bachelard ~

PROLOGUE

Howling night winds beneath a pale full moon whipped up dust devils that danced between gravestones in the four-hundred-year-old cemetery of *Infierño*, an arid and desolate realm of haunted nights and lost souls.

Infierño lay in the desert region of Aztlan del Norte, bordering the Rio Grande River, a place where generations of mixed-bloods—*mestizos* of Native, Mexican, and distant European bloodlines—lived. Vicious winds curled brown and gray dust into weird forms. They looked like taunting ghosts, their bony fingers stretching out as claws pricking the skin of still-living souls.

Grit and sharp pieces of sandstone twisted through the night like poison-tipped cactus needles set on a path of targeted violence.

Five-year-old Gabriél de LaTierra, a slight and sickly boy, clutched his mother's hand. He did not like the cemetery. His mother made him come with her when she brought flowers to the graves of old friends. She had so many friends who had died; here one day and the next swept away by the dark powers of death.

Gabriél's father was dead. His father had loved him, and he had loved his father. His heart stopped when his father died. Gabriél didn't want to live without his father. He looked into the open grave, the coffin on the dusty ground beside it, and a shudder coursed up his spine. His teeth chattered, and his head quivered with a quick chill.

He tried to step back from the edge of the grave. It was deep and dark. He couldn't see the bottom. His mother yanked him back to the grave's edge, held him in place with her steel grip on his shoulder. His chin jerked downward. He was forced to peer into the black.

Grains of sand crumbled along the edges of the grave. Gabriél feared falling into the open pit. He did not move. His mother pulled him back from the edge, into her cold and hard body.

Six women dressed in black, like his mother, let out cries and howls. *Mantillas*, delicately crafted black lace, were draped over their heads and foreheads. The stubbly black wool that covered their bodies was like the closely cropped fur of a coyote. They were his mother's friends.

The winds grew worse, and the priest's black cape flapped furiously. It looked like the outspread wings of a bat. Above the wind's roar, the priest shouted Latin prayers for the dead. The old language scared Gabriél, for it seemed like the echoes of a million voices of dead people chanting.

Hairs on the back of Gabriél's neck stood on end. A flush of fear tingled up his spine. His mother told her friends that since birth, Gabriél sensed things, presences. Others couldn't see them.

Mother saw them, and she raised her index finger with its

sharpened red nail to her lips and shushed a little boy when he spoke of them as he lay covered in blankets in his bed at home on cold autumn nights.

The old Latin language echoed through the mesa. It brought a terrible feeling. Gray clouds turned black. The priest shouted loud like a whipping wind, his face redder than autumn chiles hanging from twine, or *ristras*, their long strands like blood on a tightly wound rope, dripping slowly to the ground. His black cape stretching outward like enormous wings, the old priest stood tall as a pine tree and scary as the swirling storm clouds.

Cottonwood trees bent twisted branches downward. Like skeleton fingers, they almost touched Gabriél's head. He jerked back, afraid of the gnarly limbs. They could hurt like his mother's fingers did when she clung and dug into his back and along his neck.

Desperate, eyes wide with horror, he wanted to move away from the spindly fingers of the tree. He knew they came alive on scary and stormy days. Everything in him wanted to run, but his mother's hand squeezed his neck and forced him in place.

The eerie nighttime and harsh cold made him close his eyes. He wanted to drift away in his mind. He tried to pretend he was home in bed, warm and safe. He tried to pretend that his father hadn't died.

Tears welled. He held them back. They clogged up on the inside. His ribs hurt from the pressure. Pinpricks tingled through his stomach and across the lining of his lungs and the insides of his throat.

No tears came. They wouldn't come. They feared his mother. Gabriél couldn't cry. He needed to be alone to cry. He needed to be at home, quiet in his bedroom, wrapped under the warm covers of his bed.

The air quivered, wrinkled with waves moving up and down, twirling inside, then out. Dull light shimmered and took form. His father, with his big chest and warm arms, appeared. Gabriél stayed still. No one else could see his father. This was a strange time. Gabriél knew his father loved him, seeing him like the morning sun melting frost from pine tips.

Juana, Gabriél's mother, squeezed his hand. His knuckles cracked. He did not cry. He became like steel. Eyes glinting red, she turned and looked at Gabriél. All thoughts of his father fled from his mind. Mother was scarier than the mighty wind and whirling dust and howling women and chanting priest. She made him push thoughts of his father far away. He was never to think of his father. Only Mother's thoughts were to stay in his mind.

I love you, mijo. You are mine. My son. She placed her thoughts into his mind. As delicately as a silk thread through the tiniest of needles, she put her thoughts into his mind. She wrapped Gabriél into her black woolen dress with its coarse fabric that scratched his face, its tangled layers and woolen folds making him gasp for breath.

Three days earlier, the doctors said his father, Ernesto, had lost the will to live. Gabriél watched color and life fade from his father's face, bronze to white and pale, then ashen. His father withered away. Gabriél wanted to remember his strong and kind father. In a secret place in his mind, he would remember his strong and good father, and no one would take the memory.

Mother squeezed his hand again, harder. Bony hands and red eyes made the memory fade. Gabriél's mind went blank. He made it blank. His mind was white space, cold as a snowstorm in Aztlan del Norte.

Te quiero mucho, mijo. Te quiero mucho. Mother smiled and nodded. *I love you, my son. I love you.* Again and again, she forced her thoughts into his mind. Her thought messages made Gabriél tighten up so hard his muscles hurt. His neck felt the jabs of pain like little needles poking through his skin. His stomach twisted and curled with pinpricks, round and round and round until he felt sick, nauseated. His jaws ached from the strain of holding back the taste of bile as it rose up to his throat and coated his tongue.

Gabriél closed his eyes. *Mother loves me. It's all right. Mother loves me.* He had to say this in his mind, or else Mother would know. He had to survive.

Within his heart, his father's presence stirred and spoke, *I am with you and will appear in many ways, in many forms during your life, to instruct and guide. Listen and follow.* Dust slapped Gabriél's cheeks like angry demons.

There was a flash of light, no more than a wink. It happened again, brighter and strong. To his side, a man cloaked in light knelt next to him and touched his shoulder. *I will come in many ways, in many forms, to instruct and guide.*

Gabriél had the sight, saw into the spirit world, his mother said. At home, when she noticed his gift, she was troubled. He could tell by her furrowed brow. Her friends who gathered with her in the family kitchen nodded when she spoke of it.

They said he would be a dangerous boy to raise, strong-willed. He had to be broken early, they said, as they had done with their sons. Mother was head of the group called *Las Mujeres de Dios*, the Women of the Almighty. Mother Juana, as their leader, must set an example by disciplining her son. They spoke in Spanish because they thought Gabriél did not understand. Gabriél, tucked off in his bedroom, his door slightly ajar, heard their mean words. He followed their Spanish. Mother Juana spoke, and the women wailed their prayers in Spanish, and Gabriél understood.

He saw her cruel smile. In his mind, he saw his mother's nature because he had the mystic sight, the third eye between his brow point that his mother would touch and quickly draw away from, her hand trembling. Gabriél had the sight, and others besides Mother did not know that he saw into how things were. He would shake someone's hand, and an image would come. He would see an animal, bad or good, and it told him about the person. He had dreams, and what he dreamt would happen the next day. He sensed that something was good or bad, and smells would come, roses or incense or skunks or sewage. He often saw the screeching face of his mother, a black coyote howling and drooling and foaming at the mouth. Gabriél closed off the sight of the black coyote and made it go far away.

In his bedroom, Gabriél saw and sensed most powerfully. He loved his bedroom, his small adobe room of mysteries. He knew the word mysteries from his R.L. Stein and Goosebumps. Books helped him to trust what his mind and feelings whispered. A long wooden bookshelf held his books. He'd taught himself to read before going to preschool. And so his father gifted him with books, treasures that made him feel close to his father and quiet inside.

The day after his father's death, he read his books with his bedroom door closed, the brown adobe walls sheltering him from the sadness of the outer world. As he read, his mind quickened. The white space between his eyes opened with a flash of light. Father, draped in a white glow, stood beside the bed. He smiled and told Gabriél to read and to listen and feel. Then he disappeared.

His mother wailed again. Nighttime darkness continued to descend, and the wind stayed its brutal course at Father's funeral. Mother Juana hadn't noticed the spirit of a man cloaked in light beside Gabriél. He wasn't Gabriél's father. He was more than a man; he was everything that Father was and more. Through the corner of his eyes, Gabriél saw the white-bearded old man. *In many ways, in many forms, I will come*. The words were close as heartbeats and breath. He knew if he turned and looked directly at him, the man would disappear. The light was intense, like rays of the sun. The old man had something to say.

Suddenly, unclean sounds went into Gabriél's ears and chest—crackling and squealing voices rising from under the earth and into his body, trying to block out the lingering presence of the old man and his words. Like a god, the white-bearded man lifted his right hand, fingers spread. The noise went up from the ground into his palm, a mighty hand with powerful magic.

Gabriél's mind became silent as a windless autumn night, magic making him still inside, just like he was when in his bedroom reading alone. The old man was strong and made what was bad, cease. Even as the underworld racket stopped, the graveyard winds kept up their awful screams.

The quiet of the man and the moment wrapped strong and warm arms around Gabriél. Invisibility stood guard around the old man. Mother could not see him. No one could see him. He was there only for Gabriél. He bent down beside Gabriél and touched his shoulder. A crystal clear calm made the shrieking wind and the crying women and the priest's strange prayers seem far, far away.

Mother's red hair blew in the wind like it was on fire. It didn't scare Gabriél because of the old man, his warm and solid hands steady on Gabriél's shoulders. His kind eyes said he was ten thousand times ten-thousand-years old. His mother's red hair and shrieking prayers no longer scared him.

Then the old man spoke, and through Gabriél's mind sent a message: *LISTEN… WHEN THE DAY GOES AWAY AND THE NIGHT COMES, REMEMBER I AM HERE.* He touched Gabriél's heart. *LISTEN.*

Gabriél's mother abruptly glanced down at him. He looked into her eyes and knew she hadn't heard the old man, but she had a squint in her eyes. Her eyes glowed red, and the old man's hands did not move from Gabriél's shoulders.

Big branches from the cottonwoods cast long moon shadows over the grave. Now they looked like skinny people scratching at each other, cloaking the old man. The wind picked up its screeching.

Gabriél's heart pounded like stampeding horses.

Mother squeezed his hand. His fingers tangled together, tips burning with pain. Then she looked away and wailed more loudly than ever.

The old man continued, *TELL NO ONE ABOUT ME. I WILL HELP YOU AS A BOY. I WILL HELP YOU AS A MAN. LISTEN.* The old man motioned again to Gabriél's heart and then touched between Gabriél's eyes, the brow point.

The old man stopped and looked up.

Gabriél caught his mother's gaze.

She'd seen the old man, pointed at him, and screeched like the evil winds.

Blistering dust and grit blinded Gabriél. He pulled his hand away from his mother and rubbed his eyes and tried to clear them, but when he looked again, squinting, he saw that the light of the old man had vanished.

His mother was wrapped in a cloud of dust. Out of the

cloud came a coyote, foam curling from its mouth. It howled, and an instant later legions of dust devils took over the landscape and swallowed it in clouds of dust, trash, and tumbleweeds.

Mother reappeared beside him and picked him up. She screeched with a million hateful voices. His heart beat rapidly, fluttered like a flock of sparrows flying away. Catching his breath was hard.

"The night plays tricks," his mother seethed, her breath hot and rank.

The winds suddenly ceased. Brown and gray clouds gave way to blackness that closed in and covered the full moon. Spirits of children rose out of their graves. They pointed at Gabriél and his mother. Their hands and fingers grew and reached to grab him, take him away under the earth.

Mother swept her black shawl over Gabriél. She whispered, "I will protect you, mijo."

They escaped into the jet-black night.

CHAPTER

1

*S*ons belong to their mothers.
Their mothers birthed them.
They owe them.

Mother Juana de la Cruz listened and nodded as she knelt on the scratched and scarred hard wooden prie-dieu. It was now over twenty years since the death of her husband, her reign as Mother Superior of the most influential religious order in Aztlan del Norte firmly established. She loved the silent words from the Almighty that soothed her soul. They regularly came nightly, during times of extended prayer.

Sometimes she wondered if she was vicious, but she knew she was not. Mother was the left hand of the Almighty, one who exacted righteous standards on unrighteous souls. Hers was a mission of compassion, women of righteousness cleansing the world of stains made by those who dared defy the will of the Almighty.

The nighttime air in the little convent chapel was still,

stagnant as the underground burial chamber of a gothic cathedral. Her breathing was shallow and slow. Light-headedness expedited heavenly voices.

Kneeling was her extraordinary sacrifice. She knelt for hours, callouses thick as rubber on her knees. Intense prayers released beads of sweat down her brow and cheeks. She was hard on herself and so grew strong, the body tamed, the mind disciplined.

"The Almighty speaks consoling words to me, Sister Thea."

Sister Thea knelt beside the Reverend Mother, hands clasped in prayer. She kept her gaze fixed on the bronze crucifix set atop the altar in the small private chapel. Dozens of red votive candles flickered on either side of the crucifix. She was Mother's second-in-command, the prioress of the biggest convent in Aztlan del Norte.

"You are chosen, Mother." Sister Thea was reverential. Mother was severe, disrespect not tolerated. At night, as the nuns slept the allotted five hours, Mother entered their dreams. She tormented the dark places of the mind of those who dared defy her. Disobedient souls scratched and clawed at burlap bedding, dark dormitory hallways echoing with the nightmare cries of unruly nuns.

Legions of demons assailed the tortured nuns in their sleep, like poisonous ants swarming a body strapped to the desert floor of Aztlan. The ants bit and bit and bit, and Mother's prayers were answered. She watched from the world of dreams and dreaming. The defiant nuns saw her as she witnessed their suffering from a mountaintop as they writhed in the surreal desert valley. They screeched and howled, looked up to where Mother stood with arms folded, and beseeched her mercy. Oh, the willful nuns suffered. From

Mother's prayerful—targeted—thoughts, they suffered. And they awoke chastened, soul blistered, and forged into obedience.

The Almighty regularly spoke to Mother Juana. On nights when others slept, Mother listened. Only Sister Thea was granted entrance to the private chapel. She alone could attest to the Almighty speaking to his chosen servant.

"He talks to me about men and their ways. I have much work to do, Sister Thea. The fields of the Almighty call for threshing." Mother salivated as she spoke the words. *Threshing, threshing, threshing*—she savored the words as they silently rolled along her tongue. She loved to thresh and thresh and thresh.

"Yes, Mother." Sister Thea was two decades younger and ambitious. Mother smelled it—a rank odor. Mother, eyes closed, concentrated at her brow point, focused her energies. They were pure energies. They were a gift, a supernatural gift.

Sister Thea doubled over, clasped her hands to her ears, and screamed. It was the high-pitched wailing of the wicked. Mother saw through the soul, pierced through Sister Thea, penetrated through all things. Mother's mind controlled the wayward and the evil, bent strong spirits to execute the will of the Almighty.

Sister Thea's wailing echoed around the chapel's white plastered adobe walls and red-bricked floors like legions of howls from cracks in the century-old structure, screeching of rats turned to hideous underworld cries.

Mother's mind knew all, controlled all, the goddess of all—the goddess of everything.

◈

Sister Thea crawled toward Mother's kneeler, her forearms pressing against its frayed red velvet edge. Mother sent currents of torment into her assistant's mind. Luxurious sensations caressed Mother's memory. She relished inflicting pain. It bettered the soul.

Sister Thea looked up at the slight-framed Mother, a woman of imposing bearing. Thea's eyes were wide, stunned. She struggled to keep her composure. Her tight smile was forced, lower lip trembling. Beads of sweat dripped from her temples and brow. She knew better than to incur Mother's displeasure. Her head jerked back several times, flashes of torment rippling across her face. She was a weasel, caught by the throat, squeezed and throttled.

Mother savored Sister's Thea's barely suppressed moan. Thea's nerve endings were on fire, from toes to fingertips to the top of her head. Mother liked setting nerve endings on fire.

Crisp and frail sinews and ligaments and bones could snap and pop under the strain. Mother could force it. Merciful as she was, she refrained. But she did permit herself particular joy. Especially one delicacy—setting nerve endings on fire.

Sister Thea's eyes grew wider, and she howled and clamped the palms of her hands against her temples and rocked back and forth. A neurological affliction like hordes of stinging fire ants spontaneously arose. Mother willed it, casual as the sweep of a dark deity's hand. Sister Thea fell to the chapel floor and writhed.

Mother smiled. She drew her hands into her billowed woolen sleeves and whispered a prayer to the Almighty. She closed her eyes and gave thanks for her gift of bequeathing suffering. Mother deepened her concentration. Violent headaches marched from the back of Sister Thea's neck to her forebrain. Mother concentrated harder. Tension squeezed Thea's retinas with the force of a raven's claw. Mother opened her eyes and witnessed her minion's agony, eyes red and pleading.

Only Mother's compassionate nature held back the hand of the Angel of Death. Mother was merciful. She was a woman of discretion. "Opportunity for penance, Sister Thea. Penance."

Mother, the slight, redheaded, iron-fisted Mother Superior of *Las Mujeres de Dios*, led the religious order of one hundred nuns, the largest in the Aztlan del Norte Archdiocese of the *Ecclesia Dei*, the church of true believers. The Mother House was in Infierño, to some a haunted realm, to Mother and the nuns a province of spiritual wonder and power.

Prompted by visions and voices, Mother performed miracles, made the lame walk, the blind see, cured the incurable. Her supernatural feats ushered the religious order into renown. People from far and wide, other states, countries, continents made the pilgrimage to Las Mujeres and the Blessed Mother Juana, handmaiden of the Almighty.

Mother gave a nod to the writhing Sister Thea. Sister Thea, like an automaton, rose to her feet. She straightened her back and cleared her throat. She quickly recovered, symptoms abating. But her breathing remained guttural. She had barely survived.

Sister Thea's mind lay cradled in the palms of Mother's prayerful hands. It was a malleable bit of gray matter. Mother twisted and knotted it into a tight ball of excruciating pain.

Mother sighed, then bowed her head. Tears streamed down her ascetic porcelain cheeks. White-knuckled, she gripped her hands prayerfully.

"Thank you, Mother," Sister Thea whispered. She sounded relieved. Her breaths were smooth but hesitant. Best that the little nun drew cautious breaths. Sister Thea turned to leave the chapel and crawl off to her adobe cell in the nunnery. The creature left, knees wobbly.

Mother's tears dried quickly. Yet, she conjured empathy for everyone's sorrow and travail. Compassion was easy as smoothing butter on toast for one skilled in the business of religion. It took little to win people over. You eased their pain a little, and they were yours forever. Comforting and healing pain-riddled minds and bodies bound the distressed soul to Mother. She felt nothing.

Thoughts of how she looked in the mirror that morning brought a smile. She kept a small oval mirror at the back of a nightstand drawer. In her stark, whitewashed ten-by-twelve-foot adobe bedroom was a metal-framed bed with a straw mattress, an old pine desk with a chair, and a nightstand. It held the precious mirror. That morning, like every other morning, she had contemplated the beatific visage of Mother Juana de la Cruz, one reputed to be miraculously ageless due to sacrifice and sanctity.

During a secret ritual, young lives were sacrificed to replenish Mother's sacred vitality. Damnable beings were exited from the earthly plane of existence. Mother sent them from one world to the next. Blood sacrifice supplied energy, fresh and clean. It streamed down Mother's throat and into blood vessels, lungs, mind, and soul.

Miraculously youthful, the seventy-three-year-old nun never aged, much as the saints of old never aged. Their bodies were incorrupt, Mother's perpetually renewed. Blood sacrifice was delicious. She was radiant as an archangel.

The black wool habit pricked Mother's summer-hot flesh. Tonight, the Infierño desert—nighttime temperatures barely cooler than the hundred-degree noonday heat—was a walk in a shaded park next to Mother Juana's fury. Rage boiled and swept through her body, tips of her fingers shaky with righteousness. Her arm muscles bulged as she gripped her hands and made a fist. The iron hand of Mother ruled as a faithful and loving mother.

It was 10:00 P.M.

Eight hours earlier, her only son, Gabriél, betrayed her. Gabriél's image lit up at the center of her forehead. She clenched her teeth, disobedience a poison dagger in the heart of a pure mother. Gabriél committed an unforgivable sin.

He had married.

Years, decades, centuries ago, Mother Juana herself had married, not to decaying flesh (Gabriél's father a mortal convenience) but to the Almighty who wooed and courted her until his flaming sword, as with the mystics of old, pierced her heart, and she became handmaiden of the Almighty. As with Spanish mystics of centuries gone by, a shudder consummated the act. A flaming sword appeared before her as she prayed. It entered her heart.

Quivering and perspiring, her breathing had become laborious. Her heart nearly burst. And Mother yielded, consummated her love to the Lord of the unseen world. They had become one. Then, there came a titillating in her ears. Mother Juana listened. The pleasing sensation signaled the coming of her Beloved's voice. Ancient texts stated that he imparted a select language to extraordinary souls.

Words, a prayer in divine tongues, were a gift from the heavenly realm. They called forth her Beloved, and with the chant came eternal powers, mighty as a blinding desert wind.

She whispered, "Bagabi laca bachabe lamac cahi achababe karrelyos. Bagabi laca bachabe lamac cahi achababe karrelyos."

And mysteries unfolded year after year. Generations died off before questions could be raised. A new saint for a new era, Mother Juana de la Cruz established a new order of beings that sacrificed body, mind, and soul to the Almighty. The nuns, all widows, took a sacred vow: *My soul I pledge to Thee, Thine promises now be mine.*

Prattling townspeople claimed that under cover of night, in a deep *arroyo* surrounded by ten thousand mesquite bushes, each hung with prayer beads, the nuns recited their vows and performed their rituals. A colossal goat descended from the high country, circling the nuns as they danced, each kissing his tail. Then, a giant black snake slithered across the desert floor and embraced each member. It put its tongue in the mouth of the newly vowed—the tongue of dark mysteries and hidden knowledge. Finally, out of the silence of the desert night, four men dressed in black emerged. They carried a coffin. A child's corpse was pulled out, and the frenzied nuns fell on it like ravenous coyotes.

Through the night, the nuns danced, feasted, and made merry. They screamed, "Bagabi laca bachabe lamac cahi achababe karrelyos." Before the first rays of sun stretched over the Sangre de Cristo mountain range, the nuns dispersed, leaving a strong smell of sulfur in their wake.

Macabre powers emanated from the convent. They were the left hand of the Almighty, saving one, smiting another— ill-advised townspeople gossiped. All were awe-struck, frightened.

Ostensibly, Mother Juana tolerated those few who dared gossip, but she knew that from the instant of the first scandalous word, they would live one, maybe one-and-one-half years. The Almighty worked in mysterious ways. Believers, supporters of the nuns and their mission to minister to orphaned children and unwed mothers, never doubted or gossiped; so they and their families lived long, relatively trouble-free lives.

But now, years of prayers had been washed away by one reckless act. Gabriél knew better. He had been raised to know better. He was his mother's son.

Mother Juana prayed on, "Bagabi laca bachabe lamac cahi . . ." In centuries gone by, a son hadn't been necessary. But things had changed. Gone were the times of public infant slayings, sacrificial offerings of the offspring of cattle, and other sordid, bloody deeds. Appeasing the wrath of an angry deity toward wayward humanity now required subtlety. It demanded cover.

Nunhood was perfect. Religious people craved to believe in the Beloved Mother. They worshipped her. Nothing of ill repute would taint such beliefs. Eternal salvation depended on it.

Upping the ante, Mother Juana birthed a son to further her influence—the power of the Celestial Mother. Thirty years ago, after his father's death, Mother Juana had trained, taught, demanded that Gabriél live a single-hearted life. Sons were to do as their mothers said, not question. Work and a mother's love were sustenance enough. Nothing else. Work and a mother's love. Such was the life of one dedicated to the Divine Mother—purity of heart and devotion. It was enough. Motherlove was more than enough.

But Gabriél had defied her and kindled, then stoked a mother's wrath.

Tonight, an unholy sword pierced Mother's heart when

Gabriél uttered the vow. Women chosen bore sons chosen. Spurning the call brought consequences. "Bagabi laca . . ."

Gabriél owed her. He would pay. He would be made to learn and return to his right mind, not remain with the sordid woman who had stolen him away. Mother Juana de la Cruz enacted the Almighty's will on men and women. Men were a particular delicacy, righteous hatred demanding righteous sacrifice. Gladly, Mother performed the deed.

And would do so with her own son, by symbol, ritual, extension.

He would have a successor, one who would be the sacrifice. And Gabriél would suffer, and suffering purified the tainted soul. And the one who had stolen him away would learn and leave. Grief conjures trauma and terrible endings. Lines of power were to be kept pure. In the family. The Holy Family. Mother and son forever.

Mother Juana would see to that.

From a pocket sewn inside the left sleeve of her billowing habit, Mother removed a small plastic, airtight bag. Opening it, she withdrew a shriveled plug of flesh. Last night, at the Ritual of the Unholy Trinity—a ceremony of excising and exorcism performed on special feast days, she had consumed two round and fresh male delicacies.

Only the plug was left.

Carefully, Mother Juana drew it to her mouth. She chewed and chewed, then swallowed. The night's secret twilight vigil on the Feast of the Holy Innocents had been sheer delight. Children sinned. Impurity. Entering eternal life free of the tainted thing was a gift. The will of the Almighty worked in strange and mysterious ways.

Severing the befouled organ freed the soul. "If the eye should cause you to sin, cut it out," the Almighty had said. So much more for the tainted thing. Ingesting it destroyed it. Mother took in the vital force. Strong medicine for bad sickness.

Mother's medicine was all Gabriél needed. A son should be glad and eternally happy to return to the mother. A little sacrifice, a little suffering, and a boy would learn that a mother's love was enough—more than enough.

Wiping her lips and repocketing the bag, Mother Juana stood, genuflected and blessed herself, and left the chapel.

CHAPTER

2

It was four years since he'd married, and Gabriél's daily workload and routine was like a spike in a block of Carrara marble. Monday morning, 6:50 A.M., he was off to a day of intensive intervention at the mental health center. Every morning was hurried, work demands inconsolably heavy. Gabriél's drive to work hard for the needy children of the county required nearly all his time and energy.

Consuela, his wife, complained that work had become more important than time and passion for one another. He hated the look in her eyes when she said it, pleading, angry. He loved her, didn't feel he short-changed their relationship. Yet, what she said struck him hard. He'd work at it, at being better at love, he told himself. He always told himself he'd work at being better at love.

Crusher-fines crunched underfoot as Gabriél walked the

familiar path from the dirt parking lot to the Infierño County Mental Health Center. He was the director of the largest outpatient psychiatric facility in northern Aztlan, caring for thousands of hurting souls. Vast swaths of the populous were beyond true healing due to the ravages of a lifetime of untreated mental illness. For those, medicines offered the only relief, dulling their unending pain.

After having completed a bachelor's degree at the University of Aztlan, Gabriél worked at the Center for five years, then left to Chicago for a master's degree in psychiatric social work. He had desired to do this work since his teenage years. His professional passion was to help his people, those who suffered from ills of the soul.

It was a short time after he had returned to the Infierño Valley that Gabriél and Consuela married. They'd met one day at the general hospital where Consuela worked as a physician's assistant. They dated, and after six months, destiny called. Their relationship was sealed.

Gabriél had begun working at the center. County politicians agreed that his executive abilities were outstanding. That, together with his mother's behind-the-scenes wheeling and dealing with Infierño politicos, soon landed him the directorship.

Each day, Gabriél was the first to arrive. Early morning quiet helped him prepare for a heavy load of counseling neglected and abused children and their families. Delegating administrative tasks to the business people on staff, he could do what he loved most—care for unloved children in a place where it was desperately needed, a county rich in beauty and poor in human welfare.

Infierño, a low-rider's paradise, had a reputation for the mind-blowing beauty of the Aztlan high mountain desert, intoxicatingly pure air, and a crystalline-blue sky that arched over the city like a divine protector. But all was not as it appeared in Hell's Little Acre, as Infierño had been designated by tongue-in-cheek critiques. Dubbed the heroin capital of small cities U.S.A., Infierño was a hang-out for new-age gurus, third-world drug dealers, and rowdy gangs of pimps and prostitutes that spread like cockroaches in an outhouse and copulated as if having kids were no bigger a deal than burping after a greasy hamburger and fries.

Gabriél reached the stairs of the brown-stuccoed administration building. Hairline cracks laced their way up and down the walls like spider webs. A flight of twenty brick steps led straight up to a hard day's work.

Daily, Gabriél struggled against tiredness. It crept through his bones and into crevices of his mind like maggots set loose on a corpse. It was a terrible thought, the mental image of being eaten away. Gabriél's psychoanalytic training had taught him there was always a message in spontaneous mental images. But Gabriél had not wrapped his mind around the meaning.

He knew the body never acted without the mind. What influenced one, influenced the other. This was a psychological fact brought home every day in clinical practice and personal life.

Symptoms were worsening. Jogging every morning at 5:00 A.M. kept his slight, thirty-five-year-old, five-foot-nine-inch body well-oiled and lean. Without the run, his energy flattened out to road-kill. On most days, he fought against the tidal wave of total depletion that threatened to confine him to his morning bed. With a raw tenacity, he got himself up and forced himself on, the depletion passing eventually like gray clouds in an otherwise turquoise-blue sky.

Pausing, he looked up. Clear skies hovered over northern Aztlan. The sight filled him with refreshment that did not last. Fatigue was all in his head, he told himself. Discontent was due to tiredness. Every day he said that. Sometimes it helped.

A deep breath and he sprinted up. It was his way of pushing passed tiredness. He had other ways too. Some worked, but mostly they didn't. He rested at the top, breaths drawing hard as air forced through a constricted passageway.

The rolling Jemez Mountains peaked over the southern skyline. Scattered hawks flew across the big blue sky. Crisp and clean Rocky Mountain air carried scents of silver sage, piñon, and wet earth. It had rained last night.

Once his breathing returned to normal, he unlocked the front door and entered the building.

Inside, the seventy-five-year-old brick edifice smelled like a neglected, used-up, institutional corpus—a stomach-turning belt of monotony and despair. It hit Gabriél like a sixteen wheeler mowing down an innocent passer-by. The nostrils would gradually adjust, but it took about as much time as a hefty dose of ptomaine passing through the gastrointestinal tract.

Gabriél did his best to blow past the stockpiled emotional debris that haunted the place. He never missed a day, never wanted to. It was his place to work, to help, and try to make a difference.

The kids needed him. Good-for-nothing parents starved, beat, and took sexual advantage of hundreds of children in the county each year. Gabriél's job was to stop bad from getting worse. He loved his vocation—helping those too young, too weak, too beaten down to help themselves.

He walked down the long, dark, greasy linoleum hallways leading to his office. His pace picked up, a sure sign of energy influx. It came from being true to who he was and what he did. Getting past early morning energy lags made all the difference, helped to jump-start the day's work. Natural energy, a subtle intoxication unique to his physical and psychic constitution, pumped a stream of adrenaline so light and luxurious that all he could do was close his eyes for a second and whisper, "*Gracias a la Vida*!" Thanks be to life.

Taking a deep breath, he thought about Consuela, her worries about him working too much. His health was suffering. Each morning, she'd reiterate her concern as she gave him a goodbye kiss and swept his thick black hair off his forehead. "Those dark circles under your big brown eyes are getting worse, Gabriél." Always, he assured Consuela he was okay, but he knew something was wrong.

He cried out in his sleep, his bedsheets often wet with perspiration by morning. And daylight hit him with yawning pit-of-the-stomach fatigue, as though his soul were slowly being sloughed off. Ancient cultures spoke of soul loss. It happened with compromise, making wrong into right and right into wrong. It was a defense against truth, and people came to believe and live by the lie.

Lately, he hadn't been home for dinner more than one or two evenings a week—Sundays a sure bet for nurturing a depleted man and a marriage badly in need of time and love. Loneliness bit hard into Consuela. It showed in her green eyes—a hope, a yearning to spend more time together. Rarely was she demanding, but on this matter, she didn't waver any more than a fierce she-wolf. "I love you, Gabriél. We didn't marry to be apart." The words gripped and broke through like a Zen master slapping a dozing practitioner.

Gabriél missed Consuela, badly. Sometimes, it ripped the breath right out of him. But professional concerns inevitably forced away immediate distress. Responsibilities bore down and took their toll. Mother Juana's demands weathered no concern for personal cares or subjects as trivial as marriage. Gabriél's powers were to be concentrated on the children, the offspring of the destitute and deranged.

The Almighty would take care of his wife and child, Mother Juana emphasized with an edge thinly camouflaged by a pursed smile. Put charity first, and the rest would follow, went the mother-to-son wisdom. She lived her life by that rule and expected nothing less of her son. The strength she nurtured in him since childhood drove him forward and, he often mused, would always be a ready source of empowerment for whatever lay ahead. Morning, noon, and night, Mother's demanding voice echoed in the ears of an obedient son.

And for now, morning energy had been summoned and rode through Gabriél's body with the

hum of a finely tuned engine. He reached his office. The sight of his name and title on his office door—Gabriél de LaTierra M.S.W., Director—always brought a smile to his face. Gabriél Must Save the World de LaTierra, his graduate student colleagues had dubbed him. By far, he was the most driven of the lot, graduating first in his psychiatric social work class at the University of Chicago. Since then, the flame to help the downtrodden had been stoked into a blaze. Nothing stood in its way.

A click and he was inside his office. It wasn't large but big enough for a scarred oak desk, three metal filing cabinets, two worn blue cloth chairs he'd come across at a Saturday morning flea market, and a sand tray. The tray was a two-by-three-foot oak container filled with a few inches of sand gathered from a remote section of Aztlan desert. Reputedly, it was a realm of healing and powerful energetic vortexes. Children often commented that the sun's rays made the grains of sand glisten like tiny diamonds.

The tray was attached to a bottom cabinet on wheels that held hand puppets, crayons and pencils, papers, modeling clay, and various cultic objects. Four shelves of the same wood and width stretched midway across the wall. They held miniature toys—metal soldiers, prehistoric creatures, play food, houses and churches, cars and boats and airplanes, abstract symbols made of wood and clay and steel, and human figurines both intact and damaged.

Gabriél set his worn leather briefcase on the desk, hung his lightweight canvas coat on an antique brass butler, and walked over to the tray. Approaching the contained space, he sensed an uneasy premonition. The sand tray was a psychological instrument. He had been trained to use it during graduate school years of psychotherapeutic training. From the first, he had intuited its psychic draw and appeal. In a contained space, it symbolically constellated human emotion and powerful archetypal—spiritual—energies.

On certain days, it called to him.

For patients, emotions surfaced and were absorbed as psychological medicine. Children were surprised and intrigued, some crying after making images in the sand. All were mystified.

Gabriél ran his fingers through the cool granules and, without censor, let them trace a pattern.

Soon, a circle in the center of the tray was etched, then another smaller circle in its center, and an X inside of it. Shuddering, Gabriél drew back. The image settled in. Taken by its intensity, Gabriél left the picture in the tray, his mind absorbing the symbol's strange energy.

Stepping to the six-paned window behind his desk, he tried to let his mind wander, drift. It was early, the sun streaming through the clear glass as through a vortex, a warm and radiating brilliance in the cozy twelve-by-twelve-foot room. A beam of light shone across his desk.

He had an hour before his first appointment at the Orphanage of the Holy Innocents where he was to see Samuel Fuentes, a twelve-year-old boy with whom he had counseled for the past year. Samuel had been the last one to make something in the sand tray. The previous session, Samuel had been at Gabriél's office.

The boy had shown Gabriél a sterling silver turquoise ring, wearing it on his pinkie finger. His mother had given it to him. Yesterday, he brought it out of hiding, wore it. He hoped the nuns wouldn't take it away. They had a rule against jewelry and keeping secret gifts from family members. Gabriél assured him it was his to keep.

After a time, Samuel had gone directly to the sand tray. From the shelves, he got an eagle, a mountain, a witch, and a long black snake. The snake curled around the perimeter of the witch, guarding, ready to strike. Perched on the mountain, centered in the lower half of the tray, the eagle watched the witch and the snake. It was centered in the top half of the tray, a symbol of opposition. They were enemies.

Placement was essential to understanding. Deeper down meant hidden, unconscious. Farther up, suggested out in the open, conscious.

Between the eagle and witch, Samuel had drawn a circle and mounded sand in the middle. Samuel said the witch couldn't see the eagle but knew he was around. The eagle, because he could see a ways off, and through and into things, saw the witch. Samuel sat a few minutes, mesmerized by the scene, Gabriél with him. Neither spoke.

A sense of the ominous had filled the room, fright mixed with wondering, imminent face-off, triumph or tragedy. Nothing was said. It would have disturbed things. Feeling was enough.

Samuel was a boy in a life-or-death conflict, unconscious energies possibly seeing him through, potentially empowering him against past and present and future evils. But nothing was certain. It never was in this line of work. Some children made it. Others didn't.

Private time in his office, an hour before beginning work each day, allowed Gabriél to gather his psychological energies, prepare for a day's work. Images from the mind's depths floated up during the uninterrupted quiet. Gabriél watched for them as one spots trout lingering in the shady parts of mountain streams, set to be caught by a sensitive and unrushed fisherman.

The symbols and images whispered what the day held in store. This one—a circle in a circle with an X in the middle— warned of trouble. Its nefarious meaning laced itself through the atmosphere like a finely woven spider's web.

Turning, he opened a locked filing cabinet. It held the private records of over one hundred children, chronic childhood trauma the common denominator. They had suffered years of beatings, black and blue, bloody, burned, violated in every orifice imaginable. Samuel Fuentes had been drugged and lived through his narcotized mother trying to cut a hole between his scrotum and anus. She wanted to crank her right middle finger inside, couldn't, settled for his anus. She used her thumb knuckle to finalize her orgasm.

Crazy as a loon and arctic cold, the psychopathic mother admitted it all bold-faced to a judge who graced her with permanent quarters at the Infierño State Hospital for the Criminally Insane. Fortunately, Samuel had been rescued by Mother Juana's orphanage. He bonded to Gabriél as his therapist. The road to recovery would be long, painful, yet hopeful. Gabriél firmly believed that Samuel could be helped despite his desperate state.

And Mother Juana made the impossible possible. She had taken a particular interest in Samuel. Mother Juana was a woman strictly devoted to caring for those she called "little angels in the making." Gabriél was proud to be her son.

He decided not to pull Samuel's chart. Sometimes, merely opening the cabinet was enough to set the therapeutic wheels in motion.

The image in the sand tray tugged for attention. He looked its way again. Lingering on the image, he sensed which direction to go.

He went to his bookcase, randomly pulled from the center shelf a thick leather-bound volume by a linguist, Frederick Thomas Elworthy. It was on ancient superstitions. Gabriél read where it fell open.

> *… in the Medusa's head we have the germ of an armorial device… It is easy to see how it became adopted practically. The belief in the power of the malignant eye, especially of a furious foe, needed something to be held up before it, which should absorb the poison of the first glance. What then so effective as a strangely attractive pictorial device, to be carried in front of the warrior on his shield, on which might alight the dreaded eye?*

Talismanic drawings were used by ancient cultures to ward off curses of which the evil eye was the vilest. Gabriél took a deep breath. He looked again at the sand tray. A circle within a circle. An X in the center.

He got his things together, locked the office, and left for the orphanage.

Something terrible was brewing, and Samuel was at risk.

CHAPTER

3

Sister Thea surveyed the dining hall, keeping the fifty preteen children orderly and obedient by a look, a nod, a thought. Her head-to-toe black woolen habit was a fortress. The children believed she knew their every action, reaction, thought—pure and impure. Many whispered that she read minds, could see straight into the soul. And she permitted that thought to grow in their vulnerable minds like a divine weed never to be uprooted.

She was six feet tall. Her chalky, severe, heavily lined and frowning face had been compared to holy card pictures of Saint Gertrude of the Huns. No one dared cross her. And she liked it that way.

The wool habit felt comfortable and warm. It was the middle of summer in Infierño. Even in the hundred-degree heat, the thick cloth was excellent; it made sister Thea suffer as the Almighty suffered. Earthly penance brought eternal bliss.

It would wash away her guilt, the Archbishop of the Ecclesia Dei always said after their monthly meetings. Guilt was simply unnecessary. The Almighty understood.

"After all, we are all merely human," the Archbishop concluded with a wink. He had encouraged Thea's vocation.

After talking with the Archbishop, Mother Juana had accepted Thea into the Order. Thea had direct access to the Archbishop. Frequently, they spoke of the goings-on in the Order, Mother's old age, Sister Thea's stellar administrative abilities, and the future of the Order.

Sister Thea was next in line, the Archbishop promising to appoint her—a faithful daughter of the church—Mother Superior of the Order of Las Mujeres de Dios.

Glancing out the east windows, Sister Thea thought of the orphanage's thousand acres of barren desert punctuated only by the occasional stands of scrub oak, gramma grass, and poisonous locoweed. It was the realm of madmen and prophets, the Gerasene demoniac and the Savior, the type of desolate place that men and women of the Almighty down through the ages had haunted.

Training her eyes back on the children, she swept her gaze from one end of the plank-floored hall to another. She smiled slightly. Pain was a great teacher. The children knew to never, ever deceive the Almighty or any of his representatives on earth. Responsible only to Mother Juana, Sister Thea relished her position. Daily, she thanked the Almighty for her calling. It was untainted, perfect.

Faithful to the spirit of their patron, St. Martyrkus, a medieval crusader who championed the religious orthodoxy of the 1563 Council of Trent, church members considered themselves the one and only true believers in the one and only true faith. They were now thousands strong internationally. Their International Chancery, its cathedral in the center of Aztlan, the largest metropolis in the desert Southwest, was evidence of their powerful spiritual presence in a fallen world. Sister Thea loved her church, her vocation, her unique calling as an earthly representative of the Almighty.

Spotting something, she clapped her hands once. The burst was sudden and hard. It echoed through the high-ceilinged room. The children startled. Pointing the long and gnarled index finger of her right hand, she aimed it at one boy.

Immediately, he stood up. He was rigid, blanched, in front of a center seat on a long wooden bench. Little knees and legs quivered. Eleven other boys at the long plank table stared wide-eyed. No one moved. Frozen in place, one and all.

The boy remained in position, legs together, hands at his side, eyes straight ahead. Seconds passed. The quiet hurt.

Spiritual joy shot through the stolid nun. Sister Thea treasured her vocation. It brought so many delights. At just the right moment, milliseconds before the stinging silence faded, she curled her finger, motioned to him. Samuel Fuentes walked forward, to the wooden lectern behind which she stood. Thrill coursed through Sister Thea. Disciplining boys and girls, helping them along the path of purity, was her mission. Her heart raced.

Samuel came, stood before her, face down, guilty. Pubescence was a filth-ridden time of life. This five-foot-two, twelve-year-old *mestizo*, had to learn a spiritual lesson. He was one of the many of those of mixed Mexican, Indian, and distant European heritage. Impurity blackened the soul, a lesson that mixed-blood heathens needed to be taught and taught well.

He had been touching himself… again.

Joy vanished, and rage thickened. Sister Thea's upper lip curled, her brow furled, and her teeth clenched as her right hand twitched—the hand with which she slapped brown faces and made them red, bright red with long fingerprints.

Hands, boy's hands especially, were to be kept in full view at all times, never on one's lap—never near the occasion of sin.

Holy rage gripped tight.

Quiet deepened the terror that flooded the dining hall. All eyes were on Samuel, burned holes in his back and brain. All would suffer for his misdeed. Drops of sweat poured from Samuel's hairline and brow. A minute passed, the silence a guillotine over wide-eyed heads.

Finally, Samuel broke. Fear-laced tears streaked his dirty brown cheeks. It was a skin that never got clean, real clean, white clean. The Almighty's spirit moved through his little, tainted soul. Wetness blotted his crotch, then his pant legs, then the floor.

Sister Thea tingled with pleasure at the brown boy's misery. No one moved. Then she clapped her hands, this time more harshly. Terror-stricken, everyone stood. *So satisfying.* "At your places… kneel." *Uric air suits these never clean heathens.* Knees cracked on the hardwood. "Arms extended in front of you. Penance must be made, for when one sins, all sin. Arms straight out. Ten prayers, ten bows, ten strikes of the breast… begin."

Arms trembled, and voices wafted into the dry atmosphere then disappeared as though souls were being sucked out of bodies.

Sister Thea smiled.

Gabriél locked the door of his ten-year-old Chevy truck. The ride to the orphanage hadn't taken too long. His mind had been on his work, eager to talk with Samuel. Gabriél knew that being there for the boy session after session, week after week, would eventually thaw his frozen heart.

Although the orphanage was in pristine Aztlan desert, the place and its atmosphere felt terrible. Gabriél wondered why his mother had chosen such a vile site. Even as he gazed around, he knew that the country was not fit for man or beast. There were no animals or birds, no rustling wind, no slithering snakes or mice or lizards. Sunlight seemed lusterless, dead. Air smelled of sulfur and things long dead.

Tugging the handle, Gabriél made sure the truck was secure. Uneasiness crawled over him like ants on a cottonwood tree. It always did here. Well-worn and scarred brown leather briefcase in hand, he walked the long downhill path past tumbleweeds and patches of cacti camouflaged by layers of sand and off-white clayish soil. Each step brought a puff of white dust that rose and then disappeared as though unseen agencies had sucked it into an invisible orifice. Gabriél couldn't help but shudder at the thought, a millisecond of fright and tingling that ran up his spine like the crazed ants.

It had blown hard last night. He had barely slept once the unholy sounds started whipping through the air. Gusts screeched through northern Aztlan like crazed women gashing at themselves and pulling out their hair for reasons unknown. The image of the women, bloody and insane, pressed itself onto the white screen of his mind. He didn't know why the vile vision came, but it always did as he began his walk toward the orphanage.

A full moon, at midnight, was the only time such horrific wind ever kicked up around here. No one ever explained the nature of the event, what caused it, or where the winds originated. But sure as the night grew dark and frigid cold, religiously inclined folk secured their houses and remained close to hearth, home, and loved ones lest they be injured by or lost in violent wind storms.

The orphanage secretary had sounded a little spooked when Gabriél called yesterday to confirm the appointment. Night winds had nearly torn her trailer park home to shreds. She hadn't slept all night and was skittish.

Gabriél kept up a steady pace but couldn't yet see the orphanage. Set atop a sprawling mesa, the parking area, about a quarter-acre of desert cleared for visitors, and the buildings were a good way from the semi-cloistered compound. The nuns wanted it that way. Hidden in the bosom of the Almighty, they said. More like a windswept hellplace, Gabriél always thought.

Soon, the orphanage's front adobe wall peeked out from the distance. Its black wrought-iron archway looked like the monstrous eye of some cruel deity. Never did it cease to amaze Gabriél that not one nun, including the Reverend Mother, admitted seeing the grotesque image.

Two dried-out, wind-ripped, uprooted yucca blocked the steep path. Gabriél pulled them out of the way. Strangely light, hallow, they seemed as if their insides had been blown out, crusts of the stalk caking its tip.

Gabriél's breathing became labored. His lungs ached. His lungs always ached up here. It was a feeling of compression, then shooting pains along his ribs. He pictured a hand gripping around his chest and gradually applying pressure.

He had asked his physician about the aches and pains.

The man chuckled, shook his head, and said nothing. No evidence of coronary concerns ever showed up in his annual physical exams, so Gabriél surmised the symptoms were more than physical. His doctor didn't understand matters other than physical. So, Gabriél stopped asking and knew the answer would come at the right time, when he was ready to listen and understand.

One day when leaving his doctor's office, he remembered what his own psychotherapist in Chicago had said. After relating a dream about lung pain and difficulty breathing, Arwind, an old and wizened man, sat back in his leather chair and stroked his white beard. An eternity seemed to pass before he stated, "It's a spiritual matter, Gabriél. Air is spirit, and difficulty breathing signals a spiritually diseased state, an inner imbalance, or the workings of an outer contaminant—a malignant energy."

Gabriél deemed Arwind an incarnation of a wise man and spiritual guide—primal wisdom first encountered at his father's funeral. Even now, he pondered Arwind's wisdom, its meaning still unclear. He recalled the words of the white-bearded spirit spoken to a frightened little boy, *I WILL HELP YOU AS A BOY. I WILL HELP YOU AS A MAN. LISTEN.*

Stopping to catch his breath, Gabriél looked down from the narrow plateau on which he stood. Both sides dropped into a deep and desolate arroyo. It would easily swallow both man and beast. Earth-brown plastered adobe buildings dotted the landscape straight ahead. To his sides, the sharp drop-offs shot him through with vertigo. He looked down to the ground, focused on a rounded piece of shiny obsidian. Apache tears they were called. Rolling down either embankment a good twenty to thirty feet with sharp and pointed sandstones at the bottom wasn't his idea of a good time.

Breaths drew hard, then harder. Lungs ached. They didn't use to. Once, Gabriél could hike any trail without breaking a sweat or losing a breath. Those times were a fading memory, something he hoped would return with time and effort. But he wasn't sure time and effort would pay off. More than decency and courage were at work here. It was a realm ruled by human desolation and wayward powers.

Things came only with tremendous effort, especially here in the remote habitation of the nuns of Las Mujeres. Nothing happened without troubles for the religiously inclined, Gabriél believed. What his mother believed and how she lived was her business. He was here, at the orphanage, to help children.

But he couldn't deny that the psychic atmosphere of the area affected him, extreme depletion pouring into joints and ligaments like leeches set through the central nervous system. Perhaps, even unconsciously thinking about the nuns, their incessant work habits, and need to sweat their way to their Almighty Deity tired him. The nuns seemed to never need to sleep or eat or engage in regular human interaction. Weirdly enough, anyone in their near vicinity often complained of weariness and eventual exhaustion.

Strange but true, Gabriél often wondered if visitors didn't sacrifice energy to the nuns. It was a bizarre thought, one that Consuela had first mentioned at dinner one night. It clicked with Gabriél. Yet, he didn't know what to do about it, so it drifted off and away like so many things Consuela mentioned. He shook his head, cleared his mind, and caught his breath. The weariness eased, and he walked on.

He was skillful at overriding bodily pain. Consuela often said, "When the mind is in pain, the body cries out."

Mind-body phenomena were the subject of his master's thesis. Research shed light on the fine line between mind-body and the paranormal. Consuela would quip, "You're the therapist, Gabriél. But a little reminder about William James, father of American psychology, stating that behind everyday reality lies the influence of an unseen world." She'd turn and walk away just like she'd told him everything he needed to know in that simple statement.

Gabriél chuckled, his heart lighter as he thought of his widely read wife, and how much he loved her. Quick to truth she was, much faster than Gabriél's grasp. He scratched his head at the veiled meaning behind her message. He was a trained psychotherapist and understood the unseen world, the transpersonal unconscious. But there was something about what Consuela said—matters from an unseen reality related to his illness. Hopefully, he'd catch up with his wife's wisdom sooner rather than later.

Consuela was a twenty-seven-year-old beauty, green-eyed, sandy blonde, and bright, very bright. She loved Gabriél, and that was why his mother was put off by Consuela. Pounding her fist gently on her desk during private conversations with her son, she tried to cast doubt about Consuela's love. Status, economic stability, for one *thing* or another she had married Gabriél—but not love. To Mother Juana, only one love mattered. This much was clear to her son. Consuela cared not a whit about such rants. Mother Juana had met her match.

Consuela, for her part, never spoke ill of Mother Juana. She just never spoke of her. All that mattered, Consuela would tell Gabriél, was their love for each other. They married each other, not each other's families. Gabriél, influenced by her steadiness and sincerity, sensed a slow change *taking* place in him. He never thought anyone could influence him as strongly as his mother.

Mother Juana felt it and didn't like Consuela's attitude. When she did speak to Consuela on those rare occasions they saw each other—baptisms, weddings, funerals—she said was praying for the Almighty to soften her heart.

Consuela always smiled softly and kept her distance.

One time, at a wake, Mother whispered a snide something in Gabriél's ear. Consuela's eyes flashed white-hot. Mother Juana's head jerk back. Gabriél swore he had heard his mother's neck bones crackle and pop. Mother Juana left shortly after that, saying she had taken ill and had to return to the convent.

Once, in a heated moment, Mother Juana barked out that Consuela was a witch. Consuela merely laughed and replied, "I'm no witch—just a woman who knows how to protect me and mine." Her eyes brightened, and Mother Juana left.

Gabriél considered this normal mother-in-law and daughter-in-law tension. Consuela disagreed. It was mother love gone bad. She said no more than that. Gabriél didn't ask.

In the quiet of the night, in their bedroom alone, Consuela would voice concern that after seeing his mother, Gabriél was always drained. Their sex life was dying. It was especially distressing after Gabriél had an extended visit with Mother Juana. He'd be exhausted, unable to love.

Gabriél didn't understand.

There was so much work to do—the needy children. Regular meetings with his mother were a must. She was the Mother Superior of the order that cared for the county's indigent and homeless children. It was his job, and he had a growing family to support.

Consuela was in her third month of pregnancy, their second

child. Their first baby, Cuauhtémoc, was four years old and lively as a high-desert roadrunner on a sunshine-filled spring morning. The boy was pure joy for Gabriél and Consuela. Mother Juana called him her little angel. For months before Gabriél was able to help him feel safe, Cuauhtémoc would freeze, his eyes growing wide as though fear-stricken when he saw Mother Juana.

He would dart behind his mother's skirt when Mother approached. Consuela wrapped Cuauhtémoc in the safety of her simple cotton dress. She kept her gaze on Mother as she tried to lure the child with a smile and a piece of hard candy in the palm of her hand. Mother would sneer at Cuauhtémoc's rejection, refuse to acknowledge Consuela, then stand up abruptly and leave.

Medical complications forced Consuela to remain in bed some of each day, and Gabriél and Consuela agreed that once she delivered, she'd stay home and not return to her work as a physician's assistant until their children were school age. Then she'd return part-time.

Gabriél was solely responsible for their livelihood. Readily, he embraced his responsibility, but somehow a burden was associated with supporting his family. It ought to have been a challenge, one that energized him not depleted an otherwise vital man.

He wondered about the effect of his mother's private conversations. Somehow, they succeeded at instilling doubt in a devoted husband's heart. She planted thoughts about Consuela as a homely local girl who desired only the status of marriage to a professional gentleman. It gnawed away at a rational man's mind, depleted energy. It was nonsense, but she was his mother, and mothers never meant wrong. Mothers loved their sons and always meant well.

Fortunately, the county paid administrators more than social workers. Money for the needs of his family was sufficient, the personal drain mental, a psychic conflict with physical repercussions. Sooner rather than later, Gabriél intuited, he'd break free of this ordeal. Yet, thoughts of what had happened to his father flew through his mind like accursed flies.

He remembered what he told Consuela—things would let up. His time and energy would improve. He did his best to believe it even though it often seemed like a wild stretch of the imagination. One day he'd have uninterrupted family time, play ball with Cuauhtémoc, and take him fishing. There would be long talks and plenty of loving with Consuela. These were reasonable expectations for a man often interrupted by professional demands. Breaking free of the pernicious energy that twisted through his brain and sucked the juice out of life and love was both a challenge and a necessity.

Walking on, he realized how lost he had been in thought. Head crammed full of worries from moments earlier, he was swept into a disorienting mental whirlwind. The pristine turquoise sky above and red clay earth below flipped places, east and west tumbling over each other. A quick shake of the head righted his dizzy mind.

And then he stumbled, slipped on a loose piece of sandstone. His right ankle and knee buckled. Pain shot up his spinal column to the back of his neck. It hit hard, then stopped. He waited, right knee dropping to the ground, fingertips giving a shaky balance.

He moved a little without slipping again and finally stood upright. His kneecaps were popping-point tight. Everything in this haunted region felt outside of his control, including his own shaky body. It was a taut bundle of fibers and nerves. Nothing felt dislocated, so he continued on, cautiously.

There appeared along the white screen of his mind an image of a circle within a circle, an X in the middle. The talismanic drawing flashed bright as an Aztlan sunrise. *An armorial device. A shield on which might first alight the dreaded eye. Protection against the invisible blow.*

For Samuel and himself.

A sharp light hit his peripheral vision. Someone stood beside him, to his right. Shock and blinding desert sun sent sprays of red, yellow, and blue lights across his visual field. Squinting, he looked to his side.

No one was there, yet he'd felt a presence, seen something—a white hue, a person set into the sun's glare. Images of a young boy at his father's funeral burned alongside the edges of his memory banks. Like a watchful guardian, a white-bearded man raised his eyes and both hands to the sky, fingers spread. Ripples of bluish electric energy flew up from the ground through his core, into his palms. He then touched Gabriél's solar plexus, a psychic power center, and hot currents pulsated through his frame.

Mother Juana's son wasn't welcome here. The nuns despised unbelievers. But he came to see Samuel, and nothing or no one could keep him from that. Gabriél's solar plexus tightened, bearing straightened, and he walked on.

Lately, he'd had mishaps and weird happening on these grounds. A month earlier, two practically brand-new tires had gone flat without reason. No holes anywhere, the mechanic reported. They hadn't gone flat since. A time before, as he trekked uphill, a coyote sprang out from behind a lone silver sage. Foam curled around the edges of its mouth. It growled and snapped at him. Then it disappeared against the sun's glare, vaporized into rarefied desert air.

Eeriness—a stepping into a netherworld—always got stronger, the closer he got to the compound. Mother Juana said devils prowled the perimeters of sacred sites trying to discover a way in. Perhaps devils, foul energies, had tripped him. Gabriél was conversant with psychic phenomena, a realm of spirits both light and dark where life and death often hung in the balance.

CHAPTER

4

Out of nowhere, Sister Thea appeared at the orphanage's black wrought-iron gate. She had a way of materializing out of thin, dry high-mountain air like a burst of grit and grime on an otherwise crystalline bright day. The gate bordered a central courtyard.

As Gabriél walked toward it, he felt a sudden chill. It was a cold grip in the gut that reached to his backbone and twisted. Always, it caught him off guard. Usually, he convinced himself he had masked it—the start and twitch. Inevitably, the nun spotted the subtle and slight shoulder tension and facial wince. She was a predator swooping down on prey.

A tight-lipped sinister smile crawled across Sister Thea's face. Gabriél loathed having to see her. Her scowl reminded him of barbed wire. Harsh desert sun had dried out the perimeter of her mouth, splitting and crinkling ashy skin.

Unexpectedly, a thought shot to mind. He wondered why he bothered to help hopeless kids. Far more experienced administrators and therapists had given up on the "behaviorally indecent desert castoffs." *Behaviorally indecent desert castoffs*? He didn't think or speak of his patients in such a twisted way. The thought weighed on him like a one-hundred-pound bag of rocks set across his shoulders. He shrugged, the sinister energy dropping away, dissipating.

Sister Thea's smiled loosened and widened, eyebrows arching. Her mouth opened—a pernicious orifice. Images of her religious antics crowded into Gabriél's head, Thea yelling at children as she forced them to their knees in prayer and jettisoned sexual thoughts into their minds. In her green-linoleum classroom of forty children, she clapped loudly, startling the wide-eyed students. Exerting her formidable mental powers, the towering sister of the black cloth excited the adolescents, titillation shooting through their loins.

Then she shouted, "I know of your impurity—nasty, brown heathens. Lift your hands and arms in front of you and do not lower them." She silently paced around and through the rows of kneeling students for the next twenty minutes, arms hidden in the sleeves of her religious habit. Fidgety children trembled as they tried to comply with the fearsome nun's mandate. Gabriél could never prove his intuition about the second-in-command, but he could set his mind on doing what he could—helping the orphaned and forgotten to heal.

As he had with Samuel, he considered having the children brought to the mental health center for therapy. For the children, it would offer respite from the tyranny of the nuns. However, transporting over twenty children per week for mental health care could prove impractical, negotiating therapy time with school schedules a formidable task. He wouldn't see them as often, monthly at most. That would be like battling a mental-health hellfire with a squirt gun. The healing of the psyche required intensity, consistency, and time.

He shook loose from the confusing thoughts that always landed on him right before he reached the front gate. He did what he did for the children, otherwise they didn't stand the slightest chance to make it through life in one psychological piece. As he touched the wrought-iron gate, an icy finger traced a curlicue pattern down his neck and upper back.

One second the gateway was locked, the next it creaked open as though released by an invisible hand. It emitted a high-pitched-then-scratchy sound like in the old horror movies he watched as a kid. Many a childhood Saturday afternoon, he'd spent at the downtown Infierño movie theater when Mother was preoccupied with monthly full moon activities. She and Las Mujeres would gather late into the night at some secret location. Gabriél would stay overnight with a friend whose mother was not in the cult.

Gabriél tried to push the gate all the way open. A resistance surprised him, pushed back a little, then didn't, giving way only inch by inch. It toyed with him, had a mind of its own. This place was a haunted realm of invisible and sordid energies that afflicted flesh and blood and objects and atmosphere.

Sister Thea, forbidding and temperamental as ever, sternly posed herself ten paces behind the gate as a concentration camp guard dog. She was the embodiment of cold, mean, and ambitious. Mother Juana knew of Sister Thea's religious ambitions, did not care for the woman. She confided to Gabriél that Thea was on a tight leash. Tethered to the nunnery, Sister Thea left the convent only when the Archbishop called for her to engage in a *particular ministry*. The Archbishop had his code words, Mother said with a smirk, never questioning or intruding since giving the Archbishop his way always paid off. The thought of Sister Thea and the Archbishop turned Gabriél's stomach as he closed the gate and turned to face the stolid nun.

He nodded. Sister's Thea's face reminded him of a hideous gargoyle. He'd once seen it, peering from a rooftop, along a sizeable Infierño plaza lined by small stone homes dating to the time of the Spanish Inquisition. The nun watched, waited, and connived from afar and up close and personal, either way suiting the power-ridden sister of the black cloth. She stepped forward and stood in front of Gabriél, blocking his path.

He moved around her a few steps then stopped. A hate-filled stare burned a psychic hole through the back of his shirt, like noonday sun through a magnifying glass. A quarter-sized patch of skin throbbed in his back. He turned to meet her stare, her eyes appearing black with red irises.

Impassively, Sister Thea stood stolid and stern, arms nestled into the loose folds of her thick black wool sleeves as she glared at him, irises an inflamed crimson. This wasn't new. Unnerving encounters happened with all the nuns. They materialized out of thin air and also conjured freakish incidents. From a distance, one of the sisterhood would stare at a person who had spoken ill of the order or sneered at a nun. The unsuspecting soul quickly found themselves in a precarious situation, knees buckling as pains shot through their midriff. They would double over in agony. Other instances, Gabriél witnessed a car sideswipe an anti-cleric pedestrian, then mysteriously disappear down an alleyway, a nun inevitably watching from a safe distance. Once, he'd seen a gossiping schoolmate's mother pass out and snort like a pig. From that day on, children and parents called her *la demonia*—the nuns exacting an infernal toll.

"The dark side of the archetype," Arwind, in his sagely manner, had called it. With each passing day, Gabriél grew into the reality of the old wisdom. The nuns had their own brand of dark powers, Mother Juana the only one who stood apart.

Maliciousness curled through each encounter with all the nuns save Mother, the tiny diamond in a rubble of black coal. Mother was the reason the order lived on and prospered, her reputation far and wide that of a compassionate and generous, yet administratively, tough woman. Gabriél, thankful for her kindness, could depend on her altruistic motives. Grateful for the determination she'd taught him, he grit his teeth and shook his head at Thea.

His gaze swept past the walls of the enclosure. The air was dry, and the sun beat so hot that heatwaves curled through the atmosphere. They were like undulating blasts out of an ether sphere. He returned his focus to the matter at hand and noticed Thea's unblinking stare, a twinge of disgust flickering across his shoulders. The contrast between desert heat and her religious frigidity was stark.

This freezer-burned nun tolerated Gabriél because of who he was; otherwise, she would have long ago barred him from this secluded site. As he matched stare for stare, he noticed her right thumb twitch, a little tell perhaps. He chuckled to himself. Twitch likely was due to the strain of masking murderous impulses.

However, Gabriél was not the only target of Sister Thea's barely suppressed hate. This ready-to-pop-her-cork nun aimed for all creatures of the male species. Plainly, she didn't like men and specifically didn't like Gabriél. More than one man had expressed this opinion over long, cold sips of a favorite microbrew at Los Ojos Cantina.

Sister Thea clenched her hand and made a white-knuckled fist.

To boot, Gabriél smelled her bigotry. Like rotting alfalfa stood the white-lordly missionary to brown-skinned infidels. Mother Juana was her superior only on paper. Gabriél chuckled, shook his head, and let a strong-willed, cantankerous attitude bloom, a talent and a gift. And it was undoubtedly deemed insolence by one who considered herself beyond male contestation.

Sister Thea—stiff as a board—had a foul, if mostly silent, temper. It burned like dry ice on flesh. Her eyes did the speaking. She incinerated anyone who crossed her infernal path, most notably those of the non-white males of the species.

Las Mujeres prided themselves on their solemn, ascetic ways—The Almighty's Militia, tough as nails, impenetrable as the Vatican Bank. Sister Thea, was nearly the toughest of the tough. Word in town was some preferred intimidating encounters with Mother Juana to this stolid ax of a woman. She reigned tall, imposing, and fearsome.

The *frozenest* of the frozen chosen, Gabriél privately quipped.

He broke the stare and broke the silence. *"Buenos dias,* Sister Thea." She hated it when he talked *Mexican,* she'd snapped off one day to another nun. The second he'd spoken what was widely considered the language of love, freeze turned to whatever lay beyond the realms of blistering iciness. A hideous look rippled across her face.

"Gabriél." She nodded impassively, saying his name with a harshness that would've made Jesuits of the Inquisition bend the knee and vow servitude.

Another second's long silence. Gabriél relished enduring such quietude. It was mere seconds but cut to the bone of Thea's haughtiness. Quick twitches beneath the folds of her habit fessed up, index fingers uncontrollably flicking off mounting tension.

Gabriél smiled. "We're always at such a loss for words, Thea." He paused, smile widening, then mood-switched to hard and to the point. "So, here we are. No need to go inside to review matters. Let's get down to the issue at hand." He shot off a harsh glance and opened his satchel and rifled through for Samuel's manila folder.

Dust kicked up around the park-sized courtyard. Tiny bits of grit and gravel swirled like legions of minuscule demons. He leafed through the papers as a nun's rage curled through the atmosphere and made the air dance with devilish frenzy. Grit quickly dispersed into a handful of dusty funnel cones that lurched over the white-stuccoed wall.

Edginess ground down and bit hard, the hairs on Gabriél's arms and neck stiffening. Sister Thea's poison seeped beneath skin and into muscles and bone. It penetrated like a viper's fangs into human flesh. The mind was a powerful thing, and Thea used it like a crazed but strategic surgeon with a finely honed tungsten knife.

He couldn't find the file. His heart quickened. He distinctly remembered putting the manila folder in his briefcase after pulling it from the cabinet in his office. Heartbeats rang through his ear canals. He never left the office without the right paperwork, and now a file had vanished. Neck muscles tightened, hurt, and he grew flush, then looked up.

Sister Thea watched, didn't blink. Perhaps she never blinked, or swallowed, or breathed, or slept. The way her habit stopped centimeters short of the ground yet still hid her shoes, perhaps she didn't even walk—simply levitated and glided.

Childhood memories of parochial school classmates whispering their private musings about their ethereal teachers—the nuns—crowded into Gabriél's mind during his weekly visit. They, the nuns, relished being thought of as supernatural creatures. At night during bad dreams and the worst of nightmares, the women of the loping black cloth haunted the psyches of children. They blasted their threats of hellfire for the slightest infraction, such as chewing gum before Mass or looking too long at a pretty girl. There was no way out of damnation for those who bit that party line.

Gabriél was grateful for his father's declaration that a god who condemned people to a hot hellfire was the figment of the cruel imagination of hateful religionists. Such sordid folk took out their misery on gullible souls. That teaching, from a sincere old man, insulated a young boy's mind from religion. The teachers of the old religion espoused that a youngster indoctrinated from birth to six years of age would forever belong to the church. To that, his father replied that everything depends on the parents, their allegiance to love or ecclesia. Parents, not religion, shaped the soul, his father had taught, and Gabriél was his father's son.

A quick instant, then from the corner of his eye, a shimmer formed an image of an old man who smiled and touched fingertips to ears, lips, then heart. Pride and determination lit through Gabriél, his mother's face flickering in the far-off distance and then disappearing like an inconsequential dust mite. Both images startled him, one nurturing and the other scrutinizing.

Gabriél zipped the satchel closed, would discover later how the file had disappeared. Usually, he pulled the pink visitation slip from the folder and submitted it at the front desk. Today, Thea stood watch. The slip had to be presented to her and signed off. It was a formality. Everyone knew who he was and why he was there, but it needed to be done as a matter of record.

"I'm here to see Samuel." The words stumbled out, shouldn't have, but wasn't surprising. He was flustered. The file was not only missing, but the misstep made Thea's superiority complex swell. Prejudice was a rapacious demon.

Dust flew again, and a high-pitched screech like ravenous desert coyotes echoed through surrounding sandstone canyons. Chills rippled up Gabriél's back and arms. Bursts of sand shot up from the center of the courtyard, near the substantial concrete fountain planted with low-lying cacti. Yet, beyond this small, twelve-feet-in-circumference confine, there was no wind.

Sister Thea arched her right eyebrow and sneered. "Here to see Samuel… That won't be possible."

Gabriél grit his teeth. He had never been refused access to a child for therapy. Not only was he the son of the Mother Superior, but he alone placed over half of the orphanage's residents. To boot, county funds second to church donations sustained the orphanage. To refuse Gabriél access to one child threatened the convent's standing.

"And why is that, Sister?"

"Mr. Fuentes is no longer with us." She uttered the words with perverse delight.

Gabriél's stomach twisted.

CHAPTER

5

W aiting in his mother's study, Gabriél drummed his fingers on the arm of the badly scarred old oak chair. He wanted answers. Samuel's discharge could not have happened without his knowledge or agreement. He was the licensed behavioral health care provider whose signature was required before releasing a child. Under state regulations, Samuel Fuentes was a patient under professional treatment. Impatience intensified, fingers tapping nervously along the blackened arm of the spindly chair.

Gabriél was beyond keyed-up. None of the children under his psychological care had ever been released without his signature. It was illegal. He couldn't imagine his mother condoning such an act. *Disposed of*. Yes, that was the term that made the most sense, hit square on Thea's underlying gist—

disposed of. It was like Samuel had been done away with.

Samuel was no more than five feet tall, skinnier than a dried-out twig from a felled cottonwood, and about as needy and vulnerable as any child who had been neglected and abused by a severely deranged mother. A child in this shape wouldn't have had the emotional wherewithal or money to run away. Besides, running away would have left him with nothing and nowhere to go. The nuns, despite their meanness, offered the children a roof over their heads and piping hot meals. Lack of safety and security could wreck a child's psyche and trigger a psychological collapse.

Samuel's release was beyond Gabriél's imagining. It was traumatic for a child to be separated from his therapist, much less torn away. Gabriél's professional responsibility required that he know the whereabouts of each and every patient. He helped to ensure their stability and well-being and took this responsibility seriously, especially since those cared for by Los Mujeres de Dios were by his referral.

Sister Thea hadn't been forthcoming about any other information concerning Samuel. Dismissively, Gabriél had been directed to Mother Superior's quarters. She would clarify the matter, Sister Thea defiantly asserted. The vile nun had emotionally sideswiped Gabriél.

Evidently, Mother didn't know about this and would be as outraged as he. Mother took Gabriél into her confidence in all matters and would do nothing behind his back. They were a divinely ordained pair, church folk often quipped, and although Gabriél despised the reference, he had to admit their working together generated many a wondrous happening that helped needy children and their families. Construction projects benefiting scores of homeless, food donations feeding hundreds, and thousands upon thousands of otherwise lost dollars found their way into appropriate agencies, once Gabriél had returned from training to work with the venerated Mother Juana de la Cruz.

He looked around the bedroom-sized, white-plastered, concrete-floored chamber. The only light came from the stained-glass window near the door. It shed one shaft of intense dark red through the center of the room, inches from Gabriél. The sight of it generated a shudder, a quality of violence emanating from the dark radiance.

Images flashed hard and searing across the white screen of his mind. Ghosts, wraith-like beings, scores of children packed the room. They filtered through walls and up through stained concrete flooring. One by one, they sat in the very chair in which he now squirmed. They entered Gabriél's body, his mind, injecting him with unutterable trauma. Silent, mute, they seemed to have had no tongue or voice box. Arms and legs strapped to the chair, they fell back and over by the force of their rocking. A terror loomed, one to which Gabriél was not privy.

Faceless adults hovered around and witnessed the horror, indistinct specters. Gabriél had a way of seeing things that had happened in the past or would occur in the future. Being a seer had its moments—quite good and terribly bad. And more times than he wished, what he saw wasn't good. Seeing prepared him for what likely lay ahead, provided a clue as to what a child had gone through or would go through.

Of course, this was nothing he told anyone. No one would believe that sightedness into things past and future was a real ability; instead, he waited and pondered what he had seen. It was a way of nestling truth close and letting it cook. Then, psychic perception could silently work its magic.

Ever instructing about psychic insight, Arwind had taught

him about natural magic and said that silent knowing was the most potent of medicines when mixed with a sincere intention. An image of the old man's flickered, a surreal presence enveloping him, prompted a quick gasp. Since childhood, the Wise Old Man, archetypal presence and spiritual guide, came during times of need.

Arwind's revelation clicked inside, intuitive understanding prompting an acceptance of things unfathomable by the rational mind. Insight resonated, and its echo always kept on for days and weeks and months and years—made truth, truth.

The dynamic images of traumatized children from seconds earlier returned to front and center of consciousness, pulsed through his mind and body. Soon, a more settled consciousness took hold, psychic sensitivities regulating, calming. Gabriél took note of the fact that the rigid hardwood old student's chair was the only thing to sit on. There was not and never had been another seat in the room. Not that it had ever been different from this, but for some reason, the fact of the old chair and its history now loomed ominously.

He tried to rock on the old chair, back and forth. Strange, he had never noticed before, but it wouldn't budge. He looked down and saw that no nails or screws held it in place. Standing up, he gazed at the rickety piece of worn furniture. It tilted, angled back as though by an unseen hand. Blood surged to his face and ears, blood pressure at a high pitch, mouth dry, heart racing. He felt chilly and cold, wiped his eyes, opened and closed them.

The air was stifling, breaths forced. His head spun, nausea curling up his esophagus and into his mouth, a metallic flush of saliva inciting an instant gag. Pains spiraled across his forehead as red and yellow then white lights sprayed out at the periphery of his vision.

Then the chair sat stationary. He touched it, tried to tip it. He grabbed it hard, then harder trying to force a wobble or crack the damn thing. But as it remained eerily unmovable, the scarred-wooden seat suddenly flashed with swirling faces of abused children and screams from open mouths that made Gabriél bend over with dry heaves. Repeatedly he gagged and heaved, the body's automatic response to empathic terror and unrelenting horror.

Children had suffered for years, decades, perhaps in other places at other times for generations. The Cross and the Crown of the dark side of religion took its toll and did so without care or conscience. Wiping the back of his hand against a dry mouth and lips and steadying himself, he looked once more and saw merely scratches and deep indentations in the wood, made by frantic gestures, but simply gouges and grooves, nonetheless.

He bent down to look even closer at the old piece of wood. Never before had he noticed that the armrests also had scratches like those of human nails digging deep into the wood. He grazed the depressions with his fingers, some deep and others slight. They all emitted desperate and frenetic energy. Quickly, he lifted his fingers, removing them from the wounds to the old chair that seemed as if they would bleed, if wood bled, and would wail, if inert matter could emit sound. It was a horrid little chair of evil magic and hidden tortures. The tips of his fingers were hot and blackened as though burned by the pain of ages past and present times when no one observed, and few souls hazarded to inquire.

Fingertips throbbing, he bent down and ran the palm of his hand against the chair's spindly legs then took them by force and shook. There was no budging, and all fingertip pain ceased. Uncurling his hands from the chair and gazing at his fingers, he saw healthy pink flesh with slightly calloused tips. Eyes shifting back to the chair legs, they looked like they could be snapped in two by a person with a robust set of arms or by raising the chair and slamming it on the brick floor. The image of doing violence to this piece-of-shit furniture pressed upon him so hard, his hands and arms trembled with fury. He tried again, squeezed the legs of the chair with all his might, arm muscles bulging. He should rip it up off the floor and raise it high and crash it down. Over and over, he should slam it to the floor, destroy the shit-piece of furniture.

The seat of the chair shifted once again, took on a face, curls and swirls of wood grains twisted and mimicking. It became a single-wide mouth and grinned. And the mouth opened and there were teeth, and the teeth drooled blood. Gabriél gasped and flung himself backward, landing on his backside, mind and body trembling with rage.

Mind riveted, he saw that the edges of the chair legs were worn so that the corners gave way to roundedness. Immediately, white-hot intuition posited that they were from people rocking, violently. Image after image of horrified souls kept here, strapped down, interrogated then disposed of, lighting up bright on the white screen of his mind.

Frenetically, he scrambled back on his haunches, farther, then farther from the chair, backside dragging against worn, stained, and cold brick flooring. He shook his head, nausea starting another course from gut to mouth. The room spun, faster and faster. His head snapped back uncontrollably, sharp pains radiating down his neck, breathing labored then catching, ceasing. He passed out for a brief instant, head bobbing up, then down, waking him. He rubbed his neck and eyes and leaned against the back wall.

Surely, Mother had to know the nunnery had at one time been the site of oppression and torment, akin to the Spanish Inquisition, in Aztlan centuries ago. Perhaps Gabriél's visions had tapped into vestiges of energy from that era, haunting remnants of emotional memories trapped in floors and walls. He knew that such things happened at sites where violence had been committed.

Half of the furniture in this place dated back to times before Aztlan has been a territory of the United States. No telling how far back some of the old pieces went, but it unquestionably had absorbed the physical and mental suffering of many an innocent victim. The horror writer, H. P. Lovecraft wrote of the manner in which wood and stone in a room, beams and furniture and flooring, soak in the intense emotional reactions of the residents. Rageful and murderous acts leaving terrifying psychic traces that registered on sensitive minds.

The chair, the seat of unthinkable sorrows, torment, and tragedy was directly in front of Mother Juana's beat-up oak teacher's desk. A black foot-long steel crucifix with a silver corpus hung on the wall in back of the desk. The god on the cross hung as though having been cut and pasted into place, a thought that always ran through Gabriél's mind during times of conflict with the nuns. For purposes known only to them, they stuck everything and everyone into place. They were control freaks of the religious type. He winced, then chuckled to himself. At least his sense of humor was returning, a good thing and then maybe not. Psychological minimizing, in all its guises, never a good thing.

Hand to thigh, he got to his feet. Empathic sensitivity to people and places could be tough on body and soul. Never had this place felt so dreadful. Something needful and necessary was psychically popping in a grown man's mind, things moving from humdrum to high-pitched as the world of the unseen made its play, spun out a blazing fastball yet to hit a bull's eye.

Straightening his posture to full height, he composed himself. He had to leave without a trace of mental unsteadiness. A steady mind generated a clearer perspective, for him surprisingly accurate and symbolically spot-on. Ushering psychic sightedness forward, he knew the chair held its own ghostly life.

Mother Juana must remain in charge of this nunnery with its sordid past, help to ensure it wasn't once again overrun by a demonic will to power that had haunted its corridors for centuries. The visions of seconds earlier brought the point home—Gabriél having to stand by Mother Juana de la Cruz for the sake of the children.

Controlling others, dominating them, was all-consuming for nuns like Sister Thea. Religious power was realer than real, controlling matters of eternity and salvation. Thea's ghastly presence today had driven home this truth. Mother kept her, and those like her, on a tight leash so the good that needed to be done would not be thwarted or subverted. Few mortals could handle the power of religion and not be corrupted. Mother was such a person.

This wasn't the first and would not be the last head-to-head run-in with the *divine women of the black cloth*. They were determined to undermine Mother Juana's mission to the poor and needy. The black steel crucifix, a source of inspiration for Mother Juana, was artifice for the other nuns, an outward prop that obscured reprehensible aims.

He looked up at the religious symbol hanging on the wall behind Mother's desk. His stomach tightened. Gabriél didn't believe in a god on the wall, or in the church, or in a roll being called up yonder. Common sense had put an end to all that. No one with a whit of conscience could buy into a supposed deity that did nothing but serve the purposes of a motley crew of priests, ministers, gurus, or rishis.

Mother Juana didn't mind. Gabriél's meanderings, she called them. She said the Almighty was different things to different people, love was all that mattered, her beatific smile disarming and full of compassion. Gabriél knew she was a true humanitarian at heart, despite her outward contrivance of religion. He figured religion was what she used, a necessary means to achieve essential ends.

Gabriél glanced at his watch. 9:25 A.M. He'd been waiting ten minutes. A child had disappeared. He was hard set on a clear-cut answer. *Or else.* Gabriél de la Tierra was the son of Mother Juana de la Cruz. No one else commanded the unobstructed ear of the formidable woman. She would hear her son out and reprimand the person responsible for such an insufferable act.

His mother—an ascetic who lived on three hours sleep a night, a daily cup of milk and a slice of bread, and three or four hours a day in prayer in front of the Tabernacle of the Almighty—was a spiritually prodigious woman.

Asceticism, fasting, and prayer strengthened her tough-minded soul. She was as fierce as the desert prophets of old. To scholars of religious studies, she was reputed to be like eastern yogis lying on a bed of nails, walking on coals, meditating without end in a Himalayan cave. She drew psychic powers from severe discipline.

Confronting Mother Juana—which Gabriél rarely did—was like trying to stop the north wind's howl through the Rio Grande Gorge. It left many a tough-minded man as the fool before the sage. More than once, his internal organs twisted and knotted up after speaking his mind to Mother. It was like a darkened chamber of horrors. You wished you hadn't gone in, felt as if there was no way out. You left scathed—soul burnt.

The door creaked open.

The hairs on the back of Gabriél's neck stood on end. Quickly, he sat back on the chair. He clenched his teeth so hard his jaw ached. His heart pounded like a scattering of wild horses.

Mother walked silently into the room. There were no footsteps. It was as if she glided over the cracked and waxed concrete flooring, her body motionless. Hands nestled into the folds of her habit's black woolen sleeves, her face was obscured by the covering of the cowl.

Gabriél stilled his breathing. He did not fidget or speak. He looked forward, eyes to the floor, not turning to gaze upon the mindboggling force that was Mother. Her presence overawed even a beloved son. She stood behind Gabriél, her presence now subtle as a specter. The smell of her black woolen habit, human perspiration, slightly sour and baked-in, wafted through the atmosphere. He stifled a gag, then the reflex subsided. Beads of sweat formed across his brow.

Mother's warm hands rested on his shoulders and head. He settled in the chair, comfort permeating his frame. Mother Juana loved her son. This was her ritual. She whispered prayers, and tongues of fire danced through Gabriél's mind, flames flickering as tiny ephemeral deities. Iridescent wisps glimmered hypnotically, and he lost hold of consciousness.

His mind slipped away for three or four seconds, repeatedly, before he pulled and tugged himself back to consciousness. His head bobbed as though he were caught in a hypnotic trance. Motherlove had lulled a grown man into a stupor. She called it *slain in the spirit*, a loss of consciousness preceded by head-to-toe relaxation. It was hypnosis far more potent than any technique introduced during his graduate training. He wasn't the least bit enthralled by clinical hypnosis, considered it an intrusion into the mind, a forced entrance; but with his mother, things were different. She used her hypnotic rituals and prayers for good, not for evil.

Prayer in a mystic language and a mother's loving touch soothed Gabriél's restless soul. She knew when he was wrestling with doubt. She took care of all, and it went away. Gabriél felt quieted, assured. The hardiest of souls could not resist the allure—bliss.

Mother Juana stroked the side of his head and face. "Bagabi laca bachabe lamac cahi achababe karrelyos." The repetition was intoxicating. "Bagabi laca bachabe lamac cahi achababe karrelyos. Bagabi laca bachabe lamac cahi achababe karrelyos." Intoxication lingered then went in deeper, tailings of nervous unease dissolving.

Seconds or minutes or hours later (time stood still with Mother Juana's prayers), Gabriél was as a ship returning to port. He slowly opened his eyes. Spiritual highs had been commonplace throughout childhood and adolescence, induced by Mother's exquisite touch and prayer. It was always the prayer, the same prayer, *Bagabi laca bachabe lamac cahi achababe karrelyos*. The words were her words, her touch, entrancing—bliss.

Mother.

CHAPTER

6

M other Juana sat behind her desk, lips whispering unceasing prayers, eyes riveted on her son. Brown and piercing, the corneas glowed a luminescent black. Gabriél's studies in religious phenomenology spoke of the light emanating from the eyes of mystics, Mother's a numinous black, darkness penetrating. His neck muscles tightened and twitched.

The Ecclesia Dei did not condone the mysticism of Las Mujeres, laying on of hands, and routinely performed exorcisms, but neither did it interfere. The church hierarchy dare not intrude with the rituals of Las Mujeres, lest there be a withdrawal of spiritual protection, the women of the black habit the real powers behind the pomp and circumstance of the male-dominated religion.

Mother Juana's reputation within the Church was that of

holy woman, prophetess, and miracle worker. Families around the world claimed her spirit visited them as they slept, healing physical and mental ailments. Cripples were made to walk, blind able to see, arthritics and sufferers from common illnesses, such as chronic colds and headaches, restored to health and vitality.

Due to Mother Juana's reputed miraculous feats, the Church's Chancery Office in the city of Aztlan annually received over ten million dollars in contributions. It was an excellent source of revenue. Mother Juana's esteem in the eyes of the clergy brought power to the convent gates, the lowest to the highest of clergy and politicians doing her bidding.

Gabriél could not move or speak. Since childhood, Mother Juana's prayers exercised strange effects. Gabriél savored the moment, an unearthly delight. Tingling coursed from the top of his head through his frame, core muscles easeful, head bobbing slightly. It was a psychic intoxicant, what the old yogis spoke of as an *amrit*, a natural opiate secreted from the pituitary gland during *samadhi*—pure consciousness and bliss.

It was spirit possession, Arwind bluntly had stated. Mother Juana's prayers activated the mother complex, the old man asserted, light and dark states of bliss at times indistinguishable. Gabriél's mind resisted the old one's wisdom regarding Mother. Arwind insisted intoxication left Gabriél under her spell, a kept man.

"Decisions make the man, Gabriél," he asserted as he had many times before. Gabriél found himself always resisting the old man, his plight in life if what the sage-like therapist said was true. Making the mother cut, having what it took to do what needed doing, would demand hanging from life's edge, no way out but the unthinkable—the unbearable.

Trained by C.G. Jung in Switzerland, Arwind, a seasoned practitioner of forty years by the time of Gabriél studies, cautioned against returning to Infierño. He warned him about ongoing spiritual possession by a dominating mother. The wise-old therapist advised, "A man isn't a man until mother ties are cut. It's you or her, Gabriél. Decisions make the man."

"People have their gods. Your mother is yours. She possesses you." Never had the old man been so curt. Gabriél had wanted to run, stop treatment; but his feeling for Arwind was strong, an odd affinity with the old man, his countenance strangely familiar from the first moment they'd met. Opening the door and entering his office on the south side of Chicago was stepping into a hallowed realm of one whose eyes conveyed a no-nonsense understanding.

Even back then, Gabriél had learned to squelch his pain, the pinpricks that shot up between his legs whenever speaking of his mother. He remembered squirming in his seat many a time in the sage's consultation office. It prompted Arwind's *use 'em or lose 'em* mentality, an age-old wisdom that Gabriél recognized as freeing many a man. But one who needed no freeing had no need of such knowledge. He learned to sidestep the learned healer, but attempting to hide from the old man was like trying to hide from the sun in a searing desert.

Arwind's gaze would intensify—white light like the sun. "Kill the mother-god, and man lives. Then and only then is manhood earned." His eyes never left Gabriél's, silently conveying a still-to-be-lived-out truth. Such times shot Gabriél full of hatred for the gray-and-white haired sage, an emotion immediately quashed. Gabriél recognized transference-based hate, a dynamic he should have put into words but did not.

Gabriél asserted, "I've taken the good and let go of the bad." Words rang untrue even as they stumbled out. It was as if they had been scripted. It was a desperate attempt to cling, to hold on white-knuckle tight as though already hanging from life's edge. "I am my own man, no else's... my own man."

"No. You are not your own man. You are hers. When she calls, you run. And the god calls. And she is calling."

"She is no god."

"She is the most powerful kind. She gets into you, into your mind. Twists, pulls, consumes. By her side, you feel strong. Without her... nothing."

In their last consultation session, the old sage reaffirmed, "A man isn't a man until the mother ties are cut, Gabriél." He said it spryly. A smile crossed his face, and he cocked his head and raised his eyebrows. He sometimes did that. It was his way of saying listen, or the worst will get hold of you, surprise you when you think you're most free and clear.

Gabriél had more than a few disagreements with the old man. In his consultation office overlooking the University of Chicago, the psychotherapist would lean forward in his worn blue leather chair, eyes full of compassion and firmness. There was no doubting his sincerity, but Gabriél alone knew his mother.

Gabriél had drifted, consciousness a long way off from the convent and Mother and the room and the chair as he mused about his former therapist and teacher. Awareness returned, and with it, a subtle but definite shock at how even now the old man in all his guises called, beckoned, strove to break through mental barriers.

Vaguely, first from a distance then closer and closer, he heard Mother Juana praying louder, fervently. Her prayers called him back into the closely knitted world of mother and son. It was as comfortable as the earthen smells of Mother's adobe office. The image and feeling of his old teacher faded, and Gabriél rested in the bosom of the Almighty, as Mother Juana called the heady sense of soothing and ecstasy. He let himself be pulled back, resisting Mother fruitless. Gabriél sat in peaceful oblivion. Tingling caressed him head to toe, spring rains on a parched desert.

After a time, Gabriél slowly opened his eyes, smiled at Mother Juana. He loved her. Those who judged her ruthless were mistaken. She was a good woman, a woman with her own ways, a woman of mystery.

Gabriél glanced around the room, joy saturating his being.

Mother Juana smiled back.

Mother Juana, psychically hot from an energy influx, held Gabriél's gaze, clasping her youthful hands tightly in prayer. They glowed on the desktop. Gabriél had fed her. Beautiful, translucent skin that many said radiated the light of holiness came at a price. Gabriél helped pay that price. Unceasingly she prayed for her son, as had countless saintly mothers for their sons.

Then the sons would stay faithful and provide youthfulness for their mother. Gabriél would do as other sons of devoted mothers had done. It was inevitable, but she needed more. Mother Juana hungered for the children, their energy, the innocence that fed her vitality. It was more than her son alone could provide. Without the children, she weakened, age creaking into old bones like rats gnawing on wallboard.

In decades and centuries past (she had lived long, was an immortal, and no one could convince her otherwise), things had been harder. Sometimes, she had been able to mentally reach into the womb, suck out the essence, but not always. Her powers had been more limited then. Bloodshed had been required.

Now, the spilling of blood happened only occasionally. Unusual circumstances required brutality, and Mother delighted in cruelty—for old time sake. Samuel was such a naughty child. And Gabriél had a way with Samuel and all of them, the children. They liked him, were drawn like tiny iron fragments to the magnet.

Since Gabriél had been a child, he had brought children to his mother. She helped them. With her hands, she helped them. With the laying on of hands, she took out what she needed. They left her home quiet, obedient, no longer rebellious. Parents brought their children from far and wide, and mothers and fathers thanked her. Many doctors did. Some didn't.

Unbelieving doctors called it childhood fatigue syndrome—the loss of energy, pleasure, and desire to live. Some children became schizophrenic. A few lost the will to go on and died. These cases were hidden away, never spoken of. Secretly, believers whispered that it was the Almighty's way of sifting wheat from chaff. Good children readily took to divine grace. Bad ones didn't. So, strong ones stayed, and weak ones blew away.

And Juana de LaTierra's reputation grew. She gained followers. Las Mujeres de Dios was founded. She assumed superiorship and took a religious name—Mother Juana de la Cruz. And children instinctively feared her. Gabriél helped with that. He believed in his mother, her mission to the forsaken and lonely. Distraught, confused, little ones were convinced to be cared for, prayed over by Mother Juana.

They came to the orphanage because of Gabriél, as they had because of the mental health center administrator before him—the silly man who dared to doubt and lost everything. In times to come, Gabriél might be finished, used up, his life taken by an act of the Almighty and his own thick-headedness. There would be another to take his place.

Cuauhtémoc.

Despite Consuela's protests, Mother Juana had Cuauhtémoc at the orphanage one day each month, Gabriél forcing the issue with Consuela by insisting children needed their grandparents.

Cuauhtémoc quickly took to the other children, developed many playmates, and enjoyed his times with his grandmother. *"Mi abuela,"* he'd say, throwing his arms around Mother Juana. She nestled him close, ever so lovingly and tight, warmly squeezed in the folds of her religious garments. Cuauhtémoc, body and soul, trusted his abuela. She had plans for him, many, many plans that could shift at a moment's notice depending on turns of events and critical decisions executed at propitious times.

For now, Gabriél was Mother Juana's extension in the world. He did what she couldn't, and the children came. He loved her, believed in her. But he did not believe in the Ecclesia Dei, had witnessed clerical corruption one too many times. Mother Juana understood, the Ecclesia for her merely a vehicle, the most expeditious way to gain trust.

And as for the Almighty—belief in a higher power—-Mother was that power.

A medieval saint had said that a boy indoctrinated from birth to seven would turn into a man loyal for a lifetime.

Gabriél was such a man—Mother's man. Their bond was airtight… Or nearly. An electric thrill shot through Mother Juana, the leak of the past four years—Consuela—soon to be rectified. Mother had her ways.

Gabriél sat before her. Without her, he was nothing. He knew that. And that was good. Very good. Mother Juana towered above, Gabriél spiritually nestled in the palm of her hands. "Do not worry about your health. Poor and desperate children need you." Gabriél hadn't mentioned his fatigue. Mother Juana pierced his innermost thoughts. Reading right through people came easy, a feeling, a strong impression emanating from the center of her forehead down through her core.

Otherworldly powers were her stock-and-trade. Searing between bone and marrow, mind and soul, she cut to the quick, left no doubt who was in charge. She knew how and where to hit. "Your wife doubts your strength. Be careful."

Gabriél's brow furrowed. As she turned to walk out, Gabriél strained, "But… Samuel?"

Mother Juana stopped at the edge of her desk, the quick, sidelong glint of her eyes causing Gabriél's head to jerk. Samuel and Gabriél had gotten far too close, Gabriél too significant to the boy. And Mother didn't like that. It had to be stopped.

Gabriél was hers alone and not permitted to form particular friendships (marriage an annoyance temporarily tolerated for the sake of precious Cuauhtémoc).

"There is nothing more for you there."

"Where is he?" Gabriél pushed the issue.

"In the hands of the Almighty."

Shock snapped Gabriél back to his senses. Mother Juana peered down at him as she stood beside her desk. The fingertips of her left hand balanced delicately along the corner of the antique piece of furniture. "I trust you will be there tomorrow for the Procession of the Holy Innocents?" She'd brushed away his question casually as if shooing off a fly. What mattered to her was the next project, the coming agenda, whatever Mother's heat-seeking missile of a mind deemed pertinent.

Annually, the church held a procession on this feast day through the streets of Infierño, a parade of over thirty priests, the Archbishop, a hundred or more altar boys, and over one-hundred nuns. Celebrating the Holy Innocents—children massacred so the Savior could live—the festivity highlighted Las Mujeres and their divine work. Mother Juana would give the invocation, and donations would stream in like minnows to a stocked pond.

Even as she asked the question, Gabriél noticed her frenzied look, eyeballs zigzagging maniacally like one possessed. He had no choice, for revenues helped children obtain the needs that otherwise would go untended, something Gabriél's professional and personal conscience would not permit. He nodded affirmatively. His presence, in its own way, lent credibility to Mother and her order of religious women.

At times, he had to admit, he was struck by a distinct sense of being used by his own mother, a community leader in professional standing affirming the validity of the Order and its mission. Even now, he automatically winced at the notion, one so troubling yet so recurrent and insistent. He'd be there, he wouldn't let Mother down.

Her eyeballs abruptly quit their jagged display, Gabriél's

mind made up. She read straight through him, into his intentions, motives—an unnerving relationship with a formidable mother who had done so much for so many, including her own son. *And I am my mother's son.*

Mother Juana turned away and walked toward the door.

Gabriél remained in his seat, stunned and beside himself with the experience of Mother. Her presence proffered no escape. He didn't so much as turn his head when Mother left the room, the door clicking shut. Her presence evaporated quickly for one excelling in imposition and persistence. She was gone, the slightest psychic vestige of her dissipated.

Shaken and troubled, his thoughts returned to Samuel. Gabriél had to trust Mother, he had no choice; he was her son and had no choice. He thought of Consuela. He wondered about Mother Juana's warning. Pinpricks shot through his groin, and he tried not to think anymore. The pain refused to fade, and he thought of Consuela again. As her image grew more vivid, the feeling of the woman he loved, the pain vanished.

Clouds passed across the tiny window behind Mother's desk. The sun dimmed, and an unnatural hue stained the room. Gabriél looked down at his hands folded on his lap as a shaft of light turned them crimson.

CHAPTER

7

Samuel's breath came hard. He'd had run to the ancient red rock mountainside bordering the Chama River. Looking for his father, he had taken a chance on where he'd find him, ran to the place where his father often went to drink and think things through.

Once Samuel's mother had been institutionalized, his father had no one to drink with. So, he carried on by himself at the river, drank and cried liquor tears. It was a grassy place hidden beneath a stand of Russian olive trees and cottonwoods. Old ghosts, ancestors, talked to him there. They set his mind straight, his father said.

Samuel feared the shadowy place. But he had nowhere else to go, to run for help and safety. An hour earlier, after prayers, Sister Thea chided Samuel in front of the other children. Then, holding Samuel by the shoulder, she dismissed the wide-eyed brood. Alone with the shaken boy, she grinned. It was time to do penance.

Samuel had felt light-headed, unreal, as though he were seeing and hearing from miles away. Those who were called to penance disappeared. Sent to Mexico, some said, while others claimed horrifying things—chained in a desert dungeon, abandoned outside the orphanage gates for the devil to take, buried alive—things that made a kid never want to disobey a nun again.

In the classroom, Sister Thea had demanded penance from Samuel. She sent him to gather his things from his room. He had twenty minutes to report back. *Or run.* A dark, windowless corridor led to the quarters he shared with three other boys. There was an exit door at the end of the hall. He tried it. Locked. He went to his room. Seconds later, pacing the linoleum floor, he had an idea.

The janitor, Old Snarl-Tooth to the kids, was down the hall, whistling and mopping. The guy was older than crumbled sandstone turned to dust and slow as a backyard turtle. He was also hard of hearing and weak in the eyes as the smudge-streaked floors showed.

Nighttime ghost stories about Old Snarl-Tooth flew around the orphanage like tumbleweeds on a windy day. Mainly they said he was a medieval gargoyle brought to life. He helped the nuns run the place and keep everyone in line. Ancient as Methuselah, with a face as black-brown and wrinkled as a sun-dried catcher's mitt, he looked the part.

Some kids said the yellowish-brown slits that passed for his eyes didn't need to see, and his big floppy ears didn't need to hear. With his mind, Snarl-Tooth saw through walls. He heard things up to a hundred miles away, picked up the slightest ungodly thought.

Samuel had had to risk it.

He cranked open the tiny window in his bedroom. It was right next to the outside steel door. Reaching as far as he could, he slapped the door, banged on it. Samuel knew what the old guy would do. He'd seen him do it before. Just last week, someone let loose a couple of hard knocks, and the rickety custodian propped his mop against the wall and lumbered down the hall and cranked his head out the door.

No one was there. They had gotten impatient, and the janitor mumbled loud enough for Samuel to hear. Prankster kids figured they hadn't been heard and ran off content that they'd pulled their prank and not gotten caught. Now Snarl-Tooth surely would look up and answer the echoing whacks. It was Samuel's only hope. He needed out, knew where he'd go, and with any luck find help and refuge from the nuns.

Pulling his hand back one last time, even though it would sting badly, Samuel walloped the cold steel door. The janitor heard it this time; the whistling ceased, footsteps squeaking down the linoleum corridor. "I'm coming. Be right there," he shouted out best as a wheezing old man could. It was no more than twenty paces to the door for the strange old codger.

Samuel waited for him to pass his partially open bedroom door. Crouched low, Samuel swung around behind him, quiet as a desert mouse.

Old Snarl-Tooth unlocked and opened the door. No one there. Confused, he called out, "Come on now. Who knocked?" He pushed the door open wide, propped it open with a nearby rock, and walked outside. Hunch-backed and achingly slow, he ambled to the end of the building and poked his head around the corner. Then he rounded the left side of the building, hollering out just as he'd done last week.

Samuel dashed out, straight back, out of Snarl-Tooth's

range of vision, and into the woods. It was a little over a mile run to the deep *bosque*, a forest of gloom and lost souls.

Samuel walked up a dusty path toward the river's edge. He spotted his father drunk on a patch of grass, steps away from the Chama River. It was a place in the shade and cool where no one would bother him. The old man didn't like to be upset. He wanted to be alone with his thoughts he'd often said, alone with his misery.

Out of nowhere, a wind kicked up. It was a slap in the face, then went around with a swift kick to the backside. He lurched forward, neck snapping backward, whiplashing pain down his spine. Pebbles and rocks flew every which way, then pebbles reared up and repeatedly smacked against his groin. Time after time, they drew back and then ripped forward lightning quick. It felt like an invisible hand gripped Samuel's crotch and twisted. Consciousness flickered off and then back on like a harsh overhead light. Hands flew from crotch to eyes. Protection from the light, bad light, impure and harsh. Bad white hit and hit and hit the center of his forehead. Nausea curled up from belly to tongue. He gagged, choked. His eyes felt wide as saucers, and bile curled up his throat.

His father turned, pointed past Samuel, and looked horrified as if something were coming. Samuel didn't want to turn and look. He feared what was there, seeing it in his mind—vast and black and ready to injure, then kill.

Bolts of pain tore up from Samuel's testicles to belly, jaws, and brain. He would not turn to look. Nothing would make him turn to look. The top of his head wanted to explode. It hurt too badly to cry, and way too badly to do anything but stand there. He was paralyzed. Pain grabbed him harder and twisted and churned through his belly. His testicles were in a steel vise, the world spinning round and round. He wanted to yell, he wanted it to stop, he wanted to make the evil time and the sick feelings disappear.

Then two invisible hands, cold and hard, pressed against his jaws and forced his neck sideways. Bones cracked until muscles threatened to snap. He saw what his father was looking at, dumbstruck, had pointed to seconds ago. Black funnel clouds drew close and blocked the sun. They merged, became one gyrating and vicious beast heading directly at Samuel. It pulsed with quivering lips like a huge and weird hungry nun.

It charged forward, a giant, gaping mouth. Samuel imagined himself swallowed whole, tumbling inside—arm-by-arm, leg-by-leg, head-from-torso—ripped to shreds. Then it stopped, hesitated, curved away, and took aim for his father.

Samuel cried out, "*No . . .*" His voice was like a sprinkling of grit in a windstorm. He was nothing before the force of the big and the black.

His father backed away, stumbled to the ground. Eyeballs bloodshot and bulging, he again pointed over Samuel's head. He let out a blood-curdling scream and felt the color drain from his bronze face. His flesh rippled from horrific wind currents slapping his face.

Heat curled through the riverside place like in a sweltering sauna. A flock of crows flew out of a nearby sagebrush in three directions at once. Low-lying grasses wilted, and sharp red sandstone ledges crumbled off the mountainside. They made sounds so loud that the funnel clouds appeared to jump with delight. They made the mountain appear to crumble, the grasses die.

Samuel's voice and breath caught in his throat. A giant shadow loomed high to his side where the funnel cloud had been. It had arisen out of nowhere, out of thin air, and came at Samuel, danced in circles around him, then skittered away, targeting with a fury of the north wind on a stormy night and his father collapsed against a sandstone boulder.

Earth vibrations sent out a ghostly moan, a trail of inhuman words, *Bagabi laca bachabe lamac cahi achababe karrelyos*.

One muted voice, "Bagabi laca bachabe . . ." Then many roared, "Lamac cahi achababe, karrelyos."

Seconds later, dead silence. Electricity charged the atmosphere. Samuel's hair stood on end, as did his father's, a man sitting stunned and mouth agape. Samuel wondered if he was dead.

Jolt after jolt of testicular pain shot up his spine into his head and back down through his stomach and backside. He suddenly felt reamed through with an electric cattle prod. Curling into a fetal position on the ground, he howled.

The nuns made bad boys pay.

It thundered, and black hands big as an earthmover rumbled out of the shadow now sky-high. The hands grew long, fingers outstretched horizon-to-horizon. Then they stretched down toward Samuel's paralyzed father. Backing up farther, his father dug his heels into the ground. He scrambled on his backside toward a cave near a bend in the river.

Samuel, arms curled into chest and legs pressing against his abdomen, pulled into a tight bundle of panic. The kids at the orphanage talked about evil and the Evil One. This was the Evil One. It drew out the soul, sucked people hollow—out the top of the head. Gutted, eyeballs and cheeks caved-in from the force. Victims were said to look like wild desert boar, butchered and left to rot. Sister Thea and Mother Juana de la Cruz said the devil would get children, and anyone with them, if they ever left the orphanage.

Samuel forced himself to his feet and yelled. His voice trailed down and into the ground as if inhaled by some underworld demon. His legs locked in place. He teetered and wobbled but kept his balance. The pain between his legs grabbed hold again, an invisible hand twisting and tugging. His eyes bulged, pressure excruciating.

Then, the agony ended. He saw a black cloud of dust sweep over his father. The old man's voice cried out weak and scratchy as a played-out old record. Then it was no more.

Heat rippled out of the earth. Violent waves of sun scorched the grass. Muddy river soil buckled violently.

He heard snapping, branches broke in two. Then tearing, meat was ripped from bone. Samuel's father was being shredded, whirlwinds of pitch-black evil spit out an arm, throwing it up in the air like a half-finished chicken wing.

Samuel squirmed, grit his teeth and trembled, lips glued shut.

Blood splattered over rocks, dusty ground, and charred cottonwood trunks. Blood whipped at Samuel, stinging his eyes and cheeks. His father's blood rolled down his forehead. He screamed and buckled to the ground.

He sobbed, remembering when he had often wished his father dead. A boy needs a father, not a perfect one, just a good enough one. Uncaring and gone were all his father ever had been—so he had wished him dead. And now he was dead, and Samuel was at fault. Samuel and only Samuel, *bad, bad Samuel... bad, bad Samuel... bad, bad Samuel...* Voices did not fade or stop, they screamed and yelled, they screeched like a woman's thin fingers with manicured and sharpened nails poking and piercing eardrums until blood dripped down his neck. But there were no nails, and there was no blood, and the hovering nuns and the earsplitting voices in his head forced Samuel's mind away, far away and back in time.

Awake and asleep, at home and on drugs with his mother, or in the orphanage—Samuel had cried out for his father. And when Father didn't come, Samuel did things with his mind—made it feel bad things, do bad things, and make things dead. Father *was* dead.

Samuel was a sinful boy. The nuns were right. His father was dead. And Samuel was a sinful boy.

Tears streamed down Samuel's face, the smell of old nuns drifting up his nostrils like moldering clothes or puddled sewage. Sweat and dust from prickly clothes and bits of phlegm flung from their screeching mouths smelled like an outhouse on a hot summer day.

Suddenly, his father's head flew out of the black swirl of dust and grit. It landed beside Samuel, blood-shot blue eyes staring, mouth agape. The head cocked backward and rolled away.

Voices from north, south, east, and west, from above and below, laughed and cackled like nightmarish monstrous hens. Vomit twisted up Samuel's throat, flushed through his mouth like raw eggs and sour milk. He wanted to vomit, and the heaves were violent but dry. Jolt after jolt of lightning-quick electricity slammed between his legs. Blackness hit, and sight vanished, and consciousness fled.

The next second, he came to, flat on his back. He rose upwards, gyrating wind currents twirling him in the air like an out-of-control kite. Vomit spewed out of his nostrils and mouth. Propelled into dark and cold space, Samuel gazed down at the world, withering, dying. A tiny dot on the horizon, the earth popped, ceased, and the pain between his legs was no more.

Then evil loosened its grip, let him drop. He was a stone falling to earth. He could not fly. He was a stone falling to earth, and the earth opened its black mouth, and Samuel plunged into a pit of children, wailing and gnashing their teeth.

Mother Juana de la Cruz opened her eyes. Palpable as a rush of wind, the power of the Almighty was present. Not yet noon, Mother Juana had saved a soul from damnation—bad caught and stopped. Mother's presence in the world held things together.

Incense from morning devotions lingered in the small, grotto-like, private chapel. Votive candles flickered in red glass as the tiny, humble woman in her modern-day cave, as Elijah on Mount Carmel, redeemed a fallen world.

Mother Juana de la Cruz was rescuing humanity from a single, twisted notion.

Freedom. It was dangerous. Bad. It left little boys and men untethered. Little boys and men needed their mothers, needed to learn that Mother reigned behind the scenes, needed to know and feel and pulse with the love of Mother— She who was everything! Little boys turned little men needed Mother.

She clasped her hands tightly, breaths quick and shallow, blood flushing through her face, warmth throbbing from solar plexus to brow point.

The presence of the Almighty was palpable as the flesh on the palms of her hands. She cupped her eyes and wept as shivers swept through her slight frame. Faceless voices whispered intonations, sounding clear as fresh winds through Abiquiu canyons, *Honor the Mother*. On and on, they sang, *Honor the Mother . . .*

Mother Juana sighed, her flesh further quickening and quivering. An intimate and fiery stirring and release accompanied the sacred words, *Honor the mother... Honor the mother... Honor the mother...* She yielded to the final shudder of body and soul, then nodded in affirmation of the divine words, head bobbing back and forth in a soothing rhythm of the lingering chant.

She was a favored soul, as had been the Immaculately Conceived One two thousand years ago.

And more.

She birthed the god, and the god was she. Born without sin, Revered Mother was destined for eternal glory: "All ages shall call you blessed." The Divine Son made sure of this. He had been nailed to a tree.

Devotion to and for the Mother knew no bounds.

And now, two thousand years later, it was a new era, a new Divine Mother—-Mother Juana de la Cruz was both virgin and god, past carnal necessities repaired, body restored. She was the Incarnate One, the son to serve her. And loyal sons sacrificed for their mothers. It was not too much to ask—precedence two-thousand years set—a son's life for the good of all, and the all was Mother.

As loud as noontime, Angelus, another interior voice, proclaimed, *All ages shall call you blessed*. Mother Juana de la Cruz trembled with holy joy at the sacred words.

As in the age-old story of the Savior, Mother Juana had

raised one boy alone, and now the new little one would serve not the Heavenly Father but the Revered Mother. Nightly religious rituals with arms stretched wide, Friday fasts, walking with pebbles in his shoes, and winter sleeps without blankets would teach him the value of suffering, as they had his father. He, too, would offer up to the Almighty bodily affliction and suffering taken up for poor souls lost in a forsaken realm of motherless sons. Singularly outstripping his father, he would transcend pain and let nothing deter him from Mother's mission.

As a boy and as a man, Gabriél beamed when he gained Mother's approval. Cuauhtémoc would outstrip, outdo, outman his father. And Mother would be proud.

Only in one matter had Gabriél ever dared cross Mother. Now he had to right that damnable wrong. And there was a way, one way, to repent for one willful wrong. Cuauhtémoc was such a good boy—docile, putty in *abuelita's* skilled hands. Grandmothers were so warm and unconditionally loving with their unconditionally bound little men.

Squeezing her eyes closed, she trembled as she dropped the prayer beads tied to her belt and made a fist that was stronger than any man's. She was Mother Juana de la Cruz. She was the left hand of the Almighty and mightier than the mightiest of the males of the species.

The father that had been her mortal father would have been no match for her now. He, with his imposing ways and harsh manner, would be no match for her now. He, with his dark and haunted gaze that made a little girl's skin crawl and ripple in the most intimate of places, would be no match for her now.

Him with his ways… Him with his ways… Him with his ways… Ways that happened in the ghostly and still times…

Ways that made minutes stretch into hours… Ways that poked and jabbed and twisted… And now Mother was the pain that poked and jabbed and twisted and twisted and twisted.

Eyes closed, Mother's second sight burned at the brow point as she gazed into things from afar.

Samuel awakened. His eyes flew open. Startled, he lay where he never expected to lay. His mind shattered, body maimed, a little boy awakened to the power of the Mother.

Samuel, now looking into the face of a black angel, had been disciplined.

Mother Juana stood and adjusted her black nun's habit, the cowl realigned and centered atop her sacred head. With Samuel, she had never lifted a finger. Targeted thought imposed torment.

Samuel had been punished; a boy chastened and chaste.

And mute.

CHAPTER

8

G abriél leaned against his truck, exhausted after having met with his mother. He wanted to rest a minute and think before driving the twenty miles back to town. Tension crawled up his neck to the sides of his head. He tried to relax. Stroking the back of his neck, he gently moved his head in circular motions, then side to side.

It only made things worse. The creep and crawl of tight muscles and shooting pain was nothing new. Since he'd become director of the Center, symptoms had started and steadily worsened. *Body pain-mind pain*, as Consuela frequently reminded him. He should be able to put an end to the chronic condition. But no matter how much he focused and strained, he couldn't get insight, couldn't find his way to the heart of this horrid matter.

What he knew was that Samuel was the third boy, he was

aware of, to disappear from the orphanage over the last five years. Mother Juana and the Order of Las Mujeres, under the auspices of the Ecclesia Dei, held legal custody of each child. To the law, what was done with a child was their business. But they had to show Gabriél or prove in court, if need be, that the child was safe and sound in mind and body. The nuns documented the physical and mental health of the children, including those who had mysteriously disappeared—*been transferred*.

The nuns meticulously documented everything in reams of reports.

Twice before, the previous mental health center director, Patricio Santistevan, had subpoenaed the orphanage's files on two boys who were there one day and gone the next. As expected, Sister Thea stated they had been transferred to another facility in Mexico. Santistevan had been the one in charge of placing the boys with Las Mujeres. He saw no reason for the sudden transfer. But the files were in order.

Sent to the missionary orphanage in Piedras Negras, Mexico, the boys were ostensibly learning agricultural skills. Pictures of both boys at a farm site, dressed in the orphanage's blue uniforms and waving and smiling at the camera, were glued to the inside front cover of the report.

There was nothing unusual or suspicious.

Santistevan wasn't convinced. He complained that the photos were taken from afar. Brown-haired boys in uniform were a dime a dozen at the orphanage. Specifically, Santistevan thought Sister Thea was up to no good. He didn't hazard to guess what precisely the intrepid nun had done.

It was well known the two didn't get along.

Privately, he complained that Thea was sadistic toward the children. The staff, counselors, and administrative aides in the center confided their misgivings about the nun to Gabriél. Santistevan was out to prove that Sister Thea was up to no good. He feared she was illegally adopting out the boys, securing a hidden source of revenue for the convent. He stopped the flow of placements with Las Mujeres.

Within a month, Santistevan was gone.

Supposedly, he retired without ceremony. After twenty-seven years with the county mental health center, he walked in one day and had the secretary type up his resignation for the county commission. He cleaned out his desk and left. His face was drawn and pale, a man defeated and mute. Mind-burnt, nervous breakdown, fellow social workers gossiped.

Six months later, the remains of his buzzard-eaten body were found near the Chama River. It was at a wind-blown place of tumbleweeds, sun-bleached cow skulls, and dome-shaped hills. Legend held that witches practiced their black arts there, turning themselves into coyotes and other wily creatures. It was a place of evil.

Centuries ago, tales passed on by generations of those from Aztlan del Norte said that, at this corrupted place, a woman made *un pactado con el Diablo*. The devil pact was sealed at a midnight meeting. The woman was bequeathed immortality. In exchange, she offered infant sacrifices.

Up to the turn of the century, infants reputedly were slain in their mother's wombs. Children were decapitated, adolescents eviscerated. Superstitious townspeople held that the evil woman stoked her powers by doing the *shameful thing*—kissing the devil's posterior. In return, the evil one gave her an incantation—el *maleficio*. It was conjuring with words in another language that summoned wicked energies. She captured the souls of children, life energy sucked from innocents. She grew radiant. They died.

As an immortal, she could never know genuine feeling—pain, loss, joy, and love. An unending world of grays, sameness, and isolation was her lot. Yet, she retained eternal youthfulness and magical powers of the dark variety.

With a sharp glance—*el mal de ojo*—the witch did foul things. She envied what she did not have, could not have. The evil eye sent sickness to the healthy, misery to the happy, and strife between lovers. A sharp look could stop the heart, curdle the blood, and drive a man insane. With her incantations, she captured souls, and with her eyes, ruined lives.

Santistevan's wife of forty years said that her husband ranted unintelligibly in his sleep about *mal de ojo*, the evil eye, and the witch-woman who called forth *el diablo*. For weeks, he hadn't spoken during waking hours. Doctors diagnosed him as suffering from chronic fatigue syndrome and a loss of will to live.

Then, one morning, he left his home and walked into the desert. He never returned. Friends and relatives suspected he just vanished, molecules of psychic life evaporating into the rarified atmosphere of high-desert Aztlan del Norte.

A rustling bush of scrub oak a few feet away drew Gabriél out of his reverie. A hundred yards outside the property lines of Las Mujeres, scrub oak and clusters of sage formed a semicircle. It wasn't unusual for birds to fly out of the bushes, for roadrunners to dash past the area like hellions out of Hades. Any of them could have made that sound. But today there were none around. Nothing stirred. Not a breeze.

Gabriél's attention returned to Sister Thea. He was sure Mother Juana strove to believe only the best about people, including her second in command. A nun's malice would not easily register on one so pure as Mother Juana de la Cruz.

Eventually, Mother would see through Thea and right this most terrible of wrongs. Things always corrected themselves, returned to a natural state of balance, Gabriél intuitively believed.

Samuel, in therapy sessions, expressed fear of Sister Thea. The black-robed plastic nun on one shelf of the sand tray would be placed in a mound of sand in the middle of the tray. In the top right-hand corner was a snake curled in on itself. Samuel would swirl the snake in the sand so it would make circles around the buried plastic nun. He bound her and her energy. Gabriél never commented, simply encouraged Samuel to do whatever he was drawn to do in the sand with the little figures and toys on the shelves. Samuel tried to protect himself, and now Samuel was gone.

A snap—loud—practically at his ear, startled Gabriél, his heart picking up its beats. Again—nothing in sight. He needed to leave. Opening his truck, he got in, put the key in the ignition, turned it. Click. Click. Click. Dead.

The battery was new. Gabriél had put one in last week after a similar occurrence. He tried again. Nothing. A sharp knock on his window and he twisted his head to the side. Neck bones crackled. He looked.

Sister Thea stood there, glaring.

Gabriél got out of his truck.

He'd been lost in thought and simply hadn't noticed Thea's impassive glare. He hadn't so much as heard a light step coming his way, a nun's steps imperceptible after years of regimented training. They walked as dark angels through the night. *Angels… Right.* There were more nefarious, apropos descriptors. She had stalked him, then materialized at precisely the right second.

He knew the reality of magic, both light and dark. But the eerie nunnery jacked up the meaning to a whole new level of psychic malignance. Consuela's presence was suddenly by his side, a supportive hand on his shoulder. She had a natural intuition, an attunement to both the good and evil facets of the mystic. It bore out in spontaneous forebodings, uncanny dreams, and unnerving insights that strengthened Gabriél's sightedness and resolve.

Sister Thea's beady eyes riveted on Gabriél like a viper ready to strike. Then, unblinkingly, she spoke, "Samuel is back with us." Her fingers twitched almost imperceptibly beneath her habit, quivers of little and index fingers in unison.

Paralysis gripped hard. Gabriél's rage brought a quick flush to his face and grit to his jaw. He'd been taught to nab and kill intense reactions. Mother said she prayed nightly that the Almighty's invisible hand stretched down from his heaven to quell Gabriél's anger. She knew he had a temper since childhood, outbursts sure as summertime monsoons. His wizened therapist had countered, *Rage is in your nature. You find your rage, you find yourself.* Arwind's words, the old healer's proclamations, were solid as Aztlan granite. *Decisions, Gabriél. Decisions. Your own man or hers.*

Sister Thea was a trauma.

Rage stayed, cooked. *Don't lose it. Use it. Target temper.* A quickening of atmospheric light, rippling sunshine, off to the left and behind Sister Thea formed a doppelgänger of an old man—Arwind. He had passed three years prior, soul presence palpable. C.G. Jung wrote of psychoid visitations as issuing from the ultraviolet end of the spectrum, a bridge between psyche and matter. Consuela grinned when he *psychologized*. "Whatever, Gabriél. It's the mystic."

A strange hush settled over the dusty expanse. The quietude pressed against flesh, past muscles and tissues and tendons and bone till Gabriél ached head to toe. It squeezed against ribs, and ribs pressed against lungs, and breath became halting. Lizards scurried under rocks. Sunrays seemed caught between heaven and earth, hues of dingy gray streaking the atmosphere. Caws from flocks of crows ceased, and the ache in Gabriél's body abruptly stopped.

It was as though hidden watchers waited for Gabriél's answer to the smirking nun. He said nothing. Despite his loss of strength, he refused to be cowed by Sister Thea, would stand his ground until the waking nightmare of Sister Thea passed.

In the center of his forehead, a vision flickered faintly. Arwind, old healer of ancient wisdom, appeared once again, flashed then dissolved into an interior ether sphere. Gabriél focused his energy, shook loose of the paralysis, then turned his head and looked off into the limitless desert horizon. He intensified his concentration, sun rays blistering across the harsh landscape.

He didn't trust Thea, a woman masterful with half-truths and disregard. From the corner of his eyes, he saw her unblinking stare, arms folded and immobile beneath her religious garb.

Arwind insisted that Gabriél learn to utterly trust his feelings, cultivate intuition—flashes of insight, persistent inklings, spontaneous images. The more Gabriél listened to his intuition, the more it spoke, a spark that could be stoked into a fire. Inner sight released an image along the white screen of his mind.

Samuel was on a bed, injured and bloody, but alive. Violence had been inflicted. Unintelligibly, Samuel groaned. The center of Gabriél's forehead burned, the place of the third eye, the sight of Samuel distinct as an eagle through a crystal-clear desert sky.

Rage surged. Gabriél turned to open his truck door, get his satchel. He locked the truck, then looked back to Sister Thea.

She was gone.

He hurried back to the orphanage.

"Lucky to be alive, boy." Old Snarl-Tooth stared down at a bed-ridden Samuel. "Some beast out there nearly killed you, son. I followed you. Got you back alive and nearly whole."

A lump of something was stuck in Samuel's mouth. He gagged. Fire shot through his loins.

"Go ahead. Spit if you need to. Throw up your insides if you have to." There was a grin on Snarl-Tooth's face as he put a trashcan by the bedside.

Fogginess tinged Samuel's bedroom. Leather straps buckled him down, arms and hands tight against the hard mattress. His mind swirled with memories of being at the bank of the river, his father's cries, being lifted into the air and spit out of an evil whirlwind. Maybe it had been a dream—a nightmare. Nothing so wrong could have actually happened. Perhaps this was all a bad dream.

Panic set in. Samuel hadn't realized it—at first. His mind raced to catch up with everything. Chest tightened, breaths quickened, cold sweat formed along brows and ran down cheeks.

Fear was ramped up and raw. He needed to run far, far

away, get going so no one would catch up. But he was tied to the bed. Squirming didn't help. Yells wouldn't come out. His voice stopped somewhere between brain and vocal cords. Between his legs felt strange, numb.

The door swung open, and Mother Juana walked in. "Did you put on the salve?" Without waiting for a reply, she added, "And more anesthetic down below?"

"Yes, Mother." Snarl-Tooth stood up, head bowed. "Just like you said, the blood dried up. There's no pain, far as I can tell. There won't be none tonight, either." Snarl-Tooth paused, looked at Samuel, and smiled evilly. "His tongue is gone, just a little curlicue at the back of his throat. And only dried-up bits below."

Samuel closed his eyes and, on the inside, wailed.

CHAPTER

9

G abriél left the orphanage, frustrated he hadn't been allowed to see Samuel. Medical staff assured him the boy was safe and under medical observation. The charge nurse related, "The doctor said the child was traumatized and is in shock. He needs rest."

Gabriél needed to clear his mind, going home for lunch an antidote to a morning of surprises and stress. He walked in through the back door of his small adobe, met by a caress of warm memories and hopeful anticipations. He loved coming home, the smell of tortillas cooking on the iron griddle in the kitchen, the familiar sound of the old oak floorboards as they creaked. The screen door glided to a close.

Theirs was a three-bedroom adobe at the edge of town. Over one-hundred-years old, the plank floors were uneven. The ceilings, although reinforced with hardwood timbers, sagged in spots. The place had been designated a historical home due to the fact that one of the founding families of Aztlan del Norte had once dwelt there. Reputedly, they were a raunchy bunch of wild-west Spaniards who cared little about customs, ritual or law, be they church or civil.

Many said their ghosts haunted the premises and made sure that whoever lived in their former dwelling was of stout heart and rebellious nature. The structure had withstood decades of blistering sun and severe monsoons. Blinding snowstorms made for long and harsh winters.

It was home for Gabriél and his growing family.

He turned back to look at the warped screen door, wasn't sure it had closed. There had been no click of wood against the doorjamb. It usually shut just fine but sometimes stopped short.

One night last week, he hadn't returned home from a board meeting until after midnight. He'd forgotten to give the door a quick check before going to the bedroom. A rattler squirmed into the house, gliding between the slightly warped wooden door and the frame. Sometime later, its rattle and hiss at the foot of their bed forced an unexpected awakening.

He smiled just as the old screen door inched forward and closed.

Walking into his enclosed study, he admired the room. Formerly a porch, it was now framed in and had three wide storm windows that let in plenty of desert sun, heating up the area during the winter. There were shades for the summer. Renovation happening before his time, he hazarded no guess on how a historic site had been granted a permit. He surmised it concerned the rebellious nature of the land and place—got what it needed and did what it needed to do.

Three yellow pine bookcases and a small pine desk spanned

the two-foot thick white adobe wall at the back of the room. All the walls were impenetrable. No arrows or gunshots were getting through that barrier. Back in the day, at least a century ago, Aztlan del Norte had its fair share of outlaws and warring Natives. Few folks were civil, and fewer still gave a spitting whit about life or limb.

He placed his satchel on the desk, glancing at the half-dozen Zuni stone fetishes arranged in a semi-circle at the top center. They were carvings of bears, a healer's familiar spirit. Consuela explained the myth surrounding each one when she presented another in a tiny gift box, usually on his birthday. In Native spirituality, the bear oversaw healing practices and protected healer and patient. The exquisitely rendered pieces of turquoise, jet, jasper, pipestone, and elk antler were earth symbols of his path as a therapist.

A wide-planked, scuffed and well-worn oak floor led down a short hallway and directly into the kitchen. The clanging of pots and pans echoed from one room to the next. The oven door opened and closed, a lovely voice singing, "Que Sera, Sera… Whatever will be will be," gracing the atmosphere.

Gabriél made his way into the kitchen and watched Consuela from the threshold. She stood at the sink, looking out the window at the backyard. She was a half-step farther back from the sink than usual. Pregnancy was showing. She was a beautiful woman, cheeks a little rosy, green eyes bright, bronze skin radiant. Her sandy-blonde hair was tied back, worn in a ponytail when she was cooking. It was near lunchtime, and Gabriél never came home for lunch. Consuela was preparing early for dinner.

He stepped into the kitchen, quiet as he could for a man in hiking boots. Consuela gave a quick turn of her head.

"Gabriél." Her voice was warm as a full embrace on a snowy winter day. Chills ran up his back and neck. Wearing a red plaid apron, she left what she was doing and went to him, arms immediately around his neck. A long kiss and a quick tightening of a hug before she pulled back and looked in his eyes, arms on his shoulders.

"Qué paso, lindo?" She stroked his face with her fingers, her eyebrows arching and eyes widening. Distress must be plain as a smudge on linen. He couldn't hide a thing from a woman who was both homemaker and seer.

Gabriél swallowed hard. He didn't answer, just gave her a quick embrace and kissed her on the cheek. Looking at the tortillas cooking on the iron griddle, a delicious and calming aroma, brought a smile to his face. Fresh tortillas and distress didn't jive.

"Thought I'd get a head start on dinner," Consuela said. She kept her eyes riveted on him, concern further creasing her brow. She'd wait for him to speak just as she always did. Not one to press for something a man might not yet be ready to talk about, she was a woman of enigmatic ways and perfect timing.

Gabriél moved to the griddle and watched the brown patches form as the lovingly tended rolled flour tortilla cooked to a savory roundedness. "Smells wonderful." Gabriél reached for the tortilla, now done on one side. He picked it up with forefinger and thumb and gave it a quick flip to the other side—a well-practiced landing on the hot iron griddle executed by one trained by a patient wife.

"Let me get that. You sit down." Consuela tapped the tortilla and moved it around a little on the griddle, more out of nervousness than necessity. Then with two fingers, she flipped it onto a pile of a dozen other tortillas stacked and wrapped in a white cotton cloth. She went to the refrigerator for butter then got two small plates from a cupboard and put tortillas on each before sitting with Gabriél at their small kitchen table. "Okay, time to fess up. Just tell me what happened. You look like you're just this side of death." Her gaze was warm yet firm.

She understood that harsh realities were the stuff of Gabriél's work and took their toll. A sensitive soul, she often talked about her studies in culture and spirituality. She had learned that ancient shamans were what they were, and did what they did, because they had spouses who were also seers and healers. Consuela kept the home fires burning and helped when the healer needed healing. She assisted him to gain and maintain a clear perspective. He supported their family in a way they both felt was true and meaningful. She was a wife, full-time mother, and maker of home, and eventually would return to full-time teaching by the inspiration of intuition and dreams.

"Where's Cuauhtémoc?" Gabriél didn't especially want to talk about the troubling events of the day right away. Consuela's quick, nearly imperceptible turn of the head and squint, signaled she'd been slighted. His head didn't feel clear enough to talk. He needed things to settle a little more before talking, not wanting to dump a toxic encounter on the most sensitive and loving of women.

He looked down the hall, toward the two bedrooms. He had hoped to see his son. Last night's board meeting ended much later than he'd anticipated. The day had come and gone without ever having talked to Cuauhtémoc or Consuela, save a quick goodbye before having left yesterday morning.

Consuela raised her eyebrows. "He's with your mother today. Remember?" Her voice had an edge to it.

Gabriél cringed. His mother hadn't mentioned Cuauhtémoc when they spoke hours earlier. How strange she could be. Cares and worries for the mission of the Order must be preoccupying the renowned Mother Superior. Usually, her eyes lit up with a visit from Cuauhtémoc, or at least, Gabriél thought they did. This morning she seemed impassive, stern. He shrugged off the awareness.

Consuela and his mother were two opposing forces. They were both stock full of intense emotion and psychic charge. That they didn't get along, Gabriél typically passed off as a normal part of life, but when edginess and irritation came out one for the other, he tightened up.

Images of Cuauhtémoc playing on the orphanage grounds with the other preschool children brought a smile to Gabriél. Cuauhtémoc was a black-haired, playful four-year-old. Many said he looked like Gabriél when he was a boy. Quick with a hug and a kiss, Cuauhtémoc was happy and secure.

Gabriél felt a lump in his throat. "Huh… I guess I forgot it was today that he'd see his abuelita. Funny though, I was just at the orphanage, and my mother never mentioned him. Too much going on I guess."

Consuela didn't reply. She stood up and returned to the counter, stirred the pots of beans and chile. Gabriél watched her, the mood having shifted. He was adrift, caught between two shores. Consuela seemed far-off, yet her presence was rock-solid.

Gabriél sat back in the old oak chair and took a deep breath. "Samuel Fuentes wasn't at the orphanage like he should have been." He leaned forward and rested his elbows on top of the scarred oval oak table, upset and puzzled at the strangeness of the day and the sudden strain with Consuela.

He told Consuela that Samuel had run away from the orphanage and was then found. He had been injured, now recovering at the orphanage ICU. Medical intervention had saved a boy whose foolish actions nearly got him killed. The doctors not available for details, the charge nurse related the general issue and asserted that Mother's ministrations had saved yet another life. The curt nurse, an aged nun, brought the news to Gabriél as he paced in the orphanage's reception area. He was not allowed beyond the front desk, Mother Juana taken away by more pressing concerns. She had made sure Samuel was safe and cared for, then moved on to address other critical burdens.

Gabriél's head cleared in the presence of his wife. "When Sister Thea appeared out of thin air by my truck, she didn't fill me in on the specifics. I had to wait for the nurse. It was like Thea wanted to draw things out, make me stew in worry. The only thing my mother told me earlier was that Samuel was in the hands of the Almighty. I hate that talk. I despise religious secrecy."

He felt his blood pressure rise, ears tingling. "It sounded as if Samuel were gone for good, dead or off to Mexico like the others. He'd been stable and in good health, so I surmised it was Mexico. That's all I could figure, and then later I learned he'd gotten himself into some mischief. He ended up hurt, the medical team tending to him. That's all I learned. I'm pissed, not at Samuel but at someone or something. I'm just not sure who or what."

He paused, drummed his fingers on the table, Consuela patiently listening. "I can't put my finger on the uneasiness. There's more going on than I can figure out or see-through. But I will. I definitely will."

Consuela returned to the table and sat down. She got a

knife to spread butter over the tortilla on Gabriél's plate, then did the same for the tortilla on her plate. "Maybe he was supposed to have gone to Mexico."

"What makes you say that?" His heart clenched, Consuela's words resonating with a vague intuition he'd had hours earlier at the convent. He'd wondered the same thing but shoved the possibility aside. The thought of Samuel expedited to Mexico made him furious. But the nuns had done it before, bypassed a mental health center director. And they'd do it again despite Gabriél being Mother's son.

Consuela stayed quiet, finished buttering the tortilla, then emphasized, "Just a feeling—uneasiness—things may not be as they appear." Consuela looked at Gabriél worriedly.

Gabriél shrugged. When his wife said she had an uneasy sense about things, he listened. Her keenness of insight often struck him to the core. Truth could be the bitterest of medicines.

He continued the story, told Consuela what had happened when he first arrived at the orphanage, then later when Sister Thea materialized beside the truck. "I swear, that nun pulls together atoms and molecules, materializes then vanishes." He grimaced as though from a foul taste.

"By the time I had run back, I was told Samuel was strapped to his bed so he wouldn't further complicate existing injuries. He'd taken a bad spill during his escape and was sedated and asleep. The doctor quickly tended to him. She informed Mother that a hospital wouldn't be necessary."

"A hospital?" Consuela asked, quickly swallowing her first bite of the tortilla. Her gaze was searing. She shook her head in disbelief twice. Then she let out a deep sigh and looked at Gabriél, exasperated.

He looked down at the table, pretended he didn't notice,

then sat up straight and cleared his throat. "Well… I was finally told that Samuel had convulsed and bit off his tongue. And there was more, I could tell, but that's all the old biddy would tell me."

"Oh, Gabriél." Consuela drew back from the table, bristled. Her eyes widened, jaws clenched. She gritted her teeth and folded her arms so tight her fists clenched and forearms flexed. Her reaction was more than Gabriél had bargained for.

He didn't want to say anymore. He'd gotten himself in deep enough. What was important was his patient. He needed to ensure that the youngster was stable and cared for. He'd handle his own lack of sightedness after tending to the boy's welfare.

Consuela sensed his shift of attitude. "What else, Gabriél?" Her tone was firm. She wanted a fuller story, a fessing up of details. He'd opened up and couldn't close off so quickly. Her eyes were angry now and set on helping her husband put into words what needed to be said. She knew he gained perspective from talking. It got the bats out of his mental belfry. Despite being a therapist, he sometimes needed a little emotional coaxing.

She often reminded her therapist husband of what he knew all too well but was obscured in the rush and press of daily demands. Emotions shoved down and snuffed out were never gone for long, and when they resurrected, their ghosts were dark and fueled up. Her confident wisdom could clear the head of the most seasoned psychotherapist.

He rested his elbows on the table, tented his index fingers, and leaned toward her. "Evidently, Mr. Fuentes tried to kidnap Samuel. He talked the boy into running off with him, bolting from the convent compound. The elderly janitor, the eyes and ears of the place, spotted them running off and followed. That old guy has a lot more gumption than I thought."

"He's one of your mother's cronies." Consuela grimaced, then pursed her lips and made Gabriél think she would spit. The woman's rage with Mother Juana burned white-hot.

"He helped Samuel, Consuela." Gabriél's neck muscles tightened, eyebrows arching. His throat constricted as he searched for words, something to say to defend himself. There were no words. Gabriél wondered why he hadn't seen things more clearly and followed through more thoroughly.

She didn't reply. Her green eyes were set squarely on her husband, breathing steady and slow. Certainty in the woman was like lightning across a nighttime desert sky. It paralyzed Gabriél for a brief second before he caught hold of himself. She had a way of coming on strong with and without words.

"You know, I don't even know the old janitor's name. Mother never addresses him directly. Just calls him the janitor. The kids call him Old Snarl-Tooth." The name coming of his mouth sounded shocking the second he said it. He should have gotten the message from the beginning.

Consuela grinned, a look of wonderment crossing her face. Shaking her head, she closed her eyes in thought, then looked back at Gabriél. Fierceness radiated iris to cornea.

He couldn't retreat. "Anyway, the old guy got to the river. It was a secluded spot. He figured he needed to help Samuel."

"Did Samuel want to be helped?"

"He was being kidnapped."

"You sure?"

Gabriél's head hurt. He rubbed his forehead with the palm of his right hand. Pains shot across his brow and into his eyes. He closed them and wished the end of the day were closer. He just wanted to be home, stay home, with Consuela, Cuauhtémoc, and their new little one in the making—without misunderstandings and squabbling. He looked back at his wife. "I'm sure, Consuela. Sure as anyone can be about what the nuns report."

Irritation mounted. The headache worsened. It was a clamp on his forehead. He arched his eyebrows. It didn't help. He squinted, thought it would lessen the ache. He rubbed across his brow with his fingertips. Nothing helped, so he spoke. "Samuel needs the orphanage. His mother is locked away, and his father is an alcoholic. Without the nuns, Samuel has nothing."

Uneasiness worsened. Words didn't lessen the pain. He wasn't getting to what had to be said, didn't know what that was but guessed he'd find the words once he faced the truth.

Learn the devil's name, and you've taken the devil's power. His old therapist spoke with the authority of one tried and seasoned by those in trauma. He'd been and continued to be mentor and guide, years back in Chicago now in liminal spaces of mind and memory.

Gabriél clenched his jaw then stood and went to the refrigerator. He pulled out a pitcher of cold water. Round slices of cucumber, mint leaves, and lemon floated in the refreshing liquid. Consuela said they energized the water. He put the pitcher on the drainboard and got two glasses from the cupboard. His hand shook as he poured.

"I'm not thirsty." Consuela stood up and walked to Gabriél at the countertop, touched his hand. Their eyes met. She wanted to hear more of the story.

He drank a full glass as she stood beside him, then placed it down on the counter before continuing. "The janitor said he lost sight of father and son at first, then heard screaming. A bear had gotten into Mr. Fuente's supplies. Fuentes tried to scare him off. It was a big black thing, fast and hungry. Ripped Fuentes to pieces. The janitor grabbed Samuel. The boy went into bad convulsions. History of epilepsy."

Consuela shook her head. "Gabriél . . ." Her hand moved to his right shoulder. The look in her eyes was that of disbelief.

Gabriél pulled to the side half a step and interrupted, "Mr. Fuentes shouldn't have done what he did." Again, the words sounded off-putting, didn't gel with the feeling of the moment. Nothing was ringing true, except Consuela, her presence and words.

Consuela remained silent. She reached for him again but stopped short, let her hand fall by her side. Her gaze did not waver from Gabriél's.

"Mother said the devil struck him."

"Oh, Gabriél come on." She raised her voice and shook her head, a dire look crossing her countenance. It shifted from sadness to near despair.

Gabriél became angry, his mother's words about Consuela ringing in his ears. Maybe Consuela only loved him for what he provided. A home. Children. A husband. Perhaps that's all there was to their marriage. Maybe there was no understanding and love. That was Mother's repeated message. Maybe he needed to listen to Mother. Mother was Mother Juana de la Cruz, a woman loved by her people, those who looked to her, hurting souls who did as she said and seemed better for it.

His left eye twitched, wouldn't stop. His face flushed, mind whirling in the wrong direction. Sometimes his mind took a wrong turn, and his body spoke up. He listened because not to inevitably ended badly. Twitching stopped.

He loved Consuela, and she loved him, but he felt like a

child before a goddess. It wasn't her. She never denigrated or demeaned. It was something inside him. And it was something in the air. He'd breathed it in since he'd been a kid. It made him feel like something was wrong with him. And there was nothing wrong with him. Nothing. He was Gabriél de la Tierra, son of Mother Juana de la Cruz.

Silence.

Coldness set in. Consuela stepped a pace back, worry written across her forehead. She cupped her palms against her face, then opened her eyes wide and sighed.

The terrible feeling came and went. For an instant, Gabriél had towered above Consuela. He was Gabriél de la Tierra, son of Mother Juana de la Cruz. He didn't like the accursed feeling. It was pure machismo. He'd come to recognize it, let it pass. It was terrible, and it was not Gabriél.

A deep sigh then he spoke, "Look, Consuela, I know. I felt it too. I'm sorry. There's too much coming at me right now. I'll sort it through, but it'll take time." He looked out the window before going on, "I don't believe in the devil, Consuela, but something tore Mr. Fuentes to shreds. There's little left of him. Decapitated. Ripped limb from limb."

"Evil is real, Gabriél." Consuela paused. "And so is your naiveté."

She did it again. Gabriél clenched his jaw, face flushed. "You're agreeing with my mother?"

"Hardly. I'm simply saying that evil is real. The devil is whoever uses it."

"Well… Whatever. It's up to the police now. They've been called in."

"It's not *whatever*, Gabriél. Evil can be in what appears to be good. It's at its strongest there. Where you least expect it."

Containing himself was hard. Gabriél held Consuela's

gaze. Seconds passed.

CHAPTER

10

Consuela went on. "Last night I had a nightmare. It was about a witch, a mystic woman, and a little boy." Gabriél sat back down. The strength drained out of him. He was fighting a senseless battle—needed to listen to his wife. Consuela knew the language of dreams and could help if he let her. He sat back in the chair. Often, she dreamed of him, of his work. He listened.

"Scared and alone, a little boy ran through a dark bosque. He thought he saw his father in the distance, but as he got closer, the father turned into a scraggy, scary man with a face like dried-out leather and jack-o-lantern eyes."

Gabriél thought of Old Snarl-Tooth. Consuela's dreams zeroed in on people she'd never met, those who affected her and hers. A chill flashed up his arms and down his neck.

"Screaming, the little boy was caught in the awful man's

clutches and brought to a realm in the south, a wind-whipped place inhabited by shadowy, faceless creatures."

It was hard for Gabriél to keep quiet. He wanted to comment, but he didn't. Speaking like this only masked anxiety about his wife's wisdom, a troublesome and chronic habit.

"The boy was taken inside a fortress. A cave. It was carved into the side of a red-rocked mountain. An old witch came down into the night along a stone spiral staircase. Frothing and snapping coyotes lined the way. She was clothed in a black flowing robe—cowled." Consuela paused, eyebrows lifted.

"With her eyes, she drew out the boy's tongue. Never touching him, she did it with her mind, pulled and twisted, then opened her mouth, and bit down. The tongue flew into her hand. She disintegrated it with her eyes. It went up in smoke, right in the palm of her hand."

Shaken, Consuela paused before going on. "A little water, please." She leaned against the table, her elbows cradling her frame as she told the story of her nighttime visitation.

Gabriél filled her glass, handed it to her, and waited as Consuela composed herself. He sat back, gazed at the mysterious woman he had married. She sipped slowly, the water's refreshment evident as she sat back and sighed contentedly.

She drew a deep breath before continuing, "Then the witch did it again, but to the boy's genitals. He couldn't even cry out."

Consuela swallowed hard. "She wrapped the parts in a small satchel and hid it in the billowing sleeve of her robe. A black robe, Gabriél."

She studied Gabriél, green eyes a pulse steady and

luminescent as a full desert moon. "The boy's eyes were a kaleidoscope of disbelief and pain. I saw generations and worlds of little boys hurt, maimed. His life slipped into the evil woman's easily as masticated meat down a hungry gullet."

A morbid feeling came over Gabriél. Nausea curled up his throat. Metallic tastes flooded his tongue.

"Darkness increased, and the cave disappeared. Nothing could be seen." She looked stunned as though caught between worlds.

A brief silence steadied her before she went on. "Gradually, a magical realm of phantasmagoric nighttime opened. Its magic exceeded that of the cave. I was awe-struck by its dark beauty. It was a cavern carved out of black basalt. A hidden source of luminescence made it visible. A mystic woman of antiquity appeared. I knew she was a timeless being, my intuition sparked with immediate knowing."

Consuela's eyes were glazed, her look far off. "She wore a flowing purple robe and stood at the center of a stream of crystal clear water. Torches, serpents, daggers, and keys lined the sandstone path on either side of the stream. She was attended by numinous barking dogs, two huge wolfhounds by her side. A full moon, half-moon, and new moon hovered majestically in the nighttime sky. Her cowled robe was embroidered along the edges in gold thread. Vapors rose out of the earth. She reached her hand up, moved across space and time into the young boy's mind. Out of her right index finger came light more brilliant than this world's brightest day. It was the light of the three moons, otherworldly and unseen by those of common sightedness. It went to the boy's forehead, between the eyes."

Neon bright, the carved volcanic cave that Gabriél often

went to flashed to mind. It was the place he would retreat for silence and to listen. Secluded, it was a place of insight, dreams, and visions. The dark realm called to him, a subtle tugging at the heart when he needed to withdraw and enter its darkness and utter quietude. There, spirits visited in flickering images as he descended into a trance, voices spontaneously arose with guidance and wisdom. It called to him now, as Consuela spoke, a gentle but firm interior pull.

The periphery of his vision flickered, sprays of gray and black light along the edges of sightedness. He leaned back in the wooden kitchen chair, its legs creaking. Things stopped, the room no longer blurry or at a slight tilt. He waited for a quick couple of seconds and then reached for his glass and drank the rest of the water. Instead of being calmed and soothed, his muscles tightened and his forehead throbbed. He leaned farther back in the chair, energy shooting to his groin, muscles and testicles aching. The white space between his eyes burned.

"You need to visit my friend, the old one, Gabriél."

A centenarian, Sophia lived in Ojo Caliente, a village of sulfur, arsenic, and lithium springs. Early Pueblo Indians considered the waters sacred, the land infused with healing energy. Sophia was a recluse and a *curandera*, a healer. People flocked to her. Consuela never said how they had met, only that they had always known each other.

Gabriél always shied away from meeting Sophia, not wanting to incur Mother Juana's wrath. Natural healing practices and the Church were at odds. A visit would mean betrayal.

"Sophia can help, Gabriél. A witch is at work and could hurt us in horrible ways. There are things you alone must confront. But Sophia has wisdom. She is like the mystic woman in my dream."

Turning to stare at the hypnotic blue flames dancing beneath the griddle, Gabriél sat quietly, pensively. The flames helped to steady a frantic mind. Seeing Sophia might help, a certain comfort washing through him at the mention of his wife's old friend. She was known far and wide, her wisdom spoken of by the old ones of Infierño.

Consuela continued, "Sophia speaks of dark forces. They operate behind the scenes of everyday life. They can will a person's demise." The way Consuela spoke was as though Sophia were speaking through her, or perhaps, she was stating what she had been told and taken to heart.

Gabriél looked at her. "Bad people wish bad on good people. They do it long and hard enough, bad things can happen." His voice was grave. The ache in his groin intensified. He tried not to let it show, gritting his teeth. A flush of cold sweat formed on his brow and trickled down his temples.

Consuela's bright eyes were riveted on Gabriél. "Sophia says we need to see past appearances. Darkness hides under the cover of good. Once we spot it, then we know what we're up against. Till then, we're blind and grope in the dark."

Pinprick pains shot through Gabriél's crotch. He closed his eyes. He hated the pain that came unbidden, its force and the fact that he could not control it, could not make it subside. A black claw lit up on the white screen of his mind, a face appearing. He willed it away, just like that, forcing the image back to the psychic netherworld. The screen snapped shut, a quick shudder running up his spine.

The white screen opened once again, Arwind's image flickering vaguely. It faded, and with it the white glow of heat in the center of Gabriél's forehead. A disquieting stillness came over him, Consuela's loving gaze helping him to regain at least some sense of himself. He had to let go of what he could not control.

The pain in his groin eased, then passed. He cleared his voice, "Consuela, I figure things out in my own way." His voice was not harsh but was curt, and he felt he had hurt Consuela.

She sighed, frustrated. Her gaze shifted out the window. Moments stretched out across the mesa of sage and scrub oak.

A mouse scurried across the red Spanish tiles of the kitchen floor and darted out the partially open back door. "I thought I'd gotten rid of them," Gabriél said with exasperation.

"I guess not." Consuela stood up.

Gabriél stood up and met her gaze. "All I know is that some bad thing got to Mr. Fuentes. Maybe a bear did come out of the hills—they've been going for the campers lately." His throat became dry. He drank more water before going on. "Maybe a psycho-killer on the loose. Maybe somebody escaped out of the forensic lock-up at the state hospital."

"Oh, Gabriél." Distressed, Consuela looked away, back out the window to the great expanse of untamed nature. She walked to the griddle and turned it off. "Dreams don't lie, Gabriél. What got Samuel has hold of you and won't let go. It has you tucked away where it wants you."

Gabriél wiped perspiration from his brow.

Consuela took a deep breath. "You've had your suspicions about the nuns, Gabriél. Now's the time to follow-up."

"Thea. Sister Thea. It's her." Gabriél was drained. He hated reiterating what had been said time and again. He was a man at odds with himself—couldn't tell friend from foe.

Consuela folded her arms across her chest and leaned against the counter, bearing weary, countenance gray. Yet she stood erect, constant.

It was as though Gabriél lived in a fog, mind infested with high-pitched cackling. It was a psychic static that left his nerves frayed, sometimes burnt. Often, he pictured nighttime witches screeching behind lone desert sandstone boulders and pointing gnarled fingers toward him, his home and family. Cowled in black, their faces were obscured. It was Thea, he knew it was that cruel nun, it was her and those who followed her. No one else. His shoulders ached, tight like steel coils. Fighting with Consuela wasn't what he wanted, or had ever wanted. But he knew marriage wasn't smooth or straightforward.

Consuela's eyes said she was frustrated but determined. She caught meanings he often missed and was one to see things through. It was both blessing and bane.

Something inside Gabriél was sore, ached. His solar plexus tightened, then twisted. Secrets remained hidden in a dark mind place. The unconscious mind bequeathed its mysteries only to the ready and worthy.

One afternoon in Arwind's consultation office, the old man told Gabriél that the unconscious had its ways and did not adjust to ours. "Our puny egos refuse to see. They remain childish and filled with illusions. We demand our way. The path of the psyche beckons, then closes if we do not respond. It comes again only when crisis strikes, and stress is at a high pitch."

The remembrance startled him like a slap across the face. Black-cowled women cackled and screeched. His nerves sparked and crackled like kindling and cedar set aflame.

Consuela could see the vision, she heard the cackles, her

nerves caught fire. Silently, empathically, she shared for an instant his torment. Her arms stayed folded, then tightened. Ferocity as an antidote to worry. Her gaze became enlivened, countenance brightening, green eyes radiating luminescence. Posture remained erect, constant.

Gabriél turned to leave and walked toward the hallway. "All I know is what I've been told. Samuel was kidnapped. Had a seizure. Bit off his tongue. Got carried back. If there's more there, I'll find it." He turned her way, hoping Consuela had been listening.

She nodded. "I know you will."

He'd forgotten to kiss her goodbye. Never did they leave without a kiss. There was no excuse. He walked back to Consuela, quick pinpricks rippling from groin to abdomen. Bypassing the shots of pain, he kissed her cheek.

She smiled, eyes warm, arms folded, bearing steady, constant.

He went back toward the hallway and front door, loneliness sweeping into hallowed places. A dark psychic gust of despair caught him by surprise. He turned into the hallway and tried to catch his breath. The narrow passage seeming aslant; he swayed, knees weakening. He steadied himself along the wall. The room whipped and swirled. Vertigo had never hit in his own home. Usually, it struck after confrontational sessions with patients' dysfunctional family members. Other times, it came and went within seconds when he hadn't had enough sleep, three or four hours not enough to replenish severe energy depletion. His soul was desolate as a windy desert day with nothing in sight but rocks, bramble, weeds, and a searing noonday sun. Memories of better times and love dissipated like desert dust on a blustery afternoon.

Consuela's image flickered. Gabriél came back to himself,

leg muscles tightening, shoulders pulling back, posture erect. He called to Consuela from the hallway, "Tortillas and beans and chile for dinner tonight?"

She appeared beside him. "Will you be here?"

He started, attempted not to show it. Consuela smiled, brushed his hair away from his brow, her touch vanquishing anguish.

"I hope to be."

She didn't reply.

"I love you," he said as he walked to the back door. His voice trailed off. He wasn't sure she had heard.

Consuela's footsteps sounded softly on the scarred oak floorboards of the hallway. She stayed at the threshold as Gabriél put on his coat and made his way out the back door. "Sophia has wisdom, Gabriél."

"I appreciate what you say, Consuela, but I must find my own wisdom."

The door closed gently.

CHAPTER

11

Gabriél had two home visits before three o'clock that afternoon. They were unscheduled check-ins at two local trailer parks, making sure the home environment was safe and suitable for child-rearing. Both of the trailers were satisfactory, not ideal but not the typical hell holes of dysfunctional families of origin.

Visits completed, he returned to the Center, did paperwork, and quit early. His secretary would cover for him at the five o'clock administrative meeting. She'd also call Consuela, let her know he wouldn't be home till late. Best she called Consuela since a call from him could prove contentious or meet with a lingering, painful silence.

Time away from Consuela and Cuauhtémoc was no small decision. Missing an evening with them over a dinner of red chile, beans, and tortillas was a hard choice, one prompted by desperation. Family life was to be enjoyable and not tainted by an irritable husband and father.

And he desperately needed time alone. Typically, solitude was a sure cure for soul ailment. But there were those times when seclusion merely emptied into a black void— isolation and desolation horrid demons of dark psychic recesses. He had to risk the bad to gain the good.

He drove down the endless black band of high-desert highway toward his hermetic cave, fears of emptiness and being forsaken clamping and squeezing heart and soul. Memories of sitting, meditating in the cave for hours, ending in a cold chill, pressed to mind. Still, there was something about driving the vastness of Aztlan del Norte's high-desert mountains that swept the mind clear, steadied a shaky soul, and opened the heart to light and dark energies. He hoped for inspiration but knew he had to be ready for rude awakenings.

He needed to be at Tent Rocks. Canyon walls, eroded layers of gray-brown sand and gravel formed by seven-million-year old volcanic ash deposits, called to him. Climbing among the tapering hoodoos, set near the Native American community of Cochiti Pueblo, released ancient healing forces, energies conjured from centuries-old psychic bloodlines.

Driving, he thought of the gentle winds breathing through shoulder-width conical structures that reached to the sky. He had a place, his sanctuary, a cave once a lookout for Indian and Anglo cattlemen. Within it, listening to the silence interposed by soft flute-like sounds from mountain breezes through canyon tunnels, he readily entered a light trance state.

Over an hour, sometimes longer, was often spent in the dark cave sensing old gods, flickering visions, and whispering voices. The unconscious mind, away from idle talk and daily pressures, became highly sensitized in primitive nature. It held wisdom and healing, insight into what lay covered in darkness.

Arwind had taught him about ancient energies. Constellated at primordial sites known as luminous vortexes, they drew sensitive souls. Meditative states were intensified as a pinpoint of light through a magnifying glass generates fire.

Altered consciousness is how Arwind referred to it. Shamans called it a trance. Gabriél sought it as an interior sanctuary and oracle.

Driving through the Native American reservation, Cochiti Pueblo, its acres and acres of verdant farmland bordering the Rio Grande River drew him into quiet. It marked the mystic entrance to what lay ahead. Transpersonal forces stirred within him with slight tingling sensations up the spine. The place of the third eye, between the brow point, warmed.

Ten minutes later, up four miles of high-desert mountain dusty road, he parked, got out of his truck, and stretched. The sky was a cloudless turquoise blue. It glistened. He had come to his spiritual place, a numinous sanctuary.

Although his mother never spoke of her past, distant relatives and family friends said that Gabriél's ancestral roots came out of this hallowed realm. Strange energies coursed through Aztlan's Peralta Canyon, spirits whisking their way up through the belly of the earth, many of the old ones said.

As Gabriél walked up a sandy wash, the unseen world stirred. Sprinkles of rain graced his cheeks. There were no clouds overhead. Shrubs, desert plants, and pinion trees trembled and swayed. There was no wind. Sand swirled, human-sized figures emerging from the dust.

Giant sedimentary cones incised with multicolored striations loomed high overhead. They were the guardians of secret chambers. Here was where medicine people, witches and warlocks, *brujas* and *curanderos* agreed that underworld forces dwelt, roamed, and conversed.

Troubled, Gabriél hungered for the inspiration and visions birthed in this sacred site. He needed to open his heart, as Consuela sometimes said. Then the eyes of his soul would unseal.

Gabriél loved Consuela, and she loved him. But their marriage was growing stale. It was caught in a subtle but definite gap, now and again unbridgeable. It hadn't grown wide enough yet to warrant despair. Yet, time was of the essence.

Distance left Gabriél distracted, unhappy, unable to work. Energy was lagging. Insight failed no matter the resolve or strain. Primal sources, nature's wellsprings, would shed their light.

Moving into the curved canyon shaped by seven-million-year old pumice, ash, and tuff deposits, Gabriél hiked up a narrow, shaded passage. It opened to an amphitheater, tapering hoodoos positioned as sentinels overhead. Despite the uphill trek, Gabriél noticed he was not short of breath. It was good here.

Passing red-barked manzanita shrubs, he soon saw the cave. He entered and breathed deeply of the age-old pyroclastic atmosphere. Studies of the writings of Greek seers and visionaries revealed that the earth beneath Delphi emitted intoxicating gases. The Pythia, Grecian priestesses, breathed the heady vapors before uttering oracles. Gabriél inhaled deeply from similar volcanic vapors, then descended to a yogic full-lotus position, closed his eyes, and fell into a psychic reverie.

Whirls of phantasmagoric vapors lulled him into their embrace. White heat intensified at the center of his forehead, a quickening of visions and intuition. Images gazed into both far-off and interior regions of mind and life. Consuela and the warmth of love, marriage, and home. Mother and severity, harshness, and demands. Drifting, he crossed further into liminal states of mind, suspended between wakefulness and sleep. His head bobbed a little, then stopped as time vanished.

Mindspace glowed a surreal lapis blue, shrill winds painting ruby streaks through boundless skyscapes. Earth shook. Gabriél lingered, calm. Thin, crisp sheets of white clouds unfolded across the heavens, a presence materializing overhead, obscure at first. Energies of earth, air, fire, water, and ether coalesced and descended as a spiraling funnel.

Transfixed, Gabriél observed, overcome by awe and reverence.

From beneath the earth, a shadowy and loamy undulating terrain, there arose a dark feminine form. Wisps of gray and black clouds swirled around the statuesque deity whose form rose to the upper reaches of the heavenly vault. Grounded, she presided on a surreal earth, vast and of infinite scope, and reigned throughout the farthest reaches of the cosmos.

She was Tonantzin, dark Mother Goddess of Aztlan, Goddess of Sustenance, Goddess of Life and Death. From unseen dimensions she governed, brought what was high low and the low high, Mother of Restoration and Balance. Legend held, she appeared but once to those of sincere heart and truthful seeking, then disappeared to exercise her will undetected.

Shafts of light beamed through Gabriél's imagination, third eye pulsing white-hot. Primeval thunders rose from the bowels of the earth and entered the core of his being. Love and rage fused.

Outside of space and time, voices from north, south, east, and west, above and below, bellowed then roared. It was the lament of men, lives thwarted, lost. Cries of tormented millions echoed from humankind's collective memory.

Consuela suffered because of Gabriél. Her firm opinions, minor disagreements felt like assaults on Gabriél's manhood. Moodiness and distance frequently possessed him.

A puff of smoke and Arwind appeared. He was dressed in a flowing, sky blue, magical satin robe. Waving a wizard's staff that sprayed luminescence in its wake, he spoke. "Thwarted man—thwarted life, Gabriél. Decisions make the man." He spoke in a clipped, sagely verse. His eyes twinkled.

The vision ended.

Gabriél's heart beat erratically, fluttering like a bird with damaged wings. His chest squeezed tight, pain rippling shoulder to shoulder. Eyes flashing open, hand over his chest, he breathed deeply and waited for his heart to calm. It didn't, a bird fluttering in its shuttered cage.

He grit his teeth, groaned, and slapped his open palms on the pebbled ground. A pulsating hologram of Consuela on his right and Mother on his left became visible. Gabriél felt tormented, a weary and fraying man.

Perhaps a move would end conflict. Cuauhtémoc, Consuela, and Gabriél could leave Infierño, Consuela having few ties to Aztlan del Norte, both parents passing away by her twenty-first birthday.

Sophia, her closest friend, had often told her it was time to pull up roots. *The world is our home*, Consuela would tell

Gabriél. Moving, even at a moment's notice, was fine with her. All she asked was that they do so without a divided mind.

Emptiness opened wide, yawned. He grabbed his abdomen, pinpricks kneading deep into his stomach. Groin muscles tightened, then twisted. A flush of nausea swept through his midsection and up to his throat and mouth, bile coursing over his palate.

Life, anywhere, with a loving wife and children should be enough. But it wasn't and wouldn't be. He needed more. He vomited.

Winds rushed through the canyon, so fierce that grit blinded his eyes and slapped his cheeks. Again, he heaved. Arwind's voice sounded louder and robust as the north wind, "A man isn't a man till the mother ties are cut." A crumbling edge of the cave fell away. Gabriél braced himself. The sky outside the mouth of the cave darkened, a morgue-like hush descending over the land. Black clouds blocked out the last rays of the descending sun.

Unseasonably cool breezes swept up into the mouth of the cave from hidden tunnels, subterranean regions of earth breathing forth air fresh and otherworldly. Outside, everything looked shadowy. Inside, soft lights began a dance across white volcanic walls. Thin shafts of sunlight beamed down from above.

Gabriél looked up. Only white rock arched overhead. Yet, light descended and danced hypnotically off and around the old stone interior. Trance-like feelings again crept over Gabriél, beckoned him into their embrace. He nodded and struggled to keep his eyes open.

Then sparks jumped in front, to the side, behind. Gabriél started, then followed each playful movement. The sparks grew larger, morphing into spectral shapes. Gabriél had heard of such things.

Native American lore said that earth spirits were tricksters. They became visible through elemental forces of earth, air, fire, and water. They made breezes that whipped leaves into dancing funnels. They made dust devils rise out of nowhere to blind, gag, and disorient the arrogant. They made tumbleweeds catch fire and roll through open mesas like crazed witches. They made the skies open wide on cloudless days and dump bucketsful on the foul-tempered and stupid people. They made dark in light spaces and light in dark places. They were nature's mischief-makers, shape-shifters, wisdom-bearers.

Gabriél watched and listened before fatigue touched his eyelids. Sleep called. He slumped forward and slipped into the dream world.

From afar, he saw the Infierño graveyard. Gabriél knew he was dreaming, lucid dreams having come before. He was at the picket fence, touching the white wooden gate.

Arwind yet again became visible. Eyes sparkling, he was hundreds of years old, unblemished. He shape-shifted to a youth of ten thousand spring times. Then another shift. He was as Gabriél remembered—a seventy-five-year-old, white-haired, and bearded wise man.

At the time of his passing, Arwind came in a dream and spoke to Gabriél of his journey to the next world. Weeks later, mutual friends wrote to inform Gabriél of what he already knew. Arwind had told Gabriél that henceforth, visits from the unseen world would be cautionary. They would be about darkness and light, evil set against good—imparting resolve and courage.

Gabriél's head jerked upwards. From out of the mouth of the cave, a gigantic sharp-toothed creature whisked overhead.

It crossed through the moonless sky like a blood-red hologram. The mythic image, well known within depth psychology, loomed viciously. *Vagina dentate.* The thought was loud. He wondered if Arwind had spoken. Arwind shook his head and smiled impishly.

Surrounded by brilliance, Arwind shifted again, this time into a virile youth. He opened his mouth as though to speak but didn't. Like a fire in the solar plexus, Arwind's teaching that a man be a man lit through Gabriél's core.

A twinkle in his eyes and Arwind vanished.

Gabriél clenched his teeth, unlatched the gate, and stepped inside the graveyard.

CHAPTER

12

He walked into another realm, the cemetery vanished. The rocky region was farther up the hills of Aztlan del Norte, a lonesome mountain place where nighttime revealed things obscured by the light of day but teeming in the darkness. Decent people huddled in their lone adobe homes and drew their window shades, howls and screams from man or beast, and no one dared imagine which.

Shadows, cast by eerie twilight, descended from a distant red sandstone cave. The isolated hollow emitted an unnatural light as from a hidden inferno, grayish-white and sickly yellow tips flickering from crimson fires.

Drawing closer, Gabriél sighted between the fires at the back of the mouth of the cave a basalt spiral staircase. The rough walls were ornately chiseled with the heads of mythical beasts and naked human bodies writhing and tumbling to the earth from some distant heaven. Chanting, scores of haunting voices rang out from the cavern and into the darkness. He shuddered.

Legions of greenish-yellow energies, spirits, glided down a dark path to the deserted mesa below. Row by row, they assembled along the sides of a miles-long and unfathomably deep arroyo. Lining the precipice like mysterious guardians, they waited.

From a distance, Gabriél saw granulations of scorched earth, dusty footprints, and gnarled and bony protrusions resembling fingers that hung from the sides of each of the night creatures. He strained to make sense of the ominous scene but couldn't.

Occult rituals executed in Aztlan wilderness badlands were the never-dreamed-of stuff of by-gone cultures, of Aztec priests and voodoo practitioners, of Egyptian funerary rites and African cannibals. In Aztlan del Norte, the atmosphere reeked of psychic rot that drew the far off close and personal. Aztlan was the soul place and hallowed land of Gabriél's birth, hundreds of years of supernatural lineage infused into the desert landscape.

Then, it came to him. *Evil.* Behind the scenes of everyday life and sacred sites, it lurked and infiltrated. Jaw clenched, his blood ran cold, fingertips icy.

A low-pitched hum, as though from an underground generator, pulsed through the nighttime atmosphere. Dull pain ran through his ear canals as a grit-spewing whirlwind spun out of the cave. It gathered momentum, targeting the gathering.

A safe distance away, Gabriél stood firm. The whirlwind stopped short of the crowd. A towering being walked out of the swirl of sand and dust. In its arms was a child, squirming.

Horrified, Gabriél started forward, then stopped.

The shadowy figure, a cowled woman in an ermine-lined cloak with scores of eagles embroidered in gold thread on purple velvet, gazed his way. Laser-red eyes streaked hatred through the moonlit dark, into Gabriél's core, riveting him in place. The evil priestess grew toward the pitch-black sky, presence engulfing the surroundings as worshippers stood heads raised upward and hands clasped in awe.

Her presence stretching from horizon to horizon, she bellowed unintelligible words, "Bagabi laca bachabe lamac cahi achababe karrelyos."

Murkiness clouded Gabriél's mind. He tried but couldn't place the odd, yet familiar words.

The cry worsened, bit, and tore into Gabriél's mind. He wanted to cover his ears but couldn't move. Sharp pains burst across his forehead, down his chest, abdomen, and pelvis. He rocked on his heels, unsteady and depleted as though his soul was being drained off.

On and on the cry sounded, scores of voices joining in the stern, low-pitched hymn.

Imperceptibly, at first, the earth quaked. Then, fissures ripped over the landscape, thousands of thunderclaps charging through the airwaves. Seconds later, everything stopped.

A dreadful silence lifted out of the arroyo. Miles and miles of white and gray sulfuric smoke, turning purplish-black, rose skywards. Swirling clouds canopied the crowd. Each being in the group breathed deeply of the foul fumes that emanated from the thick mist. Slowly, each glowed a purplish-black.

Gabriél observed as though from behind a mystic looking glass. It permitted seeing, hearing, smell. But no movement, no sound, no intrusion.

Soon, the glowing masses morphed and hunched over into old crones. They sprouted the legs, snout, and eyes of a coyote. Ghostly, high-pitched wails escaped into the jet-black night sky. Frenzied, the coyotes stalked the child.

Cloak flowing, the high priestess lowered the infant tauntingly toward the snapping mouths. Inches above a sea of frothing jaws, the child was snapped back, upwards, and carried down into the arroyo. Red smoke wafted out of a hole in the arroyo's center. It dropped into the earth's molten core, white-hot clusters of stone-like chunks twisting and churning through the heaving liquid mass.

Fumes clouded the child and priestess. After a quick minute, the lava and gases receded. A basalt altar stood to the right of the foul woman and child, each glowing a neon purplish-black. Arctic air settled over the land like the death mantle of a perverse god.

Gabriél's fingertips and toes became numb, the rest of his body hot as a furnace. Fingertips purple, he willed himself to move, squeezed his hands repeatedly. Each movement sent stinging sensations from the palms of his hand to his heart. His chest heaved, stomach clenched, and bile rose to his throat again. He stood firm.

The cry of the coyotes grew louder, ear-piercingly shrill.

The child was laid on the altar and cried as the high priestess held it in place.

Out of the desert darkness, a man appeared. He walked down into the arroyo where she and the pack of coyotes clustered. He wore white linen vestments. A chasuble and alb were embroidered with black pinecones. In his right hand was a book bound with human skin. Carefully, he rested it on the altar.

In his left hand was a silver water bowl. Smells of urine

swirled through the nighttime air. He lifted his head toward the dark sky. Closing his eyes, he muttered unintelligible words. Then he lowered his gaze and placed the rank-smelling bowl beside the crinkled text.

From beneath his vestments, he removed the host—a dead toad. He placed the creature on a golden paten that lay atop the altar to the left of the hideous book. His fingertips grazed the edge of the precious round metal as he concentrated on the sacred offering.

Cowl dropping away, the man once again raised his eyes toward a swirl of black clouds that formed a perfect pattern of gnarled fingers reaching downward. His features glowed with the dark radiance of the unholy night. He was Archbishop Milton Gall of the Aztlan Archdiocese of the Ecclesia Dei.

Gabriél's cheeks were numb, and his mind crowded with confusion. Breaths came short and quick, heart racing. Tingling sensations rose from the pit of his stomach to throat and mouth, forehead beaded with drops of perspiration curling into the corners of his mouth.

Mythological studies introduced Gabriél to the reality of Satanic rituals and black masses, the presider typically a woman. She was the high priestess, the Archbishop, her chosen celebrant. Legend held that such a woman existed, always keeping over fifty priests in her stable to do her bidding. In return, she granted them small favors—a secret wish come true, forbidden delights of the flesh, and other titillating gifts. The choicest of the priests, the Archbishop, received a bag of gold, his coffers regularly depleted by a bevy of mistresses.

Now, another woman wrapped in black walked into the arroyo. She shed her clothes, white skin glistening under the night's full moon. Her long black hair was striking, concealing her face. Bowing her head before the Archbishop, she stepped on a granite block and onto the consecrated volcanic slab and lay face upwards.

Archbishop Gall reached for the infant and lifted it aloft, over the altar, his back to Gabriél. A slash to the neck silenced the screaming child. Its blood flowed over the supplicant, naked flesh colored crimson.

Voices chanted, "Bagabi laca bachabe lamac cahi achababe karrelyos."

Blood dripped from vertical indentations on the downward slanted altar into a silver chalice. Minutes passed, the child colorless, the cup overflowing. The Archbishop handed the corpse to the high priestess. She tossed it into a pack of snapping and howling coyotes. Wails of madness tore through the night, twisted human screeches out of the mouths of frothing crones turned nighttime beasts.

Then, six black-robed priests came out of the night. They carried a coffin. Approaching the creatures, they paused, looked at the high priestess.

She nodded.

Setting the seven-foot-long black enameled box on the ground, the priests twisted its locks open, then stepped back. Of its own accord, the lid clicked and crept upward.

Yelping and snapping beasts pawed the ground, wanted to lunge for the malodorous contents. The gaze of the priestess held them in check, menacing thin red rays shooting from her eyes.

The dark figures waited until the lid stopped opening. Then a priest reached down and tilted the coffin on its side. A gunny-sacked body rolled out.

The rays from the eyes of the priestess tapered away from

the chupacabras. In seconds, they bit and ripped away flesh, bone, and organs. With their spoils, they darted into the black wilderness.

One priest approached the high priestess, bowed, and held in outspread hands a palm-sized, gunny-wrapped offering. She motioned to the altar, the nude female no longer there, the Archbishop gone. Gently, the offering was laid on the altar and opened.

It was a lump of shriveled flesh.

The high priestess looked Gabriél's way, face enshrouded by her black cloak, coyote eyes bulging. Surreal, they seemed inches from Gabriél's own. They gleamed red. In them was reflected the face of Consuela.

And the priestess threw her head back, cowl dropping off, laughed hideously, and she was Consuela.

CHAPTER

13

Consumed by fury, Mother Juana shifted her gaze away from her mystified and confused son—conjuring the image of Consuela was a thrill.

She riveted her sight on the withered member on the altar. It flew into the palm of her right hand.

A howl sent tumbleweeds spinning, exploding into balls of fire. Northeasterly winds kicked up as Mother intoned, "Bagabi laca bachabe . . ." Repeatedly, she chanted the cultic verse, "Bagabi laca . . ." Her voice drowned out the now raging winds.

Lifting the tiny organ, it swelled and hardened. Fire rose out of the palm of her hand, white and blue flames scorching the swollen thing a crumbly black. "Bagabi . . ." she once again intoned. Seconds later, the chanting completed, she fixed her gaze on Gabriél. Slowly, her eyes slithered to the charred bit, and she blew.

An arctic wind came out of her mouth.

Black flecks spiraled upwards, then to the south, toward Infierño.

CHAPTER

14

G abriél pulled into his home driveway, the sixty-mile drive from Tent Rocks seeming to have passed in seconds. It was dark, the full moon hovering as a guide on his way home.

A quick stop by the Center told him he hadn't been missed. Meetings had gone on without him. Not a board membered balked at his secretary's explanation of his absence as due to pressing personal matters.

Nearly nine P.M. and Gabriél didn't feel tired. He was angry and stunned—mainly angry. Consuela's face in the vision had been shocking, a psychic intrusion. The look was Consuela's, but the presence was unadulterated hate. Consuela was tough but not hateful. At a dinner party, a fundraiser for the Center, a colleague had described Consuela as a feminine, no-bullshit woman.

It fit.

The occult priestess in a desecrated Aztlan wasteland wanted Gabriél to believe his wife was malicious. Visions and dreams spoke a symbolic language, shed light on the underbelly of illusion. They spoke to bad made to look decent, bad played out as good.

Gabriél's hours' long trance in the cave told him evil was happening under cover of night. The Church was involved. As for the Satanic high priestess, he had a good guess who that was—Thea!

Locking up his truck, he walked to the back door of his house. The heat of the day had let up. Crickets chirped. Two dogs hidden behind the coyote fences of neighboring homes barked loudly. They scratched against the enclosure.

Fast and black, something darted through the shadows, from around the front of the house. It disappeared into the moonless night, scrub brush bristling, then came a distant howling. *Coyote.* Again, the cry sounded, suddenly closer, Gabriél's skin crawling.

Uneasiness stole over Gabriél. Coyotes were common in the high desert. They wailed eerily like babies in the night, sounds echoing off distant canyons. Restlessness told him there was a pack trailing. Coyotes were wary of humans unless they were in a pack—then they were dangerous.

An image of someone hunched over and clothed in black flashed through his mind. Heartbeats picked up. Skin crawled. Fingertips ice cold. His head jerked back with the force of the quick vision.

He hurried up the few steps toward his home's front door, fumbled for the key, then put it in and turned. Nothing. Stuck.

He tried a couple more times, then tugged at the key. Stuck. Stuck. Stuck. He tried again. Nothing. *Cabron*! The lock gripped tight—refused exit. Frustrated, he knocked softly, not wanting to alarm Consuela and Cuauhtémoc. They had to be asleep.

No one answered. Knocked again, harder. Three more times. He pounded with his fist. Nothing.

Heart pounding, breaths quick, cold sweat forming across the brow, he put his briefcase next to the door. Hurrying to the front of the house, he hoped Consuela had dozed off on the sofa in the living room, listening to classical music. She tried to wait up for him, but sleep and loneliness often got the best of her. The couch was her favorite spot to curl up with a good book and soft music. It was a comfort, she said—consolation for another night alone.

Narrow and long, the house was a corridor of rooms—living room, hallway, two bedrooms, kitchen, and study. The nursery was along the side of the house. At the front were the living area and master bedroom. Sheers hung over the front picture window Gabriél looked in, the soft light of the reading lamp on. Consuela wasn't there. Consuela wasn't there.

He swallowed hard, then went to the front door. It was a massive wood piece of Spanish colonial craftsmanship. Weathered and impenetrable, it stood between him and his family. He didn't have another key. There was no way in, except to break one of the long and narrow side windows next to the door. Distress clamped down.

Seconds later, shattered glass and a chunk of sandstone littered the living room's varnished pine floor. Brushing the ledge free of shards, Gabriél squeezed sideways through the window's encasement. "Consuela," he called out, still hoping she'd answer. Silence. Soft light from the reading lamp illuminated the master bedroom threshold and hallway.

Gabriél looked in the bedroom. Empty. He went down the

hallway. Consuela could be in the nursery, asleep with Cuauhtémoc. Gabriél checked. The child's bed remained made from the morning. Curtains drawn, Gabriél saw the outside ledge of the two-foot thick adobe wall. Coyote eyes peered in, a band of the wild creatures. Gabriél moved to the window. A brazen coyote stared, then jumped down, vanishing into the desert night.

Gabriél's nerves were on fire. He went to the kitchen and then the study, turned on the lights with a shaky hand. He flicked the deadbolt, opened the back door, then tried the key. Quickly, it slipped out of the lock. He grabbed his briefcase and put it in the study.

Off the pantry, he went into the one-car garage where Consuela parked her small Toyota. It wasn't there. Near-sighted, Consuela rarely drove anywhere at night, especially with Cuauhtémoc. Perhaps she'd left a note.

Gabriél walked back into the kitchen. No note, anywhere. He sat down at the kitchen table, rubbed his forehead with his fingertips, tried to pull his thoughts together.

A few moments later, he got up and walked toward the hallway, then stopped. A cold draft blew through the darkened passage. It was summer, and the air outside was a nighttime desert cool, not cold.

He walked down the hallway and cast a glance at the living room fireplace. Months earlier, he had closed the chute. The chill once more swept through the room like a stream of unexpected and unwanted spirits. It came from the bedroom. A sense of unreality crept in. Overhead lights flickered, and hues of purple and blue clouded his peripheral vision.

Steadying himself, Gabriél touched the doorframe to the master bedroom door. He hesitated before crossing the threshold. Light from the reading lamp in the living room cast a dim glow into the twelve-by-twelve foot sparsely furnished space, a cold room of shadows, teasing and taunting.

Gabriél wrapped his arms around himself, stepped forward, then stopped. An invisible hand, a sudden regret, kept him from entering—ghosts of months past, memories of loving much, then little, then almost none. Tears filled his eyes. He and Consuela might never again touch.

Stepping into the bedroom, something appalling caught his eye. His knees weakened. In the middle of Consuela's handmade earth-toned quilt bed cover lay a foul-smelling scrap, partially obscured by the dark. Unnerved, Gabriél approached.

It was small, crumbly, and black.

A few seconds passed—a car turning into the crusher-fine paved driveway. Gabriél left the master bedroom to look out the study window. Consuela parked, Cuauhtémoc in his car seat. She saw Gabriél and waved, and Gabriél did as well, despite his uneasiness. He walked outside and lifted the garage door, a coyote cry echoing in the distance.

Consuela drove into the garage, Gabriél smiling and blowing her a kiss as he waited for the car to stop. He opened the back car door and hugged and lifted Cuauhtémoc out of his seat. Consuela got out and put her arms around Gabriél, kissing him softly on the neck. Gabriél lingered, gazed into her green eyes. "I love you."

"I love you too. What's the matter?" She wasn't used to Gabriél's focus and intensity.

"I'll tell you inside." Gabriél took Cuauhtémoc in his arms, the child nodding back to sleep.

Once in the house, Gabriél heard Consuela locking the back door. He called out softly as he walked into Cuauhtémoc's room, "I'll tuck *mijo* in, then we'll talk."

A minute later, he came back to the kitchen. Consuela was sorting through things. Cuauhtémoc's blanket, coloring book, and a small book bag were stacked in the middle of the kitchen table. "You got my note?" she asked.

"Never saw a note."

Puzzled, she looked around, then pointed behind Gabriél. "There it is." A notebook-sized piece of paper was on the floor, wedged in a thin space between the oven and yellow enamel wall. "A breeze must have blown it off the table. I left it right here." She tapped the table, the spot where Gabriél usually sat. A gust blew in from the living room. She looked down the hall. "Is the front door open?"

Gabriél took her by the hand, down the hall. He showed her the broken glass across their finely varnished living room floor, then explained his visionary experience in Tent Rocks. "Once I got home, breaking the window was my only way in." He told her everything, from Tent Rocks to minutes earlier. Then he waited, expecting Consuela's confusion to turn to disbelief.

It didn't.

"Are you all right?" Consuela asked, holding Gabriél's gaze. Her concern was comforting.

"One other thing," he said, guiding her to their bedroom. "Like I said, in the vision, the priestess blew the ashes toward Infierño." They moved to the threshold to the bedroom, and Gabriél pointed to their bed.

Consuela squinted into the semi-darkness, then walked in, eyed the center of the coverlet. There it was, cylindrical, small and black. Consuela reached toward the small Victorian lamp on her bed stand. There was no overhead light. She flicked it on.

The black object was no longer there.

"What the hell?" Gabriél stared at the bed cover, then back to Consuela.

Without a word, Consuela turned off the lamp, looked again. Now, it was there, only more vaguely as though it were disappearing. Quickly, she reached down and smoothed the quilt's surface. Delicately, she went over the now grayish-black flat space. "I don't feel anything but fabric, but I sense coldness, deadness."

"That's how the room felt just before you arrived."

Again, Consuela turned on the light. Nothing there. Silently, she sat on the bed, fingertips grazing the area.

Heaviness, sadness enveloped the room.

Switching the light off once more, they both looked. There was nothing on the bedcover, no object or play of shadows.

"It's gone," Gabriél was relieved.

A pained expression across her face, Consuela shifted her gaze to Gabriél. "I don't think so."

CHAPTER

15

It was the Feast of the Holy Innocents.

Infierño's heat had started early, since 7:00 A.M., the sun having struck its blinding, skin-searing rays as Mother Juana and thirty nuns arrived at the downtown convention center. They emerged from a fleet of gray vans in their black wool habits.

For an hour, Mother led them in prayer on their knees, then prostrate on the expansive lawn surrounding the facility. Penance was their witness to a fallen world. Inside the convention center, the air-conditioned building would have been too comfortable to accommodate monastic austerity.

Set in town, the convention center was the official gathering place today for clergy and religious. Seating one thousand, the three-story red brick structure had been modeled after a medieval monastery in Spain that Mother had once visited. Funded by Las Mujeres, the building project had been pushed through by Mother Juana's influence with the city council. It offered concerts, plays, and various cultural events, adding over one million dollars annually to the city's coffers.

Three years earlier, Mother received the Governor's Council Humanitarian of the Decade Award. Having clothed, sheltered, and medically tended thousands of children, she was a regionally and internationally recognized Good Samaritan.

At 9:30 A.M., the procession through the streets would begin. Invigorated by the hallowed ritual of the previous night, the nuns relished the thought of the three-mile religious parade encircling the historic city center. Mother Juana considered it a singular penitential delight since she completed the last quarter mile on her knees.

The previous night had proven invigorating save for one issue—Gabriél. Foolish boy had no more time for lessons. Time was up. Over.

Mother grinned.

Seven black limousines pulled into the parking area— Archbishop Milton Gall and entourage, four-dozen black-cassocked and white-collared priests. They stopped and parked in their designated shaded area beneath two-dozen uniformly spaced cottonwood trees. The first chauffeur, an officious brown-skinned clergyman, got out and opened the back passenger door.

Archbishop Milton Gall officiously stepped out, raising himself to his full six-foot-three inches of lean, cold, blue-eyed Aryanism. Sixty years old, he could easily pass for fifty. Beguiling looks mixed with devilish charisma made Gall an irresistible man-of-the-cloth.

Mother Juana saw through his ways.

Savvy older people of the north said priests offered their young flesh to the devil, their old bones to God. Not so with Archbishop Milton Gall.

Mother Juana snickered.

Staying in the cluster of priests, Gall nodded her way, then reconsidered and approached. Slighting Mother was not done. She watched him walk the fifty yards toward her, two rotund, coiffed clergy on each side. Bronze gleaming under desert rays, the Archbishop's crook was in his right hand. It was his crutch.

Mother loathed him.

Clergy were a necessary evil. Cut and dry answers to complex life questions were their stock-and-trade. It was religion: good old plastic Jesus, God-in-the box, a drive-up dispensary of salvation. Seven sacraments made the straight and narrow nothing more than an air-conditioned walk down an airport people-mover—fire insurance for the soul. Wheeling and dealing in run-of-the-mill fear, guilt, and self-doubt, priests had the high-end, High Mass, ritualized religion market all locked up.

Priests were Little Almighties on earth.

They were also the brunt of Mother Juana's private jokes. "Let the psychically impoverished, personality impaired, women-frightened come unto me... to priesthood," sayeth the Lord. All the nuns would laugh.

"There at least," Mother would state, "the rascals can do but little damage."

Charity, taught Mother Juana, was enough. Priests had their objectives. Mother hers.

Theirs was religion, and Mother's was Mother.

Eyeing the Archbishop, some fifteen feet ahead, she smirked.

He smacked of self-importance. Without Mother Juana, Archbishop Milton Gall would be nothing.

Three years ago, Mother had expedited a particular matter—the dethronement of the previous Archbishop, William Anarch. He had refused to approve Mother's ministry to unwed mothers. Infants were to remain with the nuns, not adopted out.

Mother withdrew her support. She stopped praying for William Anarch. The power behind the throne dissipated.

Within four days, Archbishop William Anarch was dead, and Milton Gall installed as Archbishop of the Cristo Rey Archdiocese of the Ecclesia Dei. The *Aztlan Crier* headline read *Religion Kills*. The antics of Archbishop Anarch, obscured by years of Mother's spiritual protection, had been exposed. He used, abused, and brutalized women. The lurid exposé was crafted into the regional tale of *The Unholy*.

Archbishop Gall stood a few feet away, a respectful distance. He didn't immediately address Mother, always held himself at a remove. Fear and trembling were good for the soul, Mother thought.

She didn't look at Gall. She looked through him. She liked it that way. *Searing*.

Gall cleared his throat and nodded. "Good morning, Mother. The light of the Lord shines in your face today."

Groveling fool. Mother grinned. She never addressed Gall directly. And never kissed the diamond-studded gold turquoise ring on his finger.

Gall never offered.

Mother Juana turned her head slightly. It was a sign for Gall to approach and listen. He did.

Bending toward her, the Archbishop closed his eyes as Mother whispered, "Gabriél, my son . . ." She went on, Gall flushed with excitement, then finished, "You will help. His fate will then be sealed." Pressing images into Gall's ever impressionable mind, Mother detailed the strategy — daughter-in-law and child targeted and kidnapped, sped to Mother's dungeon. Alibi was foolproof, a son deranged, committing a crime of passion, and wife's wanton desire for a powerful man of the cloth.

Gall grinned. Carnal thoughts, especially of another man's wife, always made him smile.

"Gabriél, wait just a minute. Cuauhtémoc's out of the bath. I'm drying him. We'll both go to kiss you goodbye." Consuela's voice was light and loving.

"Consuela, I'm late." Gabriél was in the study, ready to leave. He had to get to the Saturday morning procession, then to a full day's work at the center.

Last night he had failed. Their attempt at soothing one another after the night's torment had stopped short. They couldn't follow through—Gabriél couldn't follow through. This morning, he was touchy. Never had he been unable to love. Never.

And Consuela had understood. She said he was overly tired, nothing that rest wouldn't cure. But she had also looked worried.

Slamming the desk drawer shut, Gabriél grabbed his truck keys, then stopped. Drawing a deep breath, he rubbed his tired eyes. They felt irritated, like bits of sand swimming beneath the lids. He hadn't slept well.

Resting the palms of his hands on the desk, he looked out the window. Blinding morning sun seared through the sky, horizon to horizon, distant hills surrounding the Santa Clara pueblo soaking up its blistering rays. Depressed, Gabriél could hardly stand the day's intense desert splendor. It was alive. And he was dead. Or nearly so.

Softly came the touch on his shoulder. Cuauhtémoc, reaching out from Consuela's embrace, wrapped his little arms around Gabriél's neck and kissed him on the cheek. "Miss you, Daddy."

Gabriél turned and pulled him close. "I love you, mijo. I'll be home early. We'll wrestle tonight."

Cuauhtémoc's big brown eyes grew wide, and he squeezed Gabriél's neck again, tighter, then squirmed down and ran off to his bedroom to play.

Still in her loose-fitting sheer cotton nightdress, Consuela watched Cuauhtémoc scamper off. She smiled. Sunshine caressed her gown, the curves and folds of her bronze body stirring Gabriél, then nothing.

Grazing his cheek with her fingers, Consuela kissed Gabriél lightly on the lips.

Again nothing.

Consuela sensed it. "No worries, Gabriél," she whispered.

He wished he could believe her. Drawing away, he forced a tight smile. He went to the door and gave a glance back as if to say something, but didn't.

Consuela said something about things working out. Her words trailed off as Gabriél got in the truck and started it up. He gunned the engine and sped off to downtown Infierño.

Waiting never suited Mother Juana.

Parking at the rear of the full lot, Gabriél got out and looked for signs of Las Mujeres. Mother Juana would be at the head of the troop. Nervously, he glanced at his watch. Nine-fifteen. In twenty minutes, the procession would begin, the nuns nowhere in sight.

Every year since his return from graduate school, Gabriél had seen his mother off for the three-mile, hot, and monotonous walk. Priests had suffered sunstroke, altar boys dehydration, and the Archbishop cardiac fibrillation. The nuns—not a symptom. For Mother, the arid march purged the soul, harnessed the body. "Brother ass brought into godly submission."

Annually, hundreds of onlookers were awe-struck by the tiny, wool-covered seventy-three-year-old nun. Mother Juana de la Cruz marched in the ninety-degree heat without losing breath or breaking a sweat.

Half her vitality and Gabriél would feel like a man.

A small cluster of young women, unwed mothers, stood in the shade of a nearby cottonwood tree. They were wards of the nunnery, and they loved Mother Juana. Even before the woman awakened from anesthesia, details regarding room, board, delivery, and placement of their child were taken care of by Mother. Townspeople, news people, and grateful young women agreed no one cared for children like Mother Juana de la Cruz.

A block away, a hand waved excitedly through the crowd at Gabriél. Out of the dense mass came a short and plump man, Fortune Rodriguez, mayor of Infierño. A young woman clung to his arm. She was half his age, both smiling wide and bright. It wasn't like Fortune to have a woman hanging off him. Two beers at the local tavern and everyone in the joint would hear him singing the praises of bachelorhood.

"Gabriél, my friend." He was loud, happy, too happy.

Fortune turned to the woman. Her long black hair and translucent skin were unmistakable. Chills crawled over Gabriél's neck and arms. "Cassandra, my love, permit me to introduce you to one of my best friends, Gabriél de LaTierra."

Mischief sparked across her eyes. She nodded. There was a coldness about her.

Gabriél didn't like her.

"We're to be married. Next Saturday, amigo. Cassandra's wish come true."

By Infierño's standards, Fortune was a rich man. He was worth over half-a-million dollars. Four beers and a whiskey chaser had let that stumble out.

"Look, Gabriél." Fortune's eyes grew wide. He drew Cassandra's hand upward, a big diamond sparkling–harsh and cold.

Gabriél winced. Fortune didn't notice. Cassandra did and smirked.

A tug at his side and Gabriél turned. "*Aqui estas*, mijo." Mother Juana ignored the mayor and his catch. Gabriél smiled wide, glad to see his mother.

Cassandra disappeared with Fortune into the crowd.

"Wish me well. I'm not as young as I used to be." Mother Juana looked as spry as a coyote at full moon. And with reason. Money would pour in today, scores of believers having promised ten dollars for every block Mother walked.

"You never age, Mother. I wish I had half your energy."

Mother grinned and stared at him, in an odd reproving way as though having caught Gabriél in wrongdoing.

It made him uncomfortable. He broke her gaze.

In the distance, stood the Archbishop beneath the shade of an old cottonwood. He was whispering campily to a group of clerics. They were huddled like boys in a locker room.

Gall eyed Gabriél. Again, he said something to the priests. Laughter rang out louder than Angelus bells through the Infierño Plaza.

Gabriél blushed. He didn't know why. Then shame crept through him.

He looked for his mother.

She was gone.

An hour-and-a-half later, Gabriél put his notebook and files back in his briefcase. He had been sitting under a hundred-year-old cottonwood, waiting for the procession to come full circle. The time had seemed interminable. Lingering sparked intuitions about Mother's office, the weird chair, the haunted atmosphere. He tried to suppress the startling images, striking and unsettling because they refused to leave.

If a patient refused to listen to vital feeling states or mental images, there was a message. Sometimes it was defensiveness, other times it was about more than Freudian perspectives permitted. The psyche was more creative than notions bandied about by classical psychoanalysis. When a person was ready to see, they would see, and no amount of pressing or forcing would help. Soul has her own timetable.

Half a block away, Gabriél saw Archbishop Gall leading the pack. He was surprised the fuddy-duddy cleric made the arduous trek. Unquestionably, he wasn't in shape. Mother's smiling face lit across his mental screen, and Gabriél returned the smile and shook his head. Prayer beads swung at the sides of the officious priests as they chanted aloud. Hundreds of onlookers lining the roads joined in.

At least ninety-five degrees, the day felt hot enough to

refry beans on the cracked and pot-holed sidewalks. The closer Gall got, the more hollow-eyed and heat blistered he looked. Red welts splotched over his forehead and cheeks. The priests beside him looked like feather-wilted crows lining a barbed-wire fence. Whimpers, like the moans of sour old ladies, came from each one. Prayers trailing off, they went to the end of the procession and snaked into the shade.

Following the bone-tired and gaunt ecclesiastics, came the nuns—radiant. Not one broke a sweat or looked the least bit flushed. Countenances glowed. If Gabriél believed in halos, then they were an otherworldly spectacle.

Two nuns proudly hoisted six-foot bronze poles skyward, the magenta banner of Las Mujeres. Ten feet by ten feet and attached to the gleaming metal staves, it read, "Let the little children come unto me." A picture of the Almighty, arms spread wide, was silhouetted behind the caption.

Dozens of nuns filed by. One after the other, they glided across the hot pavement. Heatwaves curled up from the tar expanse as though emerging from an eerie underworld.

Lastly came Mother Juana. Otherworldliness cloaked itself about her like a specially fitted aura. Her sharp ascetic features seemed chiseled out of exotic translucent alabaster.

People clapped. Cameras flashed. Muffled voices streamed through the crowd. "*Era una santa… Una santa… Si, si… una santa.*"

She fingered prayer beads, lips moving, prayers unceasing. Cheers and applause meant nothing. Eyes heavenward, Mother was ecstatic. She knew Gabriél was watching. He could sense it.

To the side, a white, makeshift canvas canopy shaded the Archbishop. Clerics fanned him. He swayed as if ready to pass out, no one save the priests paying him mind.

Mother turned to the side and sharply caught Gall's eye.

Gall motioned the clerics away. They scampered off like mice. Immediately, he raised himself to full height and held his head high. He cleared his throat and jutted his chin.

Ever so slightly, Mother nodded.

The microphone on the podium at the front of the procession squealed. Twelve soft-mannered priests stepped up, closed their eyes, and intoned the *Salve*. It was Mother Juana's favorite hymn. The Beloved and Heavenly Co-Redemptrix was extolled in verse. Over a thousand joined in.

Solemnly, head lowered and hands clasped in prayer, Mother walked to the podium. Singing grew louder. Old people wept. Young people gazed, devoutly.

Thousands of dollars for each block Mother walked, and she was here to collect. Holy woman, businesswoman, a woman for all times and seasons was Mother Juana de la Cruz. Gabriél was proud to be her son, shivers running up his spine.

Sickly folk trembling on crutches, *viejitas* in their decades-old black lace mantillas wiping their tears, sour-faced businessman, and pay-check-to-pay-check families dropped their envelopes into passing straw baskets.

Three-hundred-thousand-dollars Gabriél guessed. It had come close last year. It would be there this year. Mother Juana said so.

Twenty minutes later, Mother finished a soul-stirring sermon. It was about abandoned and abused children, their tears when shown to a warm bed and assured of three meals a day. It was about the Infierño orphanage's sister facility in Piedras Negras, Mexico that taught youngsters about discipline and hard work and earning one's keep. It was about unwed mothers and adoptive parents, relief and gratitude, and tenderly cared for infants.

Silence enveloped the crowd. The hush made arm hairs stand on end. It was a holy moment that many later claimed was the Almighty ushered in by Mother's saintliness.

Mother suddenly appeared drawn. She closed her eyes, steadied herself at the podium. Ushers approached, gently helped her off stage to a nearby van. Perhaps she was overcome by hidden suffering, the faithful murmured. Others said no. It was holy exhaustion after the day's holy exertion.

Today, as always, Mother had worked hard for the Kingdom. Everyone knew it and bowed their heads and wept. Destitute children had been fed, clothed, and loved. Faith in Mother and the nuns meant grace, holiness, and salvation for all. And for each dollar given, the donor was one step closer to heaven.

Reverence continued to move through the crowd like sweet-smelling incense. A saint was in their midst. Mother stopped short of the van and turned to impart a final blessing. She intensified her gaze. She looked into the soul of each man, woman, and child. The moment was charged, pious moans swelling through the crowd.

She completed the blessing and entered the van. The teary faithful shook their heads and clapped, softly, then loud. Voices once more proclaimed, "*Era una santa… Una santa… Si, si… una santa.*"

They believed in Mother, and nothing could shake that belief.

Some yards off, to Gabriél's right, a group of priests fidgeted like schoolboys in church pews. Glancing his way, mischief in their eyes, they whispered one to another.

Glances darted Gabriél's way.

"Oooooh," sounded one taunting, squinty-eyed pastor,

then quickly patted his lips. The rest chuckled then mockingly did the same. Not one blushed, their red-eyed gaze streaked with meanness.

Gabriél approached.

Quickly, they dispersed. Save one. Purposefully, he had dropped his prayer beads. Slowly, he reached to pick it up from the lawn.

Gabriél came up on him.

He giggled and tossed Gabriél a quick sideways glance as he muttered something, then darted off.

Gabriél didn't catch what he had said at first. The words were rushed, and the fellow sounded as if he had a lisp. Then things became clear, and Gabriél was stunned.

Where was your wife last night?

CHAPTER

16

S amuel isn't here." Sister Thea's voice was harsh. Red glints shot from her squinty eyes like machine gunfire. The front black wrought-iron gate of the orphanage creaked.

Gabriél didn't turn to look, and he didn't reply to Thea. A visit with Samuel had been scheduled first thing after the procession and—nasty as a witch's cackle—Thea was saying he wasn't around. Again. Seconds passed.

Gabriél stood in the front patio area and would not be turned away a second time. He felt defiant, eyes riveted on Thea. Soon he would figure out a way to talk with Mother Juana about her second-in-command. But concrete evidence would be needed to prove Thea's wheeling and dealing in back-scene power plays set on undermining Mother.

He was confident the dark arts were involved, whatever

that meant to those who spoke in hushed tones and behind closed doors, regarding Thea's ties to legendary local witchery. Gabriél's knowledge of the human psyche assured him that bad people could constellate bad energy for evil ends. Sordid folk got what they wanted when they wanted it and how they wanted it—no matter the suffering inflicted on innocent and unwary souls.

Thea cleared her voice. It sounded like a truckload of gravel dumped into a refuse pit.

Gabriél didn't budge, kept her gaze.

"Piedras Negras. No more to say." Thea turned to open the door and walk down the red Saltillo-tiled corridor of the orphanage's administration building.

This couldn't be happening, Gabriél remaining silent—stunned. The boy had just suffered trauma. He wasn't in any shape to be shipped off anywhere except maybe the hospital ER. Bewilderment clutched at his mind like the claw of a predatory bird. It was as though he couldn't and shouldn't protest. Be damned if he'd accept the haughty nun's stupid answer and make himself no more than a shaky schoolboy before an ominous deity.

Just before entering the orphanage, Thea stopped and cleared her throat again—more gravel churning and chucked. From behind, she resembled a giant netherworld ogre.

Gabriél would never see Samuel again. Thea was responsible. He had to say something, anything, find some way to address a monstrous act.

"You're dismissed, Thea."

Pivoting on her heels, Thea spun around. If looks could kill... She turned back, slammed the door behind her. Abruptly taken, never to see a child again, was a harsh fact of professional life here in the Aztlan desert. In Infierño County,

Gabriél was responsible for their care and well-being, signed off on it. But the children were no longer in the country, much less the county.

And records were always found. The right letter from the right judge turned up at the right time if the issue was pressed. He'd seen it happen with the former director, and it could happen to him. There were reasons. Always reasons. The court backed community-backed justifications.

Housed in Mexico with the average swath of orphans were the "at-risk kids." Those children were hurried down south along with the children at the nunnery—a deal struck between the county courts and the nuns. The arrangement got hoodlum kids off the streets and to a place mysterious and unknown. They were the homicidal and suicidal, rapists, and con artists—gangster kids that made the local horror flick monsters seem like Hallmark Hall of Fame sweethearts.

Dangerous relatives and pissed-off gang members regularly threatened Las Mujeres by phone, mail, or graffiti sprayed walls at the convention center. They wanted to find the Mexican orphanage, break in, and get their "homeboys" back.

Everyone knew this. And everyone, common folk and law officers—church people one and all—stood by the secret. No one knew or wanted to know.

It was the Church's way. And it was how Mother did business. *A little compromise hurt no one and usually helped everyone.*

So, professional hands tied, Gabriél had to get on with things. Other children needed therapy. He had to trust that Mother was caring for Samuel. There was nothing else he could do. He spit, saliva sizzling against sandstone.

Outside the enclosure, he heard the squeak and click of

the black wrought-iron gate close behind him. After a few steps, he paused. A peculiar vibe sparked his nerves. Charging up like a generator during a power outage, his sixth sense—intuition—picked up on something.

An invisible oracle seemed to linger in the air—electricity before a thunderstorm.

Seconds went by. Nothing happened. No unexpected breeze. No flash of light. No disconcerting sound like a human voice trying to eke out a cryptic message.

Unseen energies, what psychologists called the collective unconscious, sometimes materialized in the everyday world. C.G. Jung wrote of spirits haunting a land, a place, a region befouled by calamity. Odd occurrences, peculiar sensations, striking coincidences were their calling cards.

Tent Rocks, the vision, flickered—something showing itself. Nothing came. Gabriél pictured a spirit struggling to appear but blocked by the foulness within and without the convent walls.

Arwind had been keen on listening to mental images. They dramatized vital feeling states, truths we couldn't otherwise see or understand. He taught Gabriél to pay attention to the unprompted occurrences. The more he listened and respected them, the more they came.

The vision of Tent Rocks dissipated. The spirit, far off now, had pressed to come forward then vanished, the sense of strangeness fading. Unforgiving atmospheres and its rank ghosts jettisoned and buried truth.

Why Mother Juana had chosen such a soulless environment, Gabriél could only speculate. Solitude Mother craved. Contact with people was a distraction. Perhaps carving out a sanctuary in an unwelcome desert had been her answer.

He waited. Again, peculiar energy drew close. It had been this way at his father's funeral. Everything had stopped, quieted. Something had gone on—someone there, yet not, words spoken, yet not—time fogging his memory.

Again, nothing happened, but the eerie pulsation persisted. Gabriél's mind vibrated at high pitch. Curiosity whetted, he walked on.

Grayish hues wafted through the atmosphere, foul specters, eyes on Gabriél's back. Hairs on the back of his neck curled up. He turned around.

Thea was at the gate. Spotted, she turned and quickly left, black habit flapping like bat wings in the wind. The air hung dry and rank. An odor of rotting meat rose out of the ground. Sand, as far as the eye could see, undulated here and there like burial mounds. A penetrating silence screamed through the desert.

Gabriél shook his head, tried to throw off the weirdness and revulsion. Walking on, his mother came to mind, her single-minded devotion to the poor, tunnel vision regarding the nuns and the mission of Las Mujeres. She was wise in many respects but couldn't see through Thea.

Mother Juana nurtured life, Thea stealing it away, meanness her weapon. She used it like Mother used love.

On the narrow stretch of road that ran between deep arroyos, Gabriél stopped, looked off to the left. Tumbleweeds clustered—seven or eight feet long and three or four feet wide. The spot was a hundred yards away.

Curiosity tugged. Down a steep embankment and around patches of camouflaged cacti was the only way there. He studied the site, desert sunlight biting into his eyes.

Light, as from a mirror, winked from the cluster of dried-out bramble. Something was there, hidden. Fireballs hit his retinas like blasts from a sawed-off shotgun.

Shaking his head, he closed his eyes, rubbed them gently under the lens. The shock left, and he opened them again. Slowly. No tumbleweeds. Nothing there. He looked harder, strained. Nothing.

Desert mischief happened out here. The old ones of Aztlan spoke of *los duendes*. They were supernatural pranksters. Making things appear and disappear was their forte.

But this was not mischief. It was a cover-up. Bad concealing itself. Or trying to.

Something was out there, and Gabriél was set on seeing what. He started down the steep slope of the arroyo. Loose dirt and sandstone shards were all there were for footing. A few steps and he slipped, steadied only by outspread fingertips. Steeper than he'd thought, the slope was tough, tricky.

Palm downs, he pushed himself up. Fingerprints in the dirt set a circle within a circle, an X in the middle. It vanished, covered by sliding sand. The talisman seemed nothing more than a conjuring of a sun-stressed imagination.

Throbbing started in the palm of his right hand, got hot, then jabbed like minuscule slivers of glass. Pulling it close, he saw tiny cactus needles, the kind that weren't felt right away, took a few seconds to do their dirty deed.

He looked where he'd seen the talisman. A small plant, hidden by a fine layer of dust, poked through the dry and whitish soil. It had one less arm. Gabriél had a hand full of pain.

He turned around. Stinging gave way to alarm. Beneath him was a ledge, unseen from the top. It dropped thirty feet, sharp-edged sandstone boulders clustered below.

Bad injuries, or worse, would have been Gabriél's lot, had he gone down. Less than a foot away, the ledge crumbled.

A deep breath, and again, Gabriél felt a presence. His eyes returned to where the marking had been. It wasn't there, but in his mind, the talismanic symbol glowed.

An eagle circled overhead, mystics writing of familiar spirits, guardians.

Gabriél backed away, slowly climbed to the top, and squinted, strained to see the ledge. Stones and dirt rolled downward, and the desert shelf broke off, dropped away, a ninety-degree slide to jagged sandstone and spiky granite.

On the ground, a way off, Gabriél's eyes latched onto something. He walked over and reached down for the little dust-covered thing.

It was a small turquoise ring.

It was a human voice. Samuel's. Gabriél heard with an inner ear. Arwind called it that.

Rumbling, from out of some phantasmagoric distance, started up, grew louder, then pitched high, and became earsplitting. Racket eked out a human cry.

It was Samuel.

I am where I will not be hurt, where I will not be cut, where I am safe.

Unmistakably Samuel. Gabriél intuited things about children under his care. Dreams and waking mental images read as an x-ray, tuned in to conflict, pain, need, and whereabouts.

Samuel was dead.

"I could not lie, Mother." Eyes set hard, Mother Juana chastened

Sister Thea as the Almighty with Adam and Eve—psychically stripped her down. Tidbit quivered, a nervous habit when cornered, wrapped, and fetalized. Spasming, she repeated the pitiful gesture, a creature in distress. Others would pity her. Mother, not so much.

Mother's patience had ended, now with Thea, and last night with Gabriél. He had been poking into Mother's affairs. Before leaving the morning procession, her eyes shamed her son. Unconsciously, he squirmed. Mother was sure of it. Then, he caught hold of himself and lifted his head, raised himself to full stature. Postured.

Skilled, her son traversed the psychic plane. He too maneuvered with the mind, paid attention to imaginal flights, and did not dismiss mental images. He was young but wizened. Once a potential ally, her son threatened Mother's dominance.

Side-stepping a mishap this afternoon while revisiting convent grounds, Gabriél had luck on his side. A fall would have killed more than his curiosity. And Mother would have paid no mind. After reasonable and necessary grieving—that would be that. Mother struck and moved on like a desert tornado.

Grandson, Cuauhtémoc, would be hers. He was next in line, and Mother had to hurry. Gabriél's independent ways and a wife's insolence had to be stopped. It was all planned out. In Mother's mind. One fell swoop. Consuela no more. Marriage over. Gabriél over. Cuauhtémoc hers.

Mother had had enough. Another few seconds of silence, an unblinking stare. Mother's thinly veiled contempt seeped into blood and bones and brain. She had rendered Thea a puddle of tears, the nun begging forgiveness. Too often, far too long, Mother tolerated Thea's shrouded impudence.

Authority was not hers. Obedience was—subjection to Mother Superior Juana de la Cruz.

Thea blurting out about Samuel had put Gabriél on the scent. He'd match things up with his vision. Questions would be asked. Unnecessary prodding. Problems.

And if Thea were lucky, the Archbishop would fault Mother. The Mother Superior of the Order of Las Mujeres would take the fall. Retirement from religious office was not unheard of. Gladly, Thea would step forward.

Rage burned through Mother Superior Juana de la Cruz. "The authority is mine alone. Gabriél should not have been told. I would have taken care of him. Speaking of the dead brings problems."

High noon sunlight warmed Mother's office, a saintly and pure room. There was no smudge or grime, no trace of dust, not a granule of sand. It was perfect.

Sister Thea was not. A sacrifice done was a sacrifice done—never mentioned. Mother alone followed up. It was understood. Thea did wrong. Bad. Sin.

Speaking of the dead, the precious sacrificial victim, by anyone except Mother Superior Juana de la Cruz, was sacrilege. Calling back the liberated soul brought trouble.

Secrets kept, secrets for decades, generations, were held because of fidelity to the vow of silence. Silence ensured longevity. It was the way of the Church. No one speaks, no one asks.

Thea had spoken.

Teetering, dizzy, Sister Thea, eyes set hard to the floor, touched the edge of Mother's desk.

Sharply. "Hands to your side, Sister Thea."

With a jerk, Thea became rigid, blanched.

"Mothers and their sons are true. Those of your ilk do not

understand."

Quiet settled. A minute or more past. Tears streamed down Thea's cheeks.

Usurpation was not on Mother's agenda, Thea having chased after her job from the start. Mother knew the part, the game—didn't play. Gall was in his place, and Thea would be in hers. Mother laughed.

Thea's beady eyes widened. A time came for each Iscariot, traitors speedily dealt with, suitably eliminated.

Red heat burned in the center of Mother's forehead. A hot laser of indignation seared the impertinent nun. Thea teetered, eyes rolling to the top of her head, only whites showing. By sheer force, she stayed kneeling, terrified of collapsing—petrified of Mother's predation.

No longer did Thea belong here—with Mother Superior Juana de la Cruz and her holy and loyal company of women. Thea had never belonged. Gall had instigated her placement. Pasty skinned Thea was Midwestern born and bred, a daughter of codified middle-American mindsets. She came from a land where white was white, black was black, and brown, an ugly smudge in between.

Sources reported that Thea was the Archbishop's informant. So, Mother had placed her second-in-command. It distanced Thea from the nuns. Mother alone controlled what and how much Thea knew.

And the time came, and Iscariot acted.

And then… Mother. "Thea, look at me."

Quivering, Thea raised her head. Eyes riveted, Mother Juana de la Cruz locked in.

Thea was hers.

CHAPTER

17

By four-thirty Saturday afternoon Gabriél had come home, hugged and kissed Consuela, and played and wrestled with Cuauhtémoc as laughter filled the household. He settled into a more relaxed state of mind, his body limbering up. Home was good, a soulful place of nourishment and love.

He and Consuela prepared dinner. Hamburgers cooked on the outdoor grill, blue corn chips with guacamole, potato salad, Dos Equis for Gabriél and Consuela, and lemonade for Cuauhtémoc, were the unanimous choice. Cuauhtémoc played on the swing set and slide on a small patch of lawn directly off the patio. He beamed and waved every so often. Sitting under a cottonwood tree, steps from the patio, Gabriél and Consuela let the hamburgers finish cooking as they enjoyed the cool desert evening. Gabriél told Consuela more about his vision, the day's twists and turns, and growing suspicions.

Thea was the dark priestess, the one of ill repute among the old ones of Aztlan. Outlandish as it sounded, Gabriél was convinced Thea sacrificed human offerings to work her wicked magic. Infants, stolen from the nunnery, records altered, kept her in regular supply of fresh energy. Mother delegated everyday tasks to Thea, her awareness of day-to-day acts limited. The second-in-command preyed on the babies like a vampire, religious garb a thin veneer. Gabriél was certain Samuel had been sacrificed and would not let the matter rest. Hardcore facts would be searched out, nailed down. Hardcore facts would be searched out, nailed down. Evidence in hand, Gabriél would inform Mother.

Uneasiness stole over Consuela. It was in the way she shifted in the green webbed lawn chair, got a faraway look, grit her teeth, jaw muscles taut. Then she turned to him, brow furrowed. "Things go from the top down, Gabriél."

"Thea's the culprit," he said firmly.

"Maybe you're too close. Facts get blurry when we're emotionally tied."

He knew what she was implying. Steel doors of his mind slammed shut.

Arwind's voice echoed, "You're a seer, Gabriél. Past, present, future you peer into. But what's near and dear remains hidden."

Deadbolt on steel door clicked tight.

Consuela went on, "Church horror is at work behind the scenes in our native land." She paused, frowned. "And the tomfoolery with the Archbishop and the priests... the whole thing smacks of deceit—religion as a cover-up, religion as a smokescreen." Her face reddened. "What do you think is going on with their gossip?"

Gabriél waited before answering, then said, "Stupidity."

Consuela drew back for a moment, then her face brightened. "Ahhh… you surprised me. So, you've got your edge. Just need to find your culprit. You're a good man, Gabriél."

Gabriél heard Consuela's words but was distressed, mind riveted on the one that needed to be exposed. There was much work to do, Thea's antics needing to be uncovered. Evidence in hand, Mother would listen, Gabriél unmasking the wolf in sheep's clothing.

Digging around that afternoon, he'd gotten the story on arrogant Thea. She had quite a colorful past. Shady afternoons along the Tesúque creek, naked with the Archbishop, tainted Thea's holier than thou life. Also, for three years, she had worked in an abortion clinic in Minnesota.

Scandal in the Order would not please Mother. Gabriél had to deal with the treachery of one nun—Sister Thea. Infants were traumatized then sacrificed under her care. Hatred was in her heart, not love for the young and innocent. Older children had mind-warping indoctrination dumped into their trusting and needy souls. Then the conniving nun propitiously disposed of them when short on infants.

Mother would take heed of her son's proof, and if not, Gabriél would force the issue. The same informant, a disillusioned former Church member working at the Infierño Gazette, disclosed evidence that Mother Juana knew of Thea's history. Gabriél needed answers. Now was the time, and mother or no mother, he had to be true to what he had witnessed and who he was.

Hills of the Santa Clara Pueblo swept up to the Jemez Mountain Range, hawks soaring overhead. An orange and vermilion setting sun eased down behind the Western slopes.

He put his arm around Consuela. Slipping his fingers under the shoulder straps of her white cotton sundress, he enjoyed the warmth of her skin. She was lovely.

Energy quickened. It was good as Gabriél felt what he feared lost. Consuela nestled closer, looking at him. Gabriél kissed her, lightly then deeply.

Cuauhtémoc giggled and clapped. "Ooooh, Mommy and Daddy… Ooooh." He pretended to cover his eyes with his hands, peek out, then hide again.

The evening passed quickly and well.

That night, in bed, things were better.

Barbed wire popped through Thea's skin, ocean sounds waxing and waning through her ear canals. The thick rope formed a noose over the sturdy branch of a fire-gutted cottonwood, and she dangled helplessly in nowhere-desert-land Aztlan del Norte. Back and forth, she swung, the upright log on which she long kicked away, each second an eternity.

Mother Juana de la Cruz had won.

Thea should have known better. Mother had secret files on everyone, Sister Thea included. Now, Thea would die with her past and the Archbishop's.

Far off, after the turn to the Chama River, she had driven to the exact place Mother had forced into her mind. Desolate, forbidding, here Thea was to die.

Mother would pay a quick visit and check.

It was for the good of the Order, would prevent scandal. It would hasten Thea's inevitable demise. Mother was never wrong and never lost a fight—Thea knew that now.

Past sins remained hidden only so long. Thea had no choice, public humiliation of the Order must be avoided, no matter the cost. It was Thea's only chance at salvation, Mother's declaration piercing her heart like a glistening sword turned blood-drenched.

Tiny drops of blood trickled from bare shoulders to barren ground as Thea wielded the honed German pocket knife provided by Mother shallowly across carotid artery. Thea had stripped, burned her clothes, and fixed the slipknot. Then there was the head in the noose, then the letting of blood, and soon the extinguishing of breath. She refused to resist or squirm. She hung—blood, breath, offerings to old gods and ancient energies. Nothing else could Thea have done.

Mother willed it so.

Harsh sunlight dulled to gray. No sound. No wind. Nothing for miles save the charred cottonwood and the buzzard infested badlands.

Soon there would be no sign, trace, bits of flesh or bone left of Sister Thea—the sacrifice of one for the protection of many. Desert wolves would soon swoop in on the fresh kill. Perhaps the Almighty would be merciful. Mother Juana offered consolation, but Thea recognized there was no last-minute absolution for one so wicked. She didn't mind dying. The getting there troubled the mind. By midnight her bones would be buried beneath shifting desert night sands.

White-robed angels would arrive and carry her to the Almighty. Even now, she whispered prayers for mercy—but supplication felt vacant. Angels, the Almighty, the promise of a sweet afterlife looked her in the face, and the gaze was unblinking, cold and severe, then gone. Emptiness and cold.

Surroundings faded. Timorously, she revived, and the world spun. Round and round it went like a rapidly altering gyroscope, whipping one direction then another. It made her dizzy and sick, blood spurting, vision blurring. Consciousness dimmed.

Far off, she saw the specters approach. She cringed. They were not as she had hoped. They bared rows of needle-sharp teeth and screeched, their black orbits unblinking, cold and severe. And the sun stopped its course. Blackness dripped from heaven to earth, and Thea struggled.

The angels would not come, nor would an ever-loving deity from his sweet heavens greet her with open arms.

The rope tightened and cut deeper through tender flesh, burned. Blood dripped from her neck wound.

She gagged. Eyes, Thea's eyes were playing tricks. The black-shrouded spirits with menacing teeth hovered, Mother Juana de la Cruz emerging from the center of the infernal pack.

Eyes, Mother Juana's eyes, red and hot, burned body away from soul. Exposed nerve endings, limp as tendrils from a dried-out Yucca, were tugged then yanked out—one by one. Through sheer mental force, Mother exacted retribution. Searing pain lit through the vestiges of Thea's fading consciousness, like a repeated scalding from white-hot needles expertly inserted into eyeballs.

Mind washed-out by futility and exhaustion, Thea's neck snapped like a dried twig. Soul departed flesh as a hand yanked out of a snug leather glove. Thea, now a disembodied presence, turned and looked, corpse flaccid as a gutted coyote.

Legions of uncannily familiar spirits sucked with an unearthly, vacuum-like noise that drew Thea into utter blackness.

Crossing Mother was not to be done.

CHAPTER

18

Fading sunlight quieted the autumn desert, iron-oxide reds slowly blending into shades of crimson amidst whitish clay deposits in nearby hills. Desert sage went from bright yellow and green to soft brown and gray. Shadows slipped over the face of the evening Aztlan wilderness.

An occasional cicada chirped, accompanied Consuela on her solitary walk. Just before dark she often went out near the river, no more than thirty yards from her home, a place for easing loneliness.

Cuauhtémoc lay safe and snug in bed. Gabriél was working and wouldn't be home before ten. A few more hours without him wouldn't be so bad if she could walk, clear her mind, and settle herself.

Anxiousness had tainted the afternoon. It arrived with a

strange premonition—Gabriél was compelled to do what he had to do, yet dread stirred. Fear did not suit Consuela. She did not shrink from altercation, but this enemy wouldn't permit a showdown, slithered from full-on confrontation.

Mother Juana lurked, did her deeds secretly, and no one was the wiser. Consuela was sure of it. Secrecy and hiddenness branded the deviltry of the superior of Aztlan's reigning religious battalion.

A woman of religious pretense and camouflage that thrived on fame, used whatever and whomever to ensure devotion and admiration. Gabriél refused to see the truth, needed to believe his mother virtuous. Any challenge to Mother's absolute purity would propel a grown man into crisis.

Gabriél needed to discover that a man is a man because of himself alone.

During Consuela's visit, Sophia, old wise woman and confidant, confirmed Mother's duplicity and also stressed that Gabriél was not the sole target of Juana's wickedness. Consuela shuddered at the remembrance, then started as a shadow darted along the periphery of her vision. A coyote—-plenty populating this lone land—shot between three-foot-high sagebrush as if its tail were on fire. At night, they howled like shrieking babies.

"Consuela." An eerie whisper snaked out from behind a lone cottonwood standing guard at the entrance to the bosque. A deathly quiet descended.

Perhaps it was no more than an animal growl or rustling that sounded like a human voice. Last evening had been good with Gabriél, but Consuela was still preoccupied, worried about what he was up against and its meaning for their marriage. Tired minds could fabricate strangeness, especially as daylight disappeared and nighttime began an ominous descent.

It was time to turn back homewards. Soon it would be darker, and the forest at near pitch- black night was not a welcoming realm.

"Consuela." No flight of the imagination, the sinister voice was a woman's.

A psychic image of Mother Juana pressed itself onto the white screen of Consuela's mind. As a young girl, she paid heed to mental impressions. They spoke to the situation at hand, of the nature of people and the presence of things invisible to the common eye.

A coyote, bits of whitish foam dripping from the corners of its mouth, peered out from behind a century-old cottonwood. Hatred fired out of its eyes. Abrupt movements by Consuela could prove dangerous, rabid coyotes easily spook, their bites fatal.

Crazier things had happened in the mountains of Aztlan del Norte, and Consuela was in no position to take unnecessary chances, especially since she was carrying unborn life. Shifting her gaze to the ground, she inched herself around, toward the house. A good-sized stick, four feet long and a few inches thick lay on the ground. Carefully, she picked it up.

The coyote howled. Instinctively, Consuela turned and looked. It was gone. Barking rang out from a patch of scrub oak ten feet off. A deep breath, a second's pause, and teeth locked into flesh and muscle. Consuela thought of the baby. Panicked, she screamed and kicked to no avail. Jaws locked, it bit beeper into her calf, searing Consuela with shooting pain.

Blood oozed to the desert floor. Nausea squeezed through

her stomach, lightheadedness rushing in. She tried to bat her stick at the crazed beast but was too weak and used it instead to remain standing.

Then, summoning reserves, she drove the end of the stick into the coyote's forehead. Dropping away, the coyote barked then wobbled, eyes bulging. Consuela jutted the staff again at the coyote. She missed, but the stick caught its right eye. The coyote yelped and ran off.

Exhausted from the struggle, Consuela gripped the stick tight and balanced herself even as the world spun. *The baby. Fall to the side. Protect…* She collapsed, the right side of her head hitting sandstone.

"We couldn't save the baby. I'm sorry." The female emergency room doctor wiped tears from her cheeks. Gabriél dropped into a cold blackness, hospital sights and sounds scattering to the periphery of his vision. Then his mind snapped back to the moment, riveted on Consuela's condition.

He stood up from the worn waiting room chair, wobbly then steadying himself with a broader stance, the room momentarily spinning in and out of focus. "And my wife?" The emergency room waiting area bustled with nurses shouting to orderlies; wall-to-wall patients hummed in the background.

The doctor rubbed her brow before clearing her throat and answering, "We're watching her, hoping she'll stabilize. She goes in and out of the danger zone. There's been a lot of blood loss. We're hoping she'll pull through."

"It was that bad?" Gabriél knew Consuela had been

severely traumatized medically. But he let nothing terrible about Consuela into his head. She was his wife, was and always would be there. Reality struck a rude wake-up call.

The doctor shook her head and detailed how the urgent care team had done everything possible for what she described as a medical nightmare. As she spoke, Gabriél's mind lit on who was responsible for *the black magic marked for me and mine*. An hour ago, he had come home earlier than expected (around 8:00 P.M.) and found Cuauhtémoc fast asleep, Consuela nowhere in sight. Footsteps in the sand, past the backyard lawn, led to the bosque. The night was cemetery silent. Eyes seemed to peer out from every scrub oak and far-off cottonwood, a crescent moon providing minimal light.

He had spotted a prone shadowy form at the forest's edge. He drew closer and saw Consuela sprawled out, limp—lifeless. Panic churned. Running hard, he reached her, bent down and gently touched the top of her head, and whispered her name. She didn't stir. He didn't dare move her, afraid to make bad worse. Forefingers on carotid, he held his breath. Pulse was weak, but there.

Consuela had fallen, hitting sideways, head landing hard against a jutting piece of sandstone. Smatterings of blood were smeared into the dusty rock. The side blow rendered her unconscious. Blood coagulated on her forehead, ran into a shallow stone recess, a small liquid pool reflecting a few night stars. Temples and cheeks were warm, Gabriél's fingertips sensing barely discernable breaths moving through her nostrils. Grazing his hand over her neck and back, he pressed against a damp spot along her lower back. Untucking her blouse, he saw teeth marks and blood dripping down, under her abdomen.

The baby. Gabriél shook off the panic.

Tracing his finger down Consuela's legs, Gabriél saw another bite. It was on her left leg—less savage than the one to the kidneys, but dangerous. Mad dogs or coyotes were known to run through the hills. Occult rites performed in the desert, a Satanic priestess, cowled figures morphing into coyote beasts. Consuela had been targeted and hit.

Rage ran through Gabriél's veins, neck and forehead burning. The woman, the one of dark legends and evil deeds, had attacked Consuela because Gabriél was getting too close. More rage surged like a dry heat gale. Cowardly, the witch had targeted Consuela and their unborn child.

A bite caught early enough could be treated. Otherwise, neurological complications—asphyxia, exhaustion, and paralysis—could end things quickly, especially in a compromised state. Pregnancy qualified.

An ambulance could have been out in twenty minutes. But Gabriél would not have left Consuela alone long enough to run back to the house and call 911. Delicately checking, nothing had appeared broken. He'd had to chance it and carry her home, then called a trusted neighbor who rushed to care for Cuauhtémoc while he slept.

The doctor detailed, "The trauma of the rabid bite and severe concussion caused the miscarriage. Again, I'm so sorry." She could barely contain herself, lower lip trembling.

"Consuela? She *will* be all right?" He knew he was asking too much.

"Don't know. The bite looks more coyote than dog. It was agitated and vicious. It had what's called furious rabies—mean and deep bites. Savage bites mean a shorter incubation period. Toxins are already churning through your wife's central nervous system. We can treat with a vaccine for rabies brain tissue inactivation." The doctor paused, furrowed her brow.

"Let's do it." Perspiration rolled down the side of Gabriél's face. He wiped it away, intent on the doctor. She had a troubled look.

"There could be problems." She bit the edge of her lower lip.

"Like what?" Cords of tension ripped across Gabriél's shoulders. His head throbbed with a pins and needles sensation pressing from behind his eyes.

"The head injury is bad. We need a CAT scan ASAP. They're prepping her right now. Miscarriage, concussion, rabies... central nervous system is in shock. In a small percentage of patients, especially in a weakened state, this vaccine can be fatal."

"Is there an alternative?"

"Duck embryo vaccine." She tapped her fingers on the counter of the nurse's station, glanced nervously at her watch.

"Well?" Gabriél's mouth was dry, irritability in his voice.

"We don't have any."

His stomach knotted.

Taking off her glasses, rubbing her temples with thumb and forefinger, the doctor added, "University of Aztlan Medical Center might have it in cold storage. If so, they'll fly it here. I'm waiting to hear from Dr. Devotío, Chief of Toxicology. I called him twenty minutes ago. He's doing a search. Wasn't sure they had duck embryo vaccine inventoried."

Phones were ringing by the second. People—medically precarious, crying with pain, heads bandaged, pale and green—sat in the waiting area, some with palms cupped against eyes, others rocking back and forth, cries heard intermittently from the critical care unit.

The sobering boundary between life and death appeared

like a specter in the night.

CHAPTER

19

Buried deep in the Sangre de Cristo mountain range sat the Hacienda of the Ecclesia Dei. Archbishop Milton Gall sat officiously at a twenty-foot-long cherry wood dining table. He was troubled. Worries buzzed through his frantic mind like flies around a days-old corpse.

An official document signed by Mother Juana informed the Archbishop of Sister Thea's permanent reassignment to Mexico. Gall knew the meaning of the act. Mother Juana de la Cruz had sounded the trumpet, vanquished foolhardy contenders, and pity the fool who doubted that fact.

Tightening his grip along the table edge, he struggled to compose himself as he laid the letter to the side. Thea meant more to him than he had admitted. Without her, he feared losing his ecclesiastical stronghold. Clerics, with feigned admiration and charming manners, plotted his overthrow.

Religion brokered power over life, love, and eternity, and countless were the pious men of the cloth who craved religious domination and rule.

Strange that for one so ecclesiastically accomplished, clerical conniving and self-doubt inflicted such a constant and ruthless toll. He was always vulnerable—Thea the antidote. Privy to backroom intrigue from trusting clerics enamored by her seductive charms, she funneled key information to Gall. Knowledge in hand, he flicked away ambition-ridden younger clerics, permanently exiling them to Aztlan hinterlands. Thea was everything, the protectress, lover and mother in every woman craved by every man.

The room spun round and round, his mind like a rickety and creaking Ferris wheel. Warped mental supports bent and groaned. Vertigo struck, and he moaned like an old man on his deathbed. Without Thea, he was nothing. He squelched the urge to vomit.

Patriarch Lucien Bigg, Gall's administrative and spiritual superior at the Headquarters of the Most Exalted Chancery, would be furious. Sister Thea had also been his friend. They too had had a special relationship.

A wispy middle-aged cleric, Father Estéfan, stood to Archbishop Gall's side, head bowed, hands delicately clasped in prayer. The news had been delivered. Scuttlebutt, following tonight's chanting and benediction at the Ecclesia Dei Cathedral and libations afterward at the Flaming Princess, would spread like a high-mountain wildfire. Sister Thea was terminated.

Status-seeking clerical predators would be licking their sanctimonious lips. He'd be toppled. The next generation of clergy, libidinously rambunctious queens and princesses, chomped at the ecclesiastical bit to see the old guy bumped off. One of their own would be installed. Their lascivious gallivanting would be cloaked via a centuries-old system of canonical smoke and mirrors.

Father Estéfan knew that withholding vital information from His Excellency was equal to mortal sin. A priest known not to pass on "libelous lies" in the offing was a favored priest no more. The Archdiocese had many an isolated outpost. They were rat-infested rectories hundreds of miles from sanity. Parishioners hardly spoke English and were so inbred that oddities of mind and behavior were commonplace. Drooling, nose-picking, flea-ridden congregants, were the errant cleric's lot in life. Typically, the wayward priests sought early retirement at the Holy Faith Psychiatric Hospital.

It was well known that Patriarch Bigg, with Archbishop Gall's blessing, was considering Father Estéfan for the bishopric of one of the smaller dioceses of Las Cruces, Gallup, or Raton. Nothing could stand in Father Estéfan's way, save perceived betrayal. Cunning, the priest would not permit such vulnerability. So, he placed the Archbishop on high alert for the inevitable—gossip propitiously leaked between nunnery and chancery.

Gabbing amidst the underground Confraternity of the Pink Cross—the Archdiocese's answer to Liberace in drag, clerical style—was always on the mark. So, the Archbishop did not interfere with the tail-swishing frolics of the pinky-fingered priests. Gossip was their forte. It paid to have them around, setting up the faithful for Gall's quashing of malicious intent. Empowerment was such a delicacy.

Flicking his diamond-studded right hand, Gall dismissed Father Estéfan.

Leaving the candle-lit dining room, Gall walked to his private chapel in the west wing of the palatial hacienda, the long hallways providing time for reflection and strategizing. Although no morsels of gossip or treachery conspicuously dropped from the cloistered dining tables of the silent company of nuns, Sister Thea remained vigilant. Mother knew she was being watched. It kept her in line, at least in the Patriarch's mind. Gall knew better. Juana de la Cruz was not one to be corralled.

Archbishop William Anarch, Gall's predecessor, had tried to depose the formidable Mother Superior. But he had been burnt to a crisp by high-mountain lightning. His body had been identified only by the Archbishop's official ring, a dazzling diamond-studded carved-gold band dangling from the bony remains of a blackened left finger.

And now, Thea had also been removed from office, reassigned—permanently. Danger lurked.

Mother had reason to turn on Gall. The Patriarch, despite his spying, was a step removed from Mother. Church law stipulated that direct jurisdiction belonged to Archbishop Milton Gall. Mother lived and worked in his Archdiocese. It was Gall, not Bigg at risk. Besides, Bigg was no fool. He watched his back, covered his tracks, and kissed whomever on whatever. Mother called, he ran.

With Sister Thea gone, Mother's wrath would be dead set. From the outset, Gall had maneuvered Thea's placement in the nunnery and affronted the crafty old woman. And now, gossip cleverly leaked, Mother meant Gall to suffer. He was the bull's eye for her white-hot vengeance. She incinerated many a disloyal cleric, left them as soulless beings quaking in their moth-eaten robes. It had taken a few years for Mother to position Gall in her sights. Now, he was a mandate away from being boxed and wheeled into an Archbishop's Requiem High Mass, like his lightning-struck predecessor.

Life-and-death hanging in the balance, he strained to concoct a plan to wheedle, bluff, or deal his way out of this hellacious trap. His mind was blank as the silk bedsheets procured for carnal delights. Not a whit of divine revelation struck the politically seasoned cleric.

It was a shame to let the old woman win. Mother played hard and straight. Her rules. Her war. Her kingdom. There was no winning for one opposed to the great Mother de la Cruz—unless Gall found a bargaining chip.

He reached the chapel, blessed himself, and entered. Scores of small red votive candles flickered along adobe, whitewashed walls. The consecrated space held twenty exquisitely polished mahogany pews, ten on each side of a maroon-veined, green-marble aisle. The altar was draped in cardinal red and surrounded by a polished brass sanctuary railing. Behind the altar, above a row of twelve tall votive candles, flickering like tiny spirits struggling their way out of Purgatory, hung the ten-foot bloodied crucifix of the Ecclesia Dei.

Halfway down the center aisle, Gall stopped and looked into the glassy eyes of the crucified god positioned above the front altar. The deity spoke, an interior whispering. *Be afraid, little priest… be afraid.* Every bone in his body shook. Sweat broke out across his forehead. The eyes, the piercing eyes of the looming god, glowed red. They were Mother's eyes.

He stepped back and to the side, but the eyes tracked each step. They peered into and through him, they made him cringe, they made him want to sob and cry, but he did not. He took a deep breath, stiffened his shoulders, stood tall, then approached.

It was nearly midnight.

He knelt at the cold brass altar railing. Then he stood and

stepped closer to the old deity. Candlelight now reflected a bluish hue in its eyes. Like Gall's. He squinted and saw they were now his eyes—Archbishop Milton Gall—the supreme leader of the Archdiocese of Aztlan del Norte. The Almighty watched and approved. Vigor flushed through the man.

Gall had needed Sister Thea, but that was then.

Still, Mother's powers were worrisome. Forces more considerable than those of Patriarch Bigg or Archbishop Gall were at Mother's disposal. Perhaps she commanded legions of fallen angels—dark principalities and powers. Nothing stood in her way.

Sister Thea, a woman imbued with mystery—Gall shivered with remembrance—had been considered a worthy match to Juana de la Cruz. Mother unseated, Sister Thea would have been the next Mother Superior. Then, Archbishop Milton Gall's clout in Aztlan del Norte would be secured.

But he had been wrong.

Eyes closed in prayer, Gall searched within himself. Bluish hues wafted through his soul. Inspiration hissed like a snake out of its den, the Almighty's voiceless voice.

Archbishop Gall opened his eyes, smiled.

Mother Juana de la Cruz wielded daunting powers. Patriarch Bigg was a minion. Unlike the Patriarch, wise men took notice, changed, ensured the future. Even the Almighty had made his alliances. Magdalene's ministrations and Joseph of Arimathea's gifts inevitably came at a price.

An adjustment was necessary. A favor for a favor. Mother's kind of business.

Gall had just the thing. A chip. An excellent, sandy-blonde, green-eyed chip.

Archbishop Gall would propose and expedite a new, improved, mother-in-law-rid-of-daughter-in-law transaction.

At the procession, Mother had made a request. Now, Gall would oblige. Marriage and daughter-in-law would end—sure as a wiggling nightcrawler in a blackbird's mouth, the hated match-up expunged.

Mother would get what she wanted, and there would be a favor for a favor. Gall would secure his standing and the pleasure of despoiling a green-eyed beauty before her eternal dismissal. He pictured it, fantasized, and salivated. The vision ceased.

A voice, sublime, whispered, *Can't beat Mother. Join Mother. Mother's boys abide by Mother's rules and keep Mother's favors.*

Gall's smile widened.

Poor Sister Thea. But opportunity knocked. And business was business. Especially church business.

An alliance formed, and soon Archbishop Milton Gall would be Patriarch Milton Gall.

Footsteps patted on Mexican-tile flooring down an adjacent hallway as Gall went to the east wing, the Archbishop's master suite. Father Estéfan, in less time than humanly possible, appeared at the intersection of the sconce-lit, east and west halls. He held a cell phone. Gall took it. "I'm listening."

"Archbishop . . ." The voice was hushed yet urgent.

It was the hospital chaplain, Father Tomás. No more than five feet tall, the slender, twenty-nine-year-old priest always spoke as if someone might be overhearing, eyes shifting nervously.

"Speak, Father." Gall was annoyed. He had enough on his

mind. Calling the Archbishop after midnight had better be for a good reason.

"Consuela de la Tierra." Father Tomás muttered anxiously.

"Go on." Gall felt himself key-up.

"At the procession, you told us to watch out for her. That she was a dangerous woman. Wandering eyes… lust-ridden, especially toward priests. We were to report if we heard anything."

Instructed by Mother Juana, Gall had set the wheels of communication in motion. The entourage of cavorting friars was just the thing. No one talked behind closed doors like priests—years of secret confessions rising up, boiling over, and setting tongues wagging like a coyote bitch in heat.

Scandal about de la Tierra would slosh around like manure on a rainy day. Marital tension would ensue, not at first, of course. Gabriél would dismiss the prattling until it refused to go away, became more significant by the day, took on a life all its own.

Gall hadn't questioned Mother Juana's request. Why she willed the demise of her son's marriage was her business. Deceit was Gall's. He loved it. And freshly inspired, he knew how to expedite marital failure and the passing of one, love-lost soul, Consuela de la Tierra. Ratcheting-up jiggling tongues and negotiating sworn eyewitness accounts of Mrs. de la Tierra's antics would be child's play. Despair and death (with ecclesiastical shenanigans thrown in) were always lovely bed partners.

Cemented, Gall's relationship with Mother was on its way to a sacred sinecure.

A little bad for a lot of good. It was Gall's motto. It furthered the kingdom.

Now, titillating news about Consuela de la Tierra might add *humph* to Gall's scheme. "Continue . . ." he urged in his most authoritative voice.

"She's comatose… could die." Ramirez, nearly breathless, related the facts, including the last-ditch effort to get help from the University of Aztlan Medical Center.

Gall thought, *Dr. Devotío is a staunch member of the Church. He would be interested to learn of Mrs. de la Tierra's wanton ways. He'd be told of her reputation for witchery. Her mother-in-law attests to her evil romping. Mother Superior wants the marriage ended—no matter the price.*

Father Tomás finished.

Gall stayed silent, the inspiration of minutes gaining brilliance. *A little bad for a lot of good.*

"Should I do anything else?" Father Tomás asked anxiously.

Gall's mouth watered. "Expect me at the hospital within thirty minutes. Tell no one."

"That's right, Mother Juana." Shivers went up Gall's spine.

Despite the hour (past midnight), Mother Juana had been summoned to the telephone. The matter was imperative, Father Estéfan had told the receptionist. She was a young, easily intimidated novice. The Archbishop could not wait until morning.

Mother was curt.

Gall finished the story.

Mother stayed quiet, and then merely confirmed that Consuela was at the intensive care unit, her life in jeopardy. She sounded disappointed.

"Mother, I trust I did right in calling you?" Gall couldn't risk an offense. "Did you already know?"

"No." She paused, then added, "I'm sure my son was too busy tending his wife to call his mother."

Gall went on. "Without the vaccine, Consuela might die. I… I might be able to *expedite* things."

Fondly, Gall remembered his missionary days in the Orient, mastering the black arts. There were herbs and tonics, hallucinogens, and poisons. Jumbling reality or packing the living off to the realm of the dead were his specialties. Shivers flashed up his spine.

"The baby was lost… now a poor soul in Limbo." Sheer delight. He moved forward, "Mother, what if I could ensure that Consuela follows the dead child?"

Silence.

Fingernails scratched against the insides of Gall's head, shifted down his ribcage. Nerves twisted and pulled. Cupped around his scrotum was a bony, cold hand. It was a woman's, stiff as a steel vise.

Shock left him mute.

Mother remained silent.

The Archbishop—numb.

Mother spoke. "Take care of things. Rewards will come. Otherwise—worse than Limbo. Sister Thea knows."

The line went dead.

Heart arrhythmic, tongue protruding, Gall's blood turned to ice. Scrotum clamped vice-tight.

Then, the pain stopped. He gasped.

A coyote howled as fierce winds tore through the hacienda walls. Another howl and the gusts ceased.

Wiping sweat from his brow, Gall drew a deep breath and had his assistant place a call to Dr. Devotí. The doctor understood. Gall ended the conversation and looked out the window of his second-story office, saw Father Estéfan with the black Mercedes waiting by the back entrance.

He left his office and descended the marble staircase to the ground floor. The butler-seminarian opened the twenty-foot-tall, hand-carved, cedar double door. He exited the hacienda and sat comfortably on the Mercedes' black leather sofa seat, Father Estéfan closing the door behind him.

A few seconds and the tinted window separating the driver and passenger areas slid closed. Total privacy was necessary. Killing in cold blood required focus.

The night was a windless pitch black. Father Estéfan parked the Mercedes in a space reserved for hospital chaplains. He turned off the engine. The tinted panel slid open.

"Bring Father Tomás. I'll speak with him here, and then I'll go in." Gall pushed a button on the armrest, closing the panel.

Estéfan left.

Excitement hit. It was like a leak in the Cochiti damn—then the burst. Afterglow would be sheer delight. It always was.

Gall sped dim wits out of their misery. They were rubbish, clogged up religious works, nothing more than gunk and junk, shrubs and weeds, carrion and sewage. Tough job, but someone had to do it.

Tonight, Consuela de la Tierra would die. It was Mother's wish. It was Archbishop's heavenly call. It was who he was and what he did. Archbishop Milton Gall, the man for all seasons and reasons. He felt a flush of excitement, a thrill up his spine. Shivers traveled like minuscule ants up his back, hairs on his arms and neck standing on end.

Impatient, Gall left the car, opened the trunk, and lifted the left corner section of carpeting. Reaching for a hidden away screwdriver, he popped loose a panel of steel flooring. Secretly, he had the original panel cut, the hollow place beneath fitted with double-gauged, corrugated steel siding and floor.

In the carved-out cubicle lay a small, thick, blackened-steel lockbox. Gall lifted it out, and with a twist of a key, heard the spring-loaded top click and creak open. Four trays held a dispensary of potions, toxic powders, needles, and pins.

A clear gummy substance applied to the tip of a pin would end de la Tierra's days in this world, germs swarming into arteries, veins, capillaries, and brain—an unrepentant female exterminated. Asian practitioners had gifted Gall with the invisible, pernicious bacterial beasts. A heat-tempered vial penned in their viciousness. There were enough microbes to clean sweep the human dregs of northern Aztlan, water supplies permanently contaminated.

A pin's touch and thousands of microorganisms would crawl onto the skin and into the bloodstream of the unsuspecting victim. The apostolic assassin would hold the tiny steel tip with a puncture-proof rubber glove. In the little toxic dynamo would go and set loose the biological viciousness of hell. The hottest fires of Gehenna would be preferable to such prolonged physiological agony.

It was a good thing to do. Elevated minds would sense its divine origin—purgation of befouled souls clearing space for celestial beings.

There was one other blessed courtesy. Babies needed their mothers—especially babies who were cold and alone in the gray abyss of Limbo. Gall was glad to oblige. Soon, mother and child would reunite.

A rush of adrenaline and quivers fluttered from head to groin. Energies of life and death pressed between the fingertips of Archbishop Milton Gall, foreplay with Sister Thea paling in comparison.

CHAPTER

20

Blood red ran through Mother's right eye. The oval mirror next to the door of her cell reflected the thin bloodshot lines, a multitude of claws traced over the cornea. Vessels had burst, cornea scratched, by the vicious nails of Consuela de la Tierra, her soon to be ex-daughter-in-law. At the last second, an instant before her fall, her hand reached out, middle and index fingers grazing coyote's cornea.

After Gall's call, Mother had made her way back to her monastic cell at the end of an isolated linoleum hallway. She unlocked the arched six-inch thick wooden door. A slot in the middle provided for messages, food, water, and waste removal. She entered her pious domicile.

Seclusion offered the detachment befitting a holy woman, so as to heal and hear the voice of the Beloved. She yielded body, mind, and soul to the unction of the Almighty. When Mother secluded herself for days, holy stirrings swelled.

The small white room held a steel-framed bed with a straw mattress, a scuffed kneeler with a prayer book, an enameled-gray steel table with a porcelain washbasin, and a small chamber pot in the corner.

A blood-smeared crucifix hung above the kneeler. As Mother knelt and gazed at the corpus, tingling coursed through her thighs and midsection. It ran deep through muscles, ligaments, and organs. Hot and familiar. Frightening.

Eyes closing, her mind spun. Time ceased then swirled backward, Juana now a young girl tormented by carnal stimulations. No more than seven-years-old and panicked, her mind jettisoned forward. Her eyes shot open. Flecks and splatters of crusty blood on the cell wall glowed and pulsed. Memories of childhood returned, late-at-night father times that tickled, and pleased, and hurt.

Father.

Mother forswore men, none worthy to the one. For expediency, she had married. But interiorly remained a virgin, one faithful and wedded to the One—Juana de la Cruz.

Mother alone bestowed pleasure and pain. Head turned upward to face the crucifix positioned on the wall above the kneeler, she picked up the foot-long, thorn-studded whip for flagellation. She loosened her garment and uttered prayers before letting the lash crack against bare skin. Blood trickled down her back. It purified once unspoiled flesh.

Nightly, she disciplined herself. The love of a man could never compare. Men do not love, have never loved, never. Once, they had hurt. Now, they obey. Or else.

Moans and groans, tears, and weeping were caresses for

Mother Juana de la Cruz's body, mind, and soul. Fire sprang from belly loins, self-inflicted lash after lash ravishing a woman's mortal frame. She sighed, slumped to the cold concrete.

Bliss.

Seconds or minutes or hours later, she opened her eyes, cement pressing against her right cheek. Reaching, she touched the bloodied tip of the whip. It was sharp.

She brought it close, kissed it.

So sweet is thy sting.

CHAPTER

21

G abriél closed the plastic curtain. Quietly as possible, he had left the waiting area and entered the ICU. He wanted to be alone with his wife. Odors of rubbing alcohol, medicines, and sickness swirled through the atmosphere, doctors and nurses speaking in muffled voices.

It was 1:00 A.M., the medical team hadn't yet heard from the University of Aztlan Medical Center. Everyone— orderlies, the attending physician, nurse—were on edge as they anxiously whispered one to the other. They stole sidelong glances Consuela's way, unaware of Gabriél's entrance, stress blocking out all save emergencies.

He kissed Consuela on the cheek. Her right index finger lifted slightly. A flush of warmth passed between them, a nearly invisible smile crossing parched lips. Gabriél lightly touched her lips, fingertips smoothly caressing center to edges.

A nurse peeked in, noted Consuela's vital statistics from the digital machine, nodded, then left. Gabriél sensed his presence wasn't of concern to doctors or staff. Health care professionals knew him, and that came with professional courtesies.

Needles and tubes kept Consuela alive. Heart rate was normal, blood pressure normal. Respiration was faint but steady.

Gabriél stroked the softness of her inner forearm. For half-a-second, she looked as if she stirred. Heartbeats in his throat, Gabriél again traced his finger over her forearm. Consuela moaned. Her right eye twitched. Ever so slightly, her right index finger moved, this time more definite.

A deep breath and Gabriél leaned over, softly kissing Consuela on the cheek. He whispered, "I love you." Desperation, then hopefulness washed through him. How wrong he had been in his priorities, and perhaps, a second chance was in the offing. Although, as a therapist, he knew second chances, like new beginnings, were no guarantee.

Never again would he tolerate distance to creep into their relationship. Never again would he crowd out marriage and family for pressing work matters. Never again would he take love and life for granted. Famous last words—perhaps. Or maybe not.

An image flickered, shimmered gray, faint yet malicious. A form of one taunting and teasing lingered. Gabriél recognized the specter, the quality of presence betraying one familiar but too distant to identify.

A tear welled out of the corner of Consuela's left eye. Gabriél cupped his hand over her cheek, the tear rolling onto his palm. He choked up. Her breaths were labored, raspy, heart racing. He swallowed, not wanting to disturb the moment or trouble one whose life hung in a precarious balance.

Mother Juana's face, a psychic image violently shot forward—commanded attention. She offered help. She always did her best for those whom she loved. She came when needed, presence forceful, advancing

Unexpectedly, Gabriél cringed. The underlying feeling of the image divulged deceit. *What appears to be is not what is*, Consuela often cautioned. There was more to those words, her look communicating more than his mind could take in. He didn't grasp the full meaning, but the energy of the image was toxic. Gabriél fought to dispel the foul feeling. But rage remained intense and focused.

Consuela groaned, and Gabriél shifted his attention. Her skin was clammy, moist, but electric. Her head moved slightly side to side, laboring.

"I'm here, Consuela. I sense it." Gently he squeezed her hand, closed his eyes, devotion concentrated. Images charged into consciousness. Sister Thea naked, hanging with barbed wire from a charred tree. And a black-robed priestess howled crazily, black lightning flashing around her. Samuel's ring in the desert, his voice crying out like an injured Mexican wolf. The Archbishop, knife in hand, lunging toward Gabriél.

Gabriél's eyes flew open. Sweat dripped onto his brow and down the sides of his face. At times, he and Consuela dreamed the same dreams. Sometimes one spoke the other's thoughts. Sometimes she touched him, or he touched her, and things came to mind sure as a flight of eagles through the Jemez Mountains. She'd seen the horrid presence, she strained against it, she clutched his hand and squeezed.

Stunned, her mind whispered *danger*. Things were not as Gabriél had thought. Thea was not the one. He had been mistaken and needed to stop his denial. The hairs on his arm stood on end, teeth clenched, jaw muscles rock hard.

Front and center along the white screen of his mind, the image of his mother once again forced itself forward. She snarled. Never had Gabriél seen her so furious and twisted. Dark energy once more descended, Gabriél's chest tight, breathing labored.

Hand still on Consuela, a thought came. *Decisions make the man, Gabriél.* Arwind appeared on the other side of the bed, his counsel stern.

Consuela's right index finger stroked Gabriél's hand.

When you find your rage, you find yourself. Then—decisions. Arwind's gaze was intense.

Consuela's presence became bright as a desert sunrise.

Gabriél's chest compression eased, mental fetters loosened, groin muscles relaxed.

Love for Consuela and Cuauhtémoc, their life together, welled. The thought of losing it, Cuauhtémoc without a mother, Consuela's tenderness gone, gripped Gabriél's stomach and twisted. He lurched forward, knees suddenly weak.

He gazed toward Arwind, the old mentor gone. Gabriél remembered his words, steeled himself, and stood erect. He would do whatever to whomever to protect his family.

He knew the source of the dark energy, how long he had denied it. It, too, would do whatever to whomever to protect itself. Gabriél knew Mother despised the Archbishop and all priests, thought them rancid. They hid their befouled natures beneath their effeminate dress. They were afraid of the opposite sex even as they privately derided women as vile seductresses, a missing rib better fed to the legions of hell's swine.

The Archbishop and Mother were comrades-in-arms in the church militant. *Nazi Ecclesia* had been the term branded on the sect by intellectuals, cultural critics, and scores of local independent-minded folks. Free souls knew the Ecclesia plied fear and guilt as psychic gas chambers, siphoning off mind, sincere thought, and open-heartedness.

And… so did Mother.

Now, the dark energy warned of the Archbishop. Gabriél had seen through his dealings in the black arts, and the images could suggest no one other than the reigning religious power broker of Aztlan. Killing Gabriél and Consuela would quickly tidy up matters. There would be no stopping the ruthless cleric.

Gall was deadly, and the black magic of the dark side of religion was his tour de force. Backup from Mother Juana to dispose of Gabriél and Consuela would strike as a monsoon flood. Cuauhtémoc would then be Mother's to keep, to mold.

Quicker than water rushing through parched arroyos, she'd crush Gall. Gabriél pictured the high-ranking prelate on a sandstone altar deep in the desert, a ripe feast for circling buzzards.

Mother's tactics were targeted and fatal.

CHAPTER

22

Consuela awoke, doctors and nurses crowding around her, Gabriél gone. Vision foggy then clearing, she strained to see the wall clock. 7:00 A.M. It felt as if wads of cotton were stuffed ear to ear and through crevices of her brain.

Morning light from the long and narrow clerestory window reflected off the steel cabinets and the angled round mirror near the ceiling. Garbled words floated out of gaping mouths. Faces, the room, faded in and out. Grayness like a rush of midafternoon clouds blocked the piercing sun of high-desert Aztlan. It descended further and, for a moment, lulled her into unconsciousness, then swept her back to a waking state.

Shouts, feet shuffling, orders barked out, rang through the hospital. Consuela turned away from the harsh sounds in her tender eardrums. She had no energy to call out. Temples and eardrums and the back of her eyes throbbed.

She had lost her unborn child, unbearable pain surging. Consuela wept, tears streaming down her cheeks. Instincts sharpened, more wickedness lurked. Grieving, a lifetime of sadness for a little one loved and lost, would have to wait. Steadying her mind, she tried to sharpen her thoughts.

But spasms, shots of dull then sharp pain, hit her eyes. Then chest and legs convulsed as if her soul wanted out of her body, hands, and fingers suddenly morphing into claws as though gripping onto life. Slipping away from this world to the next would be easy, simple as a hand coming out of a kid-leather glove. She sensed it plain as a vast Aztlan vista in spring.

Sophia said the soul departed during sleep, during illness, or trauma-induced unconsciousness. Travel to distant places, occasionally to past or future times, was possible during unconsciousness or sleep. Despite her hazy state, trauma had sharpened her psychic senses, and she sensed greater danger lurking. There was work to do, her present state affording entrée to mystic travel and otherworldly sightedness.

Life and love were at stake. Asleep, Consuela had seen the black priestess and witnessed Archbishop Gall's handiwork with the knife. Now, Gall was turned on her and Gabriél.

Consuela faded in and out of consciousness, then slipped away.

Gabriél's eyes shot open. Groaning and twisting, whereabouts blurry, he strained to lift his head. He was strapped down to a large wooden table. Thick leather belts ran across his chest, stomach, and pelvis. Hands to his sides, held in place by the lowest belt, he couldn't budge.

Memories shot forward like an unexpected cloud burst. Father Tomás hurrying into the ICU, saying that the Archbishop had been driven to the hospital and needed to speak with Gabriél. Time was short. It was a matter of utmost importance. To avoid a scene, they would meet in the prelate's car.

Gabriél sneered at the priest but saw his chance to deal with the evil Archbishop Gall. Consuela was stable, so he went.

The black Mercedes was in a dark, deserted spot in the hospital parking lot. The shadowy figure of the Archbishop sat in the back seat. Slowly, the window rolled down.

Intent on seizing the man, Gabriél immediately bent forward. A push came. Gabriél's shoulders hit steel, head diving forward into the car. The Archbishop moved to the side, and his driver turned and used his heavily muscled forearm like a wench to force Gabriél's head down. A chloroformed rag was slapped over his mouth and nose. Before Gabriél passed out, the Archbishop jabbed a needle into his carotid artery. Dazedly being led out of the Archbishop's Mercedes was the last incident he remembered.

Now, he was behind floor-to-ceiling steel bars, a skeleton-keyed door in the middle, jailed in the back half of a shadowy and cavernous basement. Neck bones crackling, Gabriél struggled against the leather straps, tried to shake away the grogginess. Seconds passed before his vision cleared. Musty and rank odors assaulted his nostrils like blasts from a formaldehyde-soaked corpse. Queasiness curled through his stomach, a taste of metal and rotten eggs whooshing over throat and tongue. He tried to spit but gagged, tongue thick and mouth dusty dry.

He sensed the press of Consuela's lips, her scent, spirit touching spirit. She wasn't dead. Worry slipped from his mind and evaporated like the thinning of Aztlan clouds. A palpable psychic presence meant one thing—the spirit world was close at hand. And in the realm of the deep psyche, nothing was beyond reckoning or possibility.

His mind cleared further, events unfolding like scenes in a movie reel. The Archbishop had him dragged down a flight of steps into an ecclesiastical hideaway. The place was ripe with rat infestation, creatures skittering across the water-stained, limestone floor. The twenty-by-twenty-foot room smelled musty, black mold staining floor corners.

Flexing chest, arms, and legs, Gabriél strained against the belts—to no avail. Three or four more times, he pressed against the thick bindings—nothing.

He groaned, head falling to the side, toward the adjoining shadowy room. Weird wooden contraptions affixed to the side limestone walls and spike-tipped instruments propped against the farthest wall equipped the forbidding place. Rumors of a medieval dungeon at the Hacienda of the Ecclesia Dei circulated among both believers and nonbelievers. Reputedly, it stored torture devices from centuries past when the Inquisition, brought by weal or woe, hundreds upon hundreds of declarations of loyalty to the Cross of the Church and the Crown of Spain.

These days, the Ecclesia Dei was the enforcer of the true faith. It demanded signed contracts of loyalty to the Church and its teachings from professors at the College of the Ecclesia Dei, from church employees, and dedicated volunteers to the missions both locally and internationally. Without the pact, a scholar couldn't sell pencils on a street corner, a secretary type another page, or an ardent missionary offer solace to a single destitute soul.

Economic, emotional, and spiritual threats and oppression were modern-day thumbscrews, whips, white-hot pokers, and torture wracks of the wide-eyed religious zealots of the Ecclesia Dei. From the look of things in the dim, dusty basement, the Church had preserved its nerve-severing, bone-breaking game-changers.

Gabriél swallowed hard. Beads of sweat formed across his brow. Fear rose from the pit of his stomach and pressed images of his arms stretched wide and hanging by his wrists from the wooden-beamed ceiling until he acquiesced to the demands of the Ecclesia.

One device stood out. Dangling from a rusted hook at the cell's far end was a pouch-sized hollow chunk of brass with teeth-like clamps. Thighs tightening, Gabriél looked away.

In the late 1990s, the Church had restored the hacienda after having been abandoned for decades. For scores of years, it had been the rectory for a wealthy order of French clergymen who considered Aztlan missionary territory. They converted maidens-in-waiting and supple prepubescent boys to a life that assuredly sent shudders through the old Native deities of Aztlan—Quetzalcoatl, wind god of creation, Zuni Katsina, rain spirits who dwell under the Whispering Water Lake, Huitzilopochtli, the god of sun and war, and Tezcatlipoca, the god of change through conflict.

A media fire, lit by a handful of scorned kissers and tellers, sent the mischievous priests scurrying back to France under the cloak of night. After time worked its memory-graying enchantment, the church returned to the palatial estate and set about a costly renovation.

Gabriél heard footsteps. Keys rattled. A door clicked open.

Shoes scraped against steel steps and echoed against stone walls and flooring. Then—silence.

After a time, two black-robed men spoke in hushed tones.

From the corner of his eye, Gabriél strained and glimpsed a long flight of black steel stairs that ran parallel to the back wall and led straight up to the first floor. The clerics talked at the bottom of the staircase. Abruptly, their talking stopped.

Footsteps commenced again, but now back up the stairway. The upstairs door clanged closed. Silence descended, heaviness pressing against his chest. Gabriél sensed spiritual contagion, compression of the chest by a destructive force, breathing labored.

He waited, heart pounding in his ears, a minute passing. Distress gripped him, and the press against his torso intensified. Breaths drew hard. He needed out of this horrid place. Danger curled through the atmosphere, ran through his bloodstream like tiny frenzied ants. Anger, protectiveness for Consuela and Cuauhtémoc, rushed into his legs, forearms, and torso.

Gabriél strained every joint, muscle, and tendon, the table shaking, the lowest leather strap snapping. Lifting his head slightly, he looked down. It had been nailed with brass studs to a four-inch wooden plank. Tarnished studs clung to the leather-like deadheads on a rosebush.

He yanked his wrists upwards, but they caught on the middle strap. Another swell of rage, and he tugged hard, then harder. The leather held.

The upstairs' door clicked open.

He stopped, held his breath, listened.

One by one, footsteps started down the long flight, each step slow, deliberate.

Concentrating—forehead, underarms, and hands drenched

with sweat-–Gabriél jerked his shoulders, arms, and hands, like a snapping whip. His body slammed back down on the wooden plank, loosed from the two top straps.

Steps became hurried.

He sat up, slowly got to his feet, lightheadedness blurring the room.

A key was jammed into the cell door's lock.

Stooped over the plank, trying to regain his balance as shades of bluish-gray rolled through the atmosphere, Gabriél saw a black-robed figure enter the jail cell, face cowled.

Gabriél gave a quick shiver as chills curled down his neck and back, a cold sweat starting, stomach twisting, vision blurred.

A voice.

"Gabriél. My love."

CHAPTER

23

Mother Juana stared at her son impassively, a leather patch over her right eye. Gabriél wasn't surprised to see her but was struck by the eye flap. Her nun's black habit framed her eyes and nose, shadows crawling across her countenance.

Loathing surged through Gabriél. He forced himself to hold his mother's gaze.

A tiny, laser-sharp, red light pulsed out of her left eye. He cringed. It shot to the center of his forehead, made his mind swirl, thoughts scatter like frenzied ants. He strained away from the horrid woman, legs threatening to buckle. Kaleidoscopic fractals of mind shot images of births and deaths, past and present, Consuela and Cuauhtémoc.

Tailings of injected drugs burned their way through Gabriél's veins. He closed his eyes, steadied himself against the plank, focused on his third-eye point. His mind sharpened.

On the white screen at the center of his forehead, Mother Juana hovered feet above him, emanating a blinding red glow. Strain crackled through his jaw and rib cage and coiled through crevices of brain. Third-eye burned white-hot.

Mother had the Archbishop kidnap Gabriél and transport him to the dungeon. She relished the thought of toying with his mind and torturing his soul before the final demise. Consuela first, then Cuauhtémoc cradled forever in her arms—for a wayward son to witness before his end. Gabriél would be left as carrion for buzzards.

Snapping him out of intuitive reverie, Mother's mental force shot up his spine. His head snapped back as he collapsed to the stone floor, pain radiating up his back. He stifled a cry. Eyes were glued shut. He was a twisted rag doll.

Mother's foot stepped on his right cheek and pressed it against the cold floor. Gabriél groaned. She muttered incantations, "Bagabi laca bachabe lamac cahi achababe karrelyos . . ."

From his mind's eye, Gabriél saw a bloody object in her hands. She raised it high and snarled, "Cuauhtémoc's." His son's scalp.

Gabriél wrested out from under foot, eyes shooting open. Cocking her head back, Mother howled like a rabid coyote. Rage rippled through his mind and body, head cleared. He sprung to his feet.

Mother was gone.

Images of Mother flickered in and out of consciousness as

Gabriél concentrated. The cell's door was left ajar in the wake of Mother's surreal departure. A small grated window of bent and rusted iron caught his gaze. It was a yard from the twelve-foot-high ceiling. He reached high to grip the middle of the two-foot-high bars, then swung his feet up to the bottom of the encasement.

The solder was uneven, bars vulnerable. An adrenaline rush—heart racing, palms sweating, breaths quick—he summoned the energy to grip and bend. And the bars squeaked back and apart. There was just enough space for a man of slight build to squeeze through.

The hospital was a three-mile run.

CHAPTER

24

Sunlight grazed Gabriél's face. A small circle of blood on the desert floor inches from the tip of his nose. After reaching the hospital grounds, depleted from the three-mile run, his nervous system crashed. He lay in the desert sand like a cast-off, side-swept dog.

Through plants and clusters of bramble and tumbleweeds, he saw the hospital parking lot bustling with people entering and exiting. Ambulances sped in. A squad of police cars was parked in the side lot near the physician's entrance. Six officers were busily talking with a team of doctors and nurses, two scribbling notes.

Camouflaged by loping sage, Gabriél rolled over on his back and gazed at the turquoise high-desert sky. It glistened, haloed mists enveloping terrain, curling like magical energy from *duendes*, supernatural pranksters of Aztlan that boded turns of fate and surprising outcomes.

He sensed the mind-fuzzing aftereffects of the injected drug and toxic Mother encounter wearing off. Crusty blood pooled on the ground sent a wave of sadness through him, like viewing an old photograph of a deceased loved one. Its eerie current lingered.

Gabriél touched the liquid. It evaporated, a desert illusion. Bolts of light ripped like shrapnel from his neck to the back of his head, then white-hot pain struck groin and gut. He pulled his knees to his chest and groaned. Pain lodged behind his eyes and throbbed, migraines knifing out a bloody image of a woman and child shrieking.

"Mr. de LaTierra?" The voice was commanding.

Groggily, Gabriél turned his head and looked up. He must have passed out. Head pain had ceased. Slowly, his eyes adjusted from sunblind bright to morning high-desert hues of piercing sky blue, soft earth brown, set off by crisp green cottonwoods and stands of piñon.

Three police officers, two with pistols in hand, encircled him. He thought he knew them but wasn't sure since—vision blurry. They looked concerned but officious. Wobbly, he tried to get to his feet.

The voice boomed, "Sir, do not move." Two of the officers were on him, quick as coyotes on fowl. Head back to the dirt, they held him down and strapped on handcuffs. "Sir, please do not resist. We will be taking you with us. Suspicion of murder—your wife and son."

Gabriél's world collapsed—a home falling in on itself.

CHAPTER

25

G abriél stood handcuffed in the middle of a thickly padded psychiatric rubber room. Two officers stood at the locked door. Dr. Fuentes, a seasoned psychiatrist and friend, looked teary as he spoke, lower lip trembling slightly. "There's no reason for tranquilizers, Gabriél—unless you act up again."

Gabriél had been disoriented and enraged when hearing about Consuela and Cuauhtémoc. Upon arrival inside the hospital, he had been released from handcuffs but attempted to bolt. He took down two officers. One suffered a broken rib and the other a bad blow to the face. Orderlies wrestled Gabriél to the floor, then ushered him into the white-padded square box.

He knew both of the injured officers and would talk to them, try to make amends. They weren't the ones at fault.

Dr. Fuentes, brown eyes warm and compassionate, went on, "You're not suicidal, and there's no indication of hallucinations or delusions. You appear to be coherent and able to exercise reason and adequate judgment. From what you've said, you were injected with a central nervous system depressant. I think its effects have about worn off."

A deep sigh, and he continued, "But I'm going to have to keep you in confinement, under observation. We'll see how it goes."

As Dr. Fuentes and the two officers left the room, Gabriél sat in the middle of the floor. Before the door closed, Jorge Montoya, Sheriff of Infierño County, walked in. He and Gabriél were close. They had worked many cases together, brought the forsaken and forlorn, the despairing and despised, into these very quarters. It was solitary confinement for the demented and dangerous.

Worry lines creased Jorge's middle-aged face. He was a good man, but as Sheriff of Infierño County, he had a job to do. The inpatient holding tank was Jorge's sole recourse. Gabriél knew that, but he still needed answers.

At least an hour had passed since hospital admittance.

Jorge cleared his throat before stating what Gabriél surmised. "Right now, circumstantial evidence links you smack-dab to the crime. We've got nothing concrete, but enough to keep you for a seventy-two-hour hold." He paused, then went on, "Motive's there, Gabriél. Crime of passion. Temporary insanity. Dissociated, then went unconscious."

He let some seconds pass. "Like I said… Archbishop swears Consuela had been coming on to him. You found out. So, you went for her, then tried to get him and couldn't. We found you out back of the hospital just where the Archbishop said you attacked him."

Another pause before continuing, "You took Cuauhtémoc to see his mother in the hospital. That was before you found out about the Archbishop. I know Consuela and don't believe it, but gossip-hungry people will and do. It was reported that you were talking to a priest, Father Estéfan, here in the hospital before the crime. He said you forced him to the Archbishop's private parking space. Archbishop Gall had just been in the hospital, ministering the Last Rites."

Jorge's eyes never left Gabriél. "Father Estéfan said he saw you as he left from a visitation to one of your neighbors. They confirmed he had brought them communion. He saw you from a distance raise a large rock and lunge at Consuela. You tripped and hit Cuauhtémoc, a boy killed by a blow meant for the mother. The hospital staff witnessed your temper, Gabriél." Jorge sighed, "You had motive and access… then took advantage of the situation. DA will line it up that way, Gabriél."

The horrid scenario painted of Consuela and Cuauhtémoc was like knifing Gabriél in the back. He closed his eyes. Again, he sensed Consuela, presence near. Tears welled. Swallowing hard, he looked straight at Jorge.

Intuition sparked by pain and trauma, he saw into Jorge's memories, a scene from two hours past. A young officer called to the Sheriff from one end of the short concrete hallway of the locked unit of the county psychiatric hospital.

"Mother Juana to see you, Sheriff."

Jorge walked down the hallway to the entrance where she stood. A gnarled finger motioned him closer, and the woman who provided spiritual ministry and millions of dollars for the care of severely disturbed patients whispered instructions. Her mind branded itself into Jorge's, and he was at her command.

"Looks bad, Gabriél." Jorge shook his head. "I'll check on you later."

Gabriél got up, walked behind Jorge to the grated door.

Jorge hesitated, waited, back to Gabriél as he reached for the door.

Gabriél took a deep breath. "Jorge, where are they?"

He didn't answer, simply opened the door and clicked it shut behind him.

Gabriél set his face into the bars. "Consuela and Cuauhtémoc?"

"Gabriél . . ." Jorge turned around, looked blanched. Seconds lingered. "I've seen nothing. But I've been told there's an arm here. A leg there. Female adult. Male child. Mutilated, then burned."

Dizziness, then things spun out of focus, went dark and black for interminable seconds.

Eerie background voices of patients ceased.

Silence.

Shadows in the hallway disappeared.

Jorge's distant voice affirmed, "Deputies are scouring your property and surrounding areas. If we find anything, prints should give a positive ID. Consuela's dress, Cuauhtémoc's shoes… have already been positively ID'd by Mother Juana."

Gabriél wailed, slammed both fists against the padded steel door, the thud reverberating down the hall like drones of thunder.

CHAPTER

26

Nothing suited Mother Juana more, in this instant, than Gabriél locked up. The key wouldn't be thrown away, didn't need to be. She sat behind her desk at the nunnery and smiled. Gabriél would be neurologically cared for. An undetectably thin and electrified needle would be inserted through his eye socket and pierce his frontal cortex. An errant son would be rendered eternally compliant—Mother Juana no longer troubled.

Mother had never really cared for her son. He wasn't malleable, as was his father. Unfortunately, in quiet moments alone, father had influenced son and helped him live out what the father could not. His father loved him, and that made a difference—too much difference. But that was that.

Gabriél was soon to be disposed of, and Cuauhtémoc was Mother's. One boy ended, another gained. Fresh blood for the

Altar of Sacrifice. And… Consuela was dead—or would be. Mother chuckled.

She drummed her fingers on her desk, delighted. For now, mother and child were jailed in the dungeon beneath the nunnery. Bones from other sacrifices had been spread around the countryside surrounding their home. Mother's influence ensured none would be the wiser. Gabriél's medical file would document uncontested sentencing to the Las Vegas Prison for the Criminally Insane. Mother had her ways.

Timorous raps from Sister Gertrude, Thea's eager replacement, stopped Mother's musing. Nuns were a traitorous bunch, so Gertrude was painstakingly under Mother's watchful gaze. Mother ruled, Mother willed, Mother got.

"Come in," Mother Juana ordered, voice exceptionally stern. Today, she seethed with wrath. Things must be ended. No delay or interference. A special treat awaited anyone who dared question or cross Mother Juana de la Tierra.

Gertrude, a mousy, stoop-shouldered woman, slowly opened the door. No more than five-feet tall and of frail figure, she deferentially crossed the threshold. Trepidation was wise since the smaller and humbler, the meaner the bite of the tiny rat, and Mother knew it.

Distance, cold-hearted glowering, said it all. *Mess with me, and you'll not be.*

Head bowed, eyes to the floor, neck covered by her black wool habit, the trembling nun closed the door. It clicked shut. She remained inches from the threshold, hands tucked inside billowed sleeves of the loose religious garb.

Mother's gaze bore straight ahead. She ached to sear the minion. It was the nature of religion to breed groveling souls, a thinly veiled, betrayal-spiked snapping and frothing, always lurking. The Judas curse lay within the religious breast.

Burning Gertrude to her spindly core would leave a messy pile of black ash. Regularly, the janitor swept away debris into an extra-large black dustpan, then disposed of it in the convent's industrial trash bin.

Mother waited. Impatient, she demanded, "Look at me." Gertrude's head jerked upward. Red indentations, an infected ring around the spoiled white flesh beneath her chin, stood out like the bites of a vicious vampire bat.

Gertrude lifted her shoulders and chin, tried to hide the exposed and crusty puncture marks. Mysteriously, they appeared during sleep on the neck of each new appointee— on the eve of her placement—during early morning devotions. Mother's nighttime visitations did carry a bite. Gertrude's cold blue eyes turned milky white and rolled to the back of her head.

Mother's gaze stayed fixated on the center of Gertrude's forehead. Nuns were cheap cloth puppets to be kicked about along a dusty and filthy Tijuana street. Gertrude swayed, legs wobbly, head bobbing up and down.

"You will do as I say. Is that understood?" Barely keeping her balance, Gertrude nodded.

"You and the janitor go to the dungeon and confirm that Gall has left my daughter-in-law, and the child is drugged and unconscious. Later, at my instructions, I will have her wrapped in a tarp and driven into the desert to the hallowed place. Leave the child to me. I will be present for the ritual tonight at the time of the full moon. The mother will be undone, flesh from bone, sinew from marrow. Again… leave the child. He is mine."

CHAPTER

27

Consciousness slowly returned from Consuela's spirit sojourn to Gabriél. She had imparted the strength of their love, spirit-to-spirit. Her touch, the scent of her husband, tenderness lingered as she made her way back from the etheric realm to harsh reality.

Despite the grogginess, she knew Mother Juana had kidnapped her. She had been transferred from a medical room to a basement cell. The dank smell and earthen walls of the dungeon made breathing hard. A drug injection lapsed her in and out of consciousness as she groped for a hold on reality.

Thoughts of escape felt futile. Consuela's heart sank, a dark mood shrouding her naturally buoyant spirit. But one thing rang true. Mother was keeping Consuela alive for a reason. Why, Consuela did not know, but what Mother needed, Mother got.

She stood up from the mattress on which she lay and caught sight of Cuauhtémoc nestled on a trundle bed in the adjacent cell. Deep inhalations and exhalations suggested undisturbed sleep. All was preparatory, Mother's agendas legendary. Chills ran up and down Consuela's spine and arms. Mother Juana de la Cruz scathed and fileted everything and everyone she hated.

What the tightly wound Mother Superior was up to was anyone's guess. But sure as the day was hot and dry, she never left a trace. Consuela was sure that her body would never be found. And Cuauhtémoc… she shuddered.

The cell was small, six-by-nine feet of gray concrete walls and flooring with evenly spaced steel bars caging in the unfortunate resident. The jail door had a skeleton key lock, rust around the edges, showing it hadn't been used in ages. She ran her fingertips along the sharp edges and centuries-old memories, horrible experiences of past inmates whipped through her mind.

Foggy minded and lethargic, she felt faint, symptoms of a drug hangover. She moved to the flimsy mattress that lay atop the concrete steel shelf bolted to the wall. Every joint in her body ached. Crackling sounded through hypersensitive ear canals, muscle fibers quivering.

Her feet touched the cold floor. The instant she set weight on her ankles, her legs felt unsteady, weak. She slumped back to a seated position.

Maybe there was a way to pick the jail cell lock. It would help if it was badly rusted and would tumble and snap free with pressure. A stray bobby pin might do the trick. She'd done it once as a rowdy teenager temporarily confined to a detention center holding cell for unruly inmates. Those days were long behind her, lessons learned, but some skills kept for rainy days and back-up-against-the-wall emergencies.

Footsteps, harsh and clunky, echoed down a set of metal stairs set against a far wall. Figuring that playing possum might be best, she lay down and closed her eyes. Someone made their way to the cell.

An old man, voice low and raspy, spoke, "Boy's out cold in the cell next to the mother. And looks like she hasn't come to. They'll stay that way till tomorrow is my guess. Injection had enough punch to take down a mule. Wonder they're alive. Maybe they aren't." He chuckled.

"We'll take him to Mother Juana later. The mother's to be dealt with first."

Consuela sensed a second person, footsteps must have been light as vulture's feathers.

The old man shuffled closer to the cell and pulled on the bars. They rattled. Sounded flimsy. "Hey, hey… you awake?" He spoke like he expected an answer.

Consuela barely breathed, not a flutter of an eyelid. Feigning sleep was essential. But if they opened the door, she'd bolt up. Adrenaline could lift cars and raise a felled tree. Man was old, she was young, him no match for fury fueled by peril and loss.

"Mama sure is sleeping," the codger affirmed. "Kid too." It was bait. Voice was testy, then, quiet. An old man's raspy breaths. Quiet, then a draft. Suddenly, a cold clammy hand gripped her neck, squeezed. Her eyes flew open.

An old African-American man with huge bloodshot eyes, a wispy nun by his side, stood next to her bed and smirked. "Guess you are awake."

She squirmed out from under his bony grip and shot to her feet, arms cocked to her side. Legs wobbling, she widened her stance.

He laughed and mockingly stepped back, hands in the air. "Ahhh . . ."

Blindness struck. The dungeon smelled rank, stale, and turned winter cold and damp. Fingertips shoved her back to the mattress. She landed rock hard. Blindness passed. She lay paralyzed.

The snarl-toothed man with skin like sun-blasted leather stood before her and smiled wickedly. There was no one else. He bent down beneath the bed and latched straps across her chest and legs. "We'll be back. Don't even think of trying anything foolish, cuz we see things far off and near." His low-toned laugh was like gravel tumbling through a steel chute.

Old guy and nun turned and suddenly appeared at the stairwell landing, shot off one last menacing gaze before trudging up the long flight of stairs. Consuela's skin crawled. The dungeon door at the top of the stairway creaked closed.

CHAPTER

28

Impatiently, Mother Juan waited, drummed her fingers on the scarred wooden desk. Old Snarl Tooth should have been back. Old Snarl Tooth had roamed realms both natural and supernatural for centuries, and ages before the orphans had been squirted into existence. He was master of dark intrigue and hidden ways. Nefarious power lit through his crusty veins like lightning across a high-desert sky.

Still, Mother was not to be kept waiting.

She heard him dragging his left foot along the long Saltillo tile hallway leading to her door. Scrape, scrape, scrape dragged the old leather shoe, constant scratching of grit and grime. Click and drag, click and drag, click and drag.

Footsteps ceased at Mother's office. A flimsy door stood between her and one who in a millisecond could tear and shred whole universes asunder, propel stars and moons into chaotic zigzags of cosmic frenzy.

Chills curled up Mother's spine, finely lacerated pinpricks of spindly fingers trailing their way up the back of seventy-two-year-old Mother Juana de la Cruz.

Always, Old Snarl Tooth waited before knocking. A full minute passed. Keeping Mother in suspense titillated the dark master of psychic scheming and tricks.

One harsh knock sounded. Mother flinched. Mother seethed.

Centuries past, she crushed the head of the snake beneath her heel, ground him into earth like refuse. Mother answered to no one.

Snarl Tooth hissed, "Come… Now!"

She did not answer. She answered to no one. She was Mother Juana de la Cruz. Her son's fidelity was the issue, and nothing took precedence. Nothing and no one.

The door blew open.

Old Snarl Tooth was no more. A swarm of flies appeared and morphed into a cloud of darkness in the form of a man. Flies disappeared. Cold and Dark hovered in the atmosphere as an ominous presence. Evil One, Father of Disorder, Disharmony, Dissonance, and Damnation—Ages Past to Ages Present—projected mind there to here without stepping outside His hell place. Old Snarl Tooth was but one of many incarnations—Abaddon, the Destroyer, Beelzebub, Mephistopheles, Lord of the Flies. Father of Darkness.

Outraged, Mother knew He whose presence had violated *Her* chamber.

Two invisible cold and heavy hands were laid on her shoulders. Left hand lifted and sharply forced her head downward, chin against chest. Neck bones crackled and cracked. Pain excruciating. Legions of demons ridiculed the great Mother Juana de la Cruz. Sulphur seeped into Mother's nostrils. She stifled a gag, suppressed moans.

Her right then left shoulders snapped like dried-out tree branches.

Evil had made good on His promise—immortality. Mother had made good on her promise—perpetual sacrifice. He permitted no demands. He answered to no one. No tolerance for Mother's wrath. Thought impressions of Father of Disorder, Disharmony, Dissonance, Damnation, and Darkness seared through her skull and into the folds and crevices of her brain. She wanted to scream.

He lifted his hands and wordlessly hissed, *Time's up, little mother*! His inner voice thundered, forcing Mother to cringe. She clamped the palms of her hands against her ears and dropped to her knees. More thought impressions seared into mind, *Mother... a sorry black-woolen bundle of old and crumpled misery.*

In desperation, Mother summoned the intonation, *Bagabi laca bachabe lamac cahi achababe karrelyos... Bagabi laca bachabe lamac cahi achababe karrelyos... Bagabi laca bachabe lamac cahi achababe karrelyos... Bagabi laca bachabe.*

Evil pressed its cold but invisible finger to the center of her forehead. Her words trailed off. Moving the finger to the small of her throat, he dug deep. Soft pink tissue pulsed. Her breaths became frantic.

She sank within herself, calling forth secret reservoirs of rage unknown to the Master of Deceit and Darkness. She seethed, *Bagabi laca bachabe lamac cahi achababe karrelyos...*

And, Mother's head snapped to the side quicker than a rattlesnake ready to strike, rattle erect and threatening. *Mother answers to no one.* She burned the rage-quickened words into the forehead of the dastardly foe.

A guttural laugh, and the invisible finger again pressed into her throat's soft tissue. And the finger dissolved. Presence faltered. Energy waned. Vigor sloughed off like radioactive tailings.

Mother stood up, shrugged her shoulders as if brushing away a fly, then flung her right hand at traces of the invisible presence. Furiously, she chanted, "Bagabi laca bachabe lamac cahi achababe karrelyos . . ." Inching upward, adding a foot to her petite frame, Mother's voice resounded, "Bagabi laca bachabe lamac cahi achababe karrelyos . . ."

She directed thoughts to residues of the hellish presence. *You measly piece of infernal shit. You ill-begotten, rotten tidbit of the Almighty's ass. You pitiful and miserable panderer of falsities.*

Red light glowed wall-to-wall, minions of red luminescent specters circled about the receding presence of her now former Infernal Master—etheric traces of the Father of Disorder, Disharmony, Damnation, and Darkness evaporating.

There were no new stories, only old ones retold, and now the Indomitable Mother had once again crushed the head of the snake beneath her heel and, by the power of her mind and might, made him nothing but a foul odor dispersing on a windy Aztlan night.

She was Mother—-Mother Juana de la Cruz, and Mother was not to be crossed.

CHAPTER

29

Chains rattled as the upstairs door to the dungeon creaked open. Consuela looked from her mattress to the iron chains hanging from the surrounding walls. Rust suggested antique instruments that bound hands and feet to rollers at both ends of a steel frame. They had been used to stretch and dislocate joints.

Hundreds of years before, during the Inquisition held by the Cross and the Crown of Spain in Aztlan, torture racks forced religious compliance. If victims did not yield, they suffered a drawn-out and agonizing death.

Footsteps made their way down the long flight of steel steps. Consuela counted each one. A chain, one dragging from each hand, echoed off each stair.

After fifteen steps, the sounds ceased. A rattling began, the chains held in midair, shaken with words echoing through the cold cell. "Bagabi laca bachabe lamac cahi achababe karrelyos."

The words resounded as though from an unearthly realm. Lyrics, a nerve-wrenching incantation, were like razor wire wrapped across the human heart. They were the dark magic feared throughout Aztlan, seasoned curses of the oldest of Mother witches. She was reincarnated in each generation, intoning the formula from *Libro Negro*, the black book of arcane magic.

Bagabi laca bachabe lamac cahi achababe karrelyos.

Consuela groaned as the vibrations buried themselves in the folds of her brain and down her spine. Waves of heat and cold triggered sweat and shivers. The chant rang on, forcing her arms, hands, and fingers to tremble.

Any instant, flesh could turn to flames. Her heart pounded and thumped from sternum to sacrum. White-hot electricity streamed down her left arm and into her core and pelvis.

Never had pain been so excruciating. She refused to yield, rejected the pull to despair. She curled into self. Electric currents grew hotter behind eyeballs and temples. Strands of sandy-blonde hair stood on end, electromagnetic energy burning from core to skin.

She imagined roots from an ancient world tree growing into surreal earth. The tree branches extended upwards to realms transcending space and time. Consuela, nearing her pain tolerance, wanted to cry out but stifled the urge.

Straining her body upward to break the leather straps, beads of sweat dripped, then poured down her forehead and temples. White heat from her core intensified—swirling circles of white light. Psychic energy at the center point of her brow propelled power outward—mind to mind.

Abruptly, the racket ceased. Chains dropped to the steel stairs, a tortured shriek merged into legions of screams, generations of tormented women.

Heat from the center of Consuela's brow drew energy deeper within. The wailing of women dissipated as dust devils scattering into the horizon. Quiet descended over the room. And the footsteps staggered back up the stairs, a door slamming shut.

Inner energy morphed into a miniature sun. An inch above Consuela's brow and an inch deep into her forehead, it pulsed.

Consuela drifted deeper within her mind, into a realm liminal and transcendent.

Her spirit left the cell.

CHAPTER

30

Chokeholds worked.

It was midnight, and things seemed quiet in the locked psychiatric corridor.

Gabriél was set.

Jorge, his old friend and chief of police, had stayed on graveyard shift. He knocked on the steel cell door, clicked the lock, and walked in. Gabriél paced back and forth. Insomnia scattered ragged energy through Gabriél's skull like the gnarly fingers of a lightning bolt.

"You doing okay?" Jorge asked, not expecting an answer. Then, he turned sideways as if to check outside the window. A fellow high school wrestler, Jorge never let down his guard. Gabriél made his move, wrapped, yanked, and held his forearm across Jorge's neck—squeezed.

Jorge struggled, but not much. Gabriél had tried more than

once to pin him to the mat during rounds of friendly sparring—never succeeded. Now, Gabriél applied pressure to the carotid with bicep and forearm. Cerebral hypoxia set in, and Jorge quickly went limp. He slumped to the concrete floor. Keys dangled from the chain hooked to his thick leather belt.

Gabriél unlocked the handcuffs, and keys in hand, he touched Jorge's forehead. Images formed. Eyes mirrored the soul, experiences and memories. Mother had summoned Jorge. After whispering instructions, she intimidated that refusal would compromise the lives of orphans. Her eyes were fearsome and hypnotic.

Shaken by the potency of raw evil masked as sanctity, Jorge was disoriented. He was compelled to temporarily appease malevolence to safeguard innocent lives and that of a friend. He carried out Mother's orders—in his way.

Gently, Gabriél laid Jorge's head on the floor, then unlocked the cell door. He hurried down the short hallway, looked out the wire mesh window in the center of the main entrance. The outer office was empty, 1:00 A.M. by the wall clock. He shoved the key in the door, and faster than a rattler through grass and underbrush, he was out the back door.

For too long, Gabriél had been blind to truth.

CHAPTER

31

Dazed from Consuela's unexpected display of psychic might, Mother opened her eyes.

She had never left her desk chair, spirit projection a simple task. Chains in hand, footsteps and all, she had been making her way down the dungeon stairs. Particles, waves, atoms coalescing across time and space were a well-honed supernatural skill. Except this time, she had encountered a startling turn of events.

She would settle the score with her haughty daughter-in-law later.

Right now, finishing off her son was priority. Energetic shifts tell all to a hovering mother. Gabriél had done the unforeseen. Mother expected him to show up, kick out the door hinges to her office if necessary. She anticipated no less from the male she had suckled and disciplined.

He'd attempt a replay of the Father of Evil and try to outwit Mother. But she was Mother—Mother Juana de la Cruz.

She was livid, antipathy a narcotic soothing to her wicked veins. A red-tipped fire rushed through her petite frame.

Footsteps crept craftily down the hallway. Gabriél had escaped from the county psychiatric facility on the outskirts of the city. Less than an hour earlier, Mother's intuition flamed bright as a noonday sun. A vision exposed Gabriél dashing out the back door of the holding tank. Quite a stealthy man was he—Mother's son. *Mother's*. The only man capable of meeting and holding her gaze, the only man capable of thinking himself a worthy contender. Gabriél de la Tierra was his mother's son.

She sensed a presence outside her office door—waiting. This wasn't like Gabriél, one not prone to hesitancy with Mother. If it was him, then a pitiful change had taken place. Marriage had softened the man. Unfortunate.

She lightly drummed her fingertips on her desktop, a smile ear to ear, saliva tingling against tongue and cheeks.

Quiet lingered. Seconds on end, silence agitated Mother's nerves like buzzing mosquitoes during nighttime prayers. Her breathing ceased, listening intensifying.

More silence.

Heartbeats steady, breaths light, Mother traced an invisible circle of magic on her desk. It was a few inches in circumference—an X in the middle. Days past, she had seen from a distance her son's mystic ward. Training about the unconscious mind had taught him the art of spontaneous conjuring.

Circling and circling with her middle finger, she completed the seventh rounding. Then she placed the palm of her hand in the middle of the circle and hissed, "Bagabi laca bachabe lamac cahi achababe karrelyos… bagabi…"

Seventh incantation complete, and Mother transformed. Molecule by molecule, she became no more than a hologram, and then vapor, then a vortex—dry and cold.

The door banged against the back wall, etheric Mother shocked.

She-creature entered, wildcat on the attack.

And Mother prey had vanished.

Traces of Mother hung in the air. Once before, Consuela had entered the guarded sanctum of Mother Juana. Instantly, she sensed its wickedness.

Instincts stood on high alert.

The room was meat-freezer cold.

It suddenly struck her—Cuauhtémoc had been taken. Her son had been stolen away as she lay spiritless in her cell. Mentally, Consuela had escaped from the confines, anger targeted, and now Mother had disappeared—in an instant gone to Cuauhtémoc, absconded with him.

She knew of this conjuring—its pernicious ways. And she knew the magic that happened by the setting of a woman's intent. She knew more than Mother imagined.

Consuela pivoted toward the fireplace behind her, in front of Mother's scarred wooden desk. Ashes swirled in the shallow recess as though caught in an upward draft, a prolonged dance that sent a shudder through Consuela.

A puff of smoke burst into the room, obscuring the surroundings. Confusion lit through Consuela's mind like noxious gases. Her spirit weakened, faltered. To die out, apart from the body, would be disastrous. There would be a corpse in the dungeon cell. Cuauhtémoc would be motherless.

Consuela concentrated, white light radiating from core to extremities.

The room returned to normal temperature.

Consuela's senses sharpened.

She was compelled to remember days gone by.

The day before their elopement, Gabriél surprised Mother Juana with his bride-to-be. Officiously seated behind her desk, Mother's eyes burned a smoldering dry-ice white as they surveyed the young beauty from head to toe.

It was loathing at first sight.

Unblinking with fingertips steepled, Mother spoke two hungry words to the couple as she gazed heavenward, "Grandson. Mine." Dismissively, she then turned in her swivel chair, eyes upraised to the steel crucifix centered on the wall behind her desk.

Mother Juana de la Cruz had not known Consuela was one month pregnant. Gabriél had not told her.

Secrecy kept safe what power could spoil.

Gabriél confided to Consuela that power, not religion, was Mother's god. He spoke of the crucifix behind her desk symbolizing that power.

And now the crucifix was gone. Mother had taken it—for one terrible purpose.

Town gossip held that the nuns committed vile acts in a lone desert sanctuary. They engaged in obscenities with bleating animals and screaming men and children, orifices violated with steel crucifixes. Those thought relocated to Mexico were butchered limb by limb as sacrifices.

Cuauhtémoc was being taken there, kidnapped by Mother. Consuela felt it to her core. Fury further sharpened

Consuela's focus, mystic third eye burning. Mother's plan for Cuauhtémoc had changed from guardianship to sacrificial victim. It was spite, a vicious act to be witnessed by mother and father.

Consuela's powers burned from solar plexus to third eye, woman's intent—set.

Mind returning from memories and sightedness, Consuela noticed the rank smell of Mother's office had yielded to scents of mountain sage and blowing dust, bits of sand pelting Consuela's cheeks.

Intention set, a moment passing, and she stood camouflaged behind scrub oak and sage. She saw the slight figure of Mother Juana de la Cruz, deep in an arroyo, wrapped in the swirls of a dust storm, her back to Consuela.

Mother Juana de la Cruz cried out, "Bagabi laca bachabe lamac cahi achababe karrelyos." Legions of nuns screamed forth, "My soul I pledge to Thee, Thine promises now be mine." In the darkness of the nighttime desert along the arroyo, surrounded by mesquite bushes hung with prayer beads, the nuns proclaimed their vow.

A colossal goat descended from the high country. It entered the arroyo and circled the nuns as they danced. Each kissed his tail.

Then a giant black snake slithered across the desert floor, coiling around each nun. Its tongue entered the open mouth of Mother Juana de la Cruz.

Consuela was horrified.

Out of the silence of the desert night, four men dressed in black emerged. They carried a coffin. A child's corpse was carefully taken out, and the frenzied nuns fell on it like ravenous coyotes.

Consuela's presence crackled through the atmosphere, white lightning from shoulders to the tips of her hair.

And Mother turned her way, in her arms another child—Cuauhtémoc.

CHAPTER

31

S hort of breath from running at least three miles, Gabriél abruptly stopped. Consuela's presence ripped through the air like atmospheric electricity. Panic.

She was near. Gabriél listened. Silence. There was no rustling of brush or whispers of breezes. Mother was also near.

As a boy, he knew about his mother and her friends, how they gathered and enacted secret rituals in the mountains. One midnight many years ago, a sleeping youngster babysat by one of Mother's followers in the recess of a sandstone cave, squinted his eyes open. He heard and saw animals bleating and women shouting and Mother chanting. Thunder raged and rains pounded the desert floor.

He thought he was dreaming and drifted into sleep. The next morning, he told his mother about the nightmare. She laughed and said that a child's mind made up bad things so that bad things would not happen.

Now his mind corrected the lie.

To the east, he saw the red sandstone cliffs. He felt Consuela's rage and desperation, its force knocking him back like a blast of wind. He regained balance and rushed up a narrow passageway flanked on either side by jagged rock.

Steps from the top of the cliff, there came a jolt. He slipped and grabbed hold of a jutting stone, lodged cliffside. Pebbles and rocks swept downward. Heartbeats were quick, breaths shallow, mouth dry, hands clammy.

In an eyeblink, coyotes appeared just below his feet, bits of flesh hanging from their bared and bloodied teeth.

Mother Juana had moved from arroyo to cliffside. She gazed downward over a hundred yards—a skull-crushing distance. Cuauhtémoc slept in her arms, a child's extra-strong dose of morphine having tranquilized the fractious tike.

There to here in the blink of an eye. From office to dungeon, Mother had gone quicker than a daughter-in-law's ethereal presence caught on. Urgent problems birthed unforeseeable solutions.

Cuauhtémoc, coveted grandson, was safe—for now. He was a tool to terrorize. Mother moved inches away from the edge of the cliff, sandstone chunks crumbling downward.

Haughty daughter-in-law had caught Mother unawares. She had shifted, quite a feat for one so young in supernatural battles. Troublesome creature picked up on Mother's psychic tracks clear as muddy prints along an etheric passageway.

But the daughter-in-law was an easy catch. Mother and a

company of holy sisters had, within seconds, intuited her approach. Speedily, Consuela was caught and bound by nuns hiding in Mesquite bushes. Ropes entwined with red amaranth leaves were expertly wrapped around her slight frame, restraining her psychic energies.

Eyes bulging, Consuela fought against the nuns while they slipped a noose around her neck, bound her arms and secured her ankles. An old rag was stuffed in her mouth.

Mother laughed, then turned and again looked down the side of the cliff, jagged with sandstone outcroppings. She grabbed Cuauhtémoc by an ankle and dangled him upside down over the edge.

Mother's gaze shifted to Consuela. Mind to mind, she communicated. Either Consuela nice and easy goes over the edge. Or baby boy drops head first. Consuela's son—Consuela's choice.

Consuela flinched but held her gaze.

Amaranth oils imbued Mother Juana with unearthly strength. Mother let the boy slip a bit from her grip. She quickly grabbed hold again then swung him side to side over the edge.

Violently, Consuela squirmed, screams muffled.

And Cuauhtémoc cried.

Gabriél's gaze shot upwards.

Mother looked down at him, with her foot knocking small sandstones on his head. She sneered, two red beady eyes piercing full moon night.

Gabriél kept his gaze riveted on his mother. Let go of her with his eyes, and she would drop his son. It was mind-to-mind,

244 ◈ GODDESS OF EVERYTHING

mother-to-son threat.

Mother's eyes were searing. Gabriél's groin ached, pain radiating through his testicles. He faltered. From within his heart, he heard the words of the wise man—old man. *Decisions make the man*, *Gabriél*.

He slammed his boot heel at the pack of coyote bitches biting at his legs, landed a blow that cracked against a jaw, and they scattered like cockroaches.

Consuela was shoved into sight, gagged and bound by nuns at Mother's side. Her eyes bulged at the sight of her husband. He quickly swung his gaze back to Mother.

He scrambled up the cliff like a Mexican wolf on the hunt.

CHAPTER

32

With Cuauhtémoc's cries and Gabriél close, Consuela's core superheated. Her hair streamed electric blue, tips standing on end. Carotid arteries bulging, she spit the rag from her mouth and screamed. And the winds howled.

A tree from a surreal underworld arose out of the earth, its trunk her body, her hair woven into its branches. Fire rippled from her core to the soles of her feet to legs and head, white and blue bursts of electricity shooting from the tips of her hair and fingers. Cheeks and forehead burned like the fiercest of blazes.

The nuns cowered, crumpled to the ground. The sky exploded with thunder and sheets of forked lightning. Consuela charged forward, pulled Cuauhtémoc out of a stunned Mother Juana's grasp.

Immediately, Mother's attention riveted on her son, and she spun to the ground and whirled like a frenzied dust devil.

Consuela's presence hovered from earth to sky.

Mother's eyes shot upward and hissed.

Gray clouds formed around the full moon.

Gabriél pulled himself onto the ledge.

Mother Juana lashed out. She pointed her index finger at her son and seethed her incantation, "Bagabi laca bachabe lamac cahi achababe karrelyos… bagabi…" Streams of snakes appeared from between densely packed rocks. They raised their heads, hissed, and lunged at Gabriél. Forked tongues penetrated hands, arms, and legs.

Mother Juana became a dark witch looming in the sky. Earth and its atmosphere swelled and heaved with blue and white electrical currents rolling across the nighttime desert landscape. Shadows gathered round Mother.

Consuela hovered even higher, hair streaming electric blue, her body fully transformed into a surreal world tree, her hair woven into its branches.

Mother Juana lowered her head and shielded her eyes; surrounding shadows dispersed. She faltered, head nodding and eyes closing, then opening. She appeared to weaken, then caught herself and intoned, "Bagabi laca bachabe lamac cahi achababe karrelyos… bagabi…" Over and over the words sounded.

Consuela's brilliance became blinding.

Mother's voice quivered, words fading, specter screeching—dying.

Black morphed to empty space like an atmospheric dot— there, then gone.

All was silent, then was no more.

CHAPTER

33

I t's over, Gabriél," Consuela said, stroking his brow. She sat beside him on the hospital bed, Cuauhtémoc cradled in her left arm. The snake bites had taken a life-threatening toll.

The room was hazy, gray with foggy patches of lights and forms. Sharp pains pressed from the back of his head and shot through his eyes, tears streaming down his cheeks. He remembered everything before losing consciousness, Consuela updating him on the specifics of what had transpired during his emergency medical transport.

The sheriff scouted out Gabriél's whereabouts, Native deputies keen on spotting trails by day or night. No sooner had the battle been fought and done than a squadron of officers, sheriff in tow, scrambled up the embankment and discovered the battle-worn family. Consuela sat nestling

Cuauhtémoc in her arms, Gabriél lying at her side in the dirt, eyelids drooping and barely breathing.

Mother's intimidation and extortion of Sheriff Jorge Montoya constituted criminal assault on an officer of the law by one capable of executing harm. An emergency search warrant found the orphanage abandoned by the nuns, no trace of the nuns or Mother Juana de la Cruz. The children were immediately secured.

Any legal charges against Gabriél were not pursued by the District Attorney's Office. They stated extraordinary circumstances as exculpatory. Sheriff Jorge Montoya's persuasive conviction about his own temporary loss of judgement, due to Mother's threats potentially impacting the lives of children, closed the DA's investigation of Gabriél.

Consuela's voice was a healing balm, her fingertips warm and soothing. She placed Cuauhtémoc next to Gabriél. Father and son lay cheek to cheek. With her fingertips, she traced warmth across the brows of father and son. Cuauhtémoc touched Gabriél's face and eyes, and Gabriél looked at Consuela, a woman, healer, warrior, and seer—one whose eyes spoke of love, loss, and knowing the heart of a man.

CONNECT WITH PAUL DEBLASSIE III:

www.pauldeblassieiii.com

Twitter: @pdeblassieiii
Facebook: @pdeblassieiii

www.ingramcontent.com/pod-product-compliance
Lightning Source LLC
Chambersburg PA
CBHW051425170626
46809CB00006B/2324